I0722377

SEEKING IN ROMANCE COLLECTION 1-6

SEEKING IN ROMANCE SERIES

KEKE RENÉE

304 Publishing Company

Copyright@2020 KeKe Renée

Published by 304 Publishing Company

All Rights Reserved. Except for use in any review, no portion of this book may be performed, reproduced, published, sold or distributed by any means, or quoted in any medium. Including on any website, without prior written consent from the owner. This is a work of fiction. Names, characters, places, and incidents are either the product of the author's imagination or are used fictitiously, and any resemblance to actual persons, living or dead, business establishments, events or locales is entirely coincidental. This book is licensed for personal use only.

For questions and comments about this book, please contact 304 Publishing at 304publishing@gmail.com. Visit the official website at www.304publishing.com

ACKNOWLEDGMENTS

I CAN'T MENTION ENOUGH the support and dedication of my author buddies for keeping me uplifted. My behind-the-scenes team of beta readers, editors, designers, and more.

ARE YOU SIGNED UP?

Join today and find out all the latest in new releases, contests, giveaways, sneak peeks and more.
https://BookHip.com/ZXCKSSF

DISCLAIMER

THIS WORK OF FICTION contains strong language and explicit sexual content and is only intended for mature readers. This story may contain unconventional situations, language, and sexual encounters that may offend some readers. I would recommend selecting another book. This book is for mature readers (18+).

INTRODUCTION

This is a continuation of the *Wet Heat Series* called "Seeking in Romance." This series deals with different couples, and some you've met. Steamy, suspenseful and fun.

SYNOPSIS

Maya

I've worked hard to earn my senatorial position. I'm deter- mined to do what's right, and I keep my life free from scandal, but that proves difficult when one night out at Club Seek threatens my career and reputation.

Mason

I've accomplished a lot not using my family's last name. I'm a business owner, and the son of the most powerful man in the state of Tennessee. I find myself on opposite ends of drama when photos leak out about my club after spending time with a sexy woman who's powerful in her own right. Some fun play and a few pictures later, life becomes complicated.

When those scandalous photos are leaked, Maya's life is turned upside down. With everything on the line, including our growing feelings for each other, I wonder if we can rein in the chaos and avoid political suicide for her career?

Every Time We Touch (Wet Heat Series)

"I CAN'T WAIT TO SEE you in what I bought you tonight," Mason groaned over the phone, causing a shiver to run down my spine. I'd received a package at my door, hand delivered and wrapped. I wasn't expecting anything at all. With our lives being as busy as they were, we'd made a deal to not keep in touch. The rules were simple. We met up, we fucked, and then we went our separate ways.

"Mason," I sighed. The sound of his voice alone caused my clit to throb. I ran a hand between my thighs, imagining it was his lips. I ran a hand over the red lace corset, thong, and red five-inch heels laid on top of a black box. A black engraved invitation next to the pile requested my presence tonight.

"Am I hearing distress in your voice, Miss Hill?"

"No, you're hearing the sound of a woman who hasn't had pleasure in a while because of work. It seems your voice is doing something to me, and now I'm running a hand over my breast as I talk with you on the phone."

"You know I don't like it when you touch yourself."

"I guess you'll have to remind me tonight as I wear my new lingerie for you."

"Mhmm. Maya, you know the last thing you want to do is defy me," Mason growled through the phone.

I hung up the phone, leaving him anticipating what our night would be like after the last time we met up. We had tried anal play and brought in new partners.

He made the standard arrangements for me to be picked up and escorted through the back alley of the club, so no one would notice me. The dark-tinted windows of the vehicle were always a must have whenever we planned to meet up. As the newly elected senator in Tennessee Congress, it would be all over the media about a state senator seeking pleasure from a sex club. I would never apologize for my lifestyle, since I was a single woman. But I knew it would hinder me from getting things done correctly for the people who voted me into office. It didn't make the situation any better that the son of the speaker of the house in Congress was the one who owned the club.

SENATOR HILL

Xavier, calm down; he was helping me before I tripped," Chelsey said, caressing his arm. That seemed to bringthe tension down a little, and I released the breath I was holding.

"Sorry, I get a little crazy when I think someone is hurting her," Xavier spoke as Mason's glare seemed to fall, and he nodded when I ran a hand across his arm. Bad enough we took the risk of being out in the front area of the club. I usually would be in our room, away from the crowd. But tonight, I wanted to try something different and watch a little before we sauntered off to be alone.

"Senator—" I raised my hand to cut her off. I didn't want anyone bringing up my name and causing any confusion.

"I like to keep my identity under wraps." I motioned around the room, and she smiled in acknowledgment. Mason started Club Seek as a place to get away and explore all your desires. When approved for membership, you were guaranteed discretion. Everyone signed a non-disclosure agreement during the vetting process. Having the price tag of fifty thousand to join came with significant perks from private drivers to and from the club.

"Sorry, I was just shocked to see you here," Chelsey said, and I waved her off.

"No worries, I need to get back to my evening. Please keep this between us, Chelsey," I said. She raised her hand and crossed her middle and index finger in gesture. I chuckled and walked off with Mason behind me. He placed his hand on my lower back and escorted me to our room as the live entertainment finished. Everyone mostly congregated to a corner or went to a room after getting a key.

"Who was that?" Mason questioned, placing his fingers on the lower part of my back and escorting me through the private area of Seek and down the hall to his room. I looked over my shoulder at Chelsey as she continued to explain the situation. As we approached the door, he leaned up against my back while sliding the key inside. His strong, musky aroma invaded my nose. I told myself this would be a one-time thing over and over again in my head, and now I looked at myself in the mirror and realized that lie wouldn't last any longer.

"Walk inside." His lips pressed against my shoulder. Feeling my stomach drop, I peered up, looking around the room.

I felt a chill run down my arm when he locked the door, knowing all my fantasies would come true tonight, and we'd both be in heaven from the games we liked to play. His large hands, wrapped around my stomach, held me in place. All my senses heightened with just his presence surrounding me. He decorated the room in brown and black trimming from the king-size bed, throw pillows, to the Picasso art piece hanging on the wall, to the silk robes he had custom-made with our initials. Our little getaway from the outside world, where I liked to escape and be Maya instead of Senator Hill.

"Pull the stress away." I covered my hand over his. "Mmmmm... I want to kiss you, lick you, make you mine all over again." Mason ran his hand up my chest, gripping my neck.

"I missed you." His left hand pulled the spaghetti strap down.

I moaned, "Ahhh... Prove it."

"Undress," Mason demanded as he stalked over to the bar in the corner and poured his usual glass of cognac and stared at me. Removing my dress slowly like he usually liked, I kept my heels on and swished over to the bed, peering over at him as he gave a curt nod.

"You've kept her away from me." Mason ran his finger around the rim of his glass, guzzling the last drop. Strolling to the dresser drawer across from the bed, he pulled out the feather, a small bullet vibrator.

"Am I being punished?" I questioned, raised my right brow. "Tonight is about your pleasure. I can tell by your voice youcan't handle anything else."

"Come here." I reached for his hand, letting him kiss the back of my palm. I scooted back in the bed against the head- board as he tossed the pillows on the floor.

"Touch yourself." Mason's husky voice echoed throughout the room, watching him remove his jacket, shoes, and shirt as I pulled my thong down. Gripping my left breast, I tweaked my nipple, licking my lips as we stared at each other. Seeing the lust in his eyes of what we were about to do only compelled me even more, pushing my right hand down to my stomach playing with my sex. Wetness dripped down my legs already before he could even touch me.

"Mason... Uhhhh." Goosebumps broke out, imagining his tongue gliding up my slit.

"You're stunning, Maya," Mason called out, leaning down and pressing kisses on my left and right ankle, up my leg to my inner thigh and teasing, avoiding my essence. Mason's large body hovered over me, capturing my mouth, dizzying me with his tongue. He gripped my hands, pushing them over my head.

"Mmmmm... Yes, baby," I moaned, squeezing my eyes tight. He held my arms up with one hand and pushed his index finger into my entrance.

"Are you ready to be pleased?" Arching off the bed, I bit his bottom lip and pulled back.

"Mason... Uhhhh," I moaned, wanting to taste myself on his lips.

"Don't move." He pecked me on the mouth again, removed his hands, and reached over for the feather, slowly caressing it across my heavy breasts, down to my stomach. Closing my eyes again, I savored the time we had together. I heard the buzz of the vibrator turn on and popped my eyes open. He hovered it over an inch away from my throbbing mound.

"Please," I groaned, opening my legs wider.

He held the vibrator against my clit, while sucking my dark nipples into his mouth. Squirming from the double intensity, I felt my chest rise, and my head tossed and turned, fighting the temptation to touch him back. My hips subconsciously rocked back and forth, and my eyes grew heavy.

"I need you now."

"Do you want to come, baby?" Mason asked me, using his tongue to penetrate the deepest core of my soul.

"Yes, please... Oh, God!" It was demanding, letting me know that no one would ever compare.

"Soon." Hearing the zipper of his pants, Mason paused, reaching to the nightstand for a condom. A long time ago, we agreed we didn't want any accidents separately from protecting against any diseases even though I wasn't seeing anybody else. Kids weren't in the plan for my future, with my schedule only growing.

Tapping his dick against me, I tried to grip his shaft, and he smacked my hand away.

"No touching, Senator Hill," Mason grunted, thrusting forward. Sweat beads dripped across my forehead. As the room spun, my eyes grew blurry from processing the overwhelming passion coming off his large body. Feeling his hands run through my hair, I tilted my head back.

◈

TWO HOURS LATER, THE DOOR WAS HELD OPEN FOR me, and I walked away wearing my same clothes, feeling satisfied. The car pulled up for me to get inside. Tony started to open the door to come to help me, and I held my hand up to stop him.

"I got it."

A flash of light came across, and I looked around, trying to see where it was coming from. The security guard behind nudged me into the limo.

"Everything all right, Senator?" he said. I looked behind me, standing in the middle of the door with my leg halfway inside.

"Uh, yeah. I thought I saw something." I shook my head and got into the car, and Tony pulled off, staring through the back window. I tried searching the buildings and alleyways for the flash again.

Picking up my phone, I opened a text message thread, looking for Mason's name.

Me: Did you have security do a sweep tonight? Mason: I always do a sweep.

Me: I think I was followed.

Mason: Are you sure you want to be alone?

I gnawed on my bottom lip.

Me: Tonight was great, but I need to work early in the morning. Mason: All right, I want to see you soon.

Me: I'll get back to you.

Turning my phone off, I laid my head on the back of the seat, closing my eyes, wondering if my secret was out. This was the little peace I enjoyed where I could be myself and not a senator in demand for someone else. The car pulled up to the house, and Tony started to get out. I placed my hand on his shoulder.

"It's fine, Tony. I can make it from here."

"I'll wait out here to make sure you get inside comfortably."

Opening the door, I wave good night and head to the front door, sliding the key in my one-story, ten-thousand-square- foot home. Becoming a senator afforded me a nice, well-off place for my family to visit with three bedrooms, four baths.

I dropped my keys in the cup holder, kicking off my heels and coat. I jogged upstairs to my bedroom to end the night with a hot bath before work tomorrow.

SENATOR HILL

The senate meeting finally finished, and I left the room and walked back to my office with my assistant next to me, still feeling the effects of a night out at Club Seek.

"Senator Hill, you have lunch with Congressman Dole today," Jennifer spoke, running down my calendar of events.

"Anything else major? I was trying to leave early today." I checked my watch as we approached the door to my office. She pushed it open, walked inside, and I headed to my desk. As she sat on her own, I noticed a large manila envelope addressed to me.

"A few calls with the local newspapers and then another meeting with the speaker of the house." Jennifer crossed her legs, briefing me on the day. I flipped the envelope open, removing the contents, raising my hand to my mouth in shock. There were pictures of me at Club Seek, one of me standing with the security guard and one of me laughing with Mason. There was even one of his bedroom with me dressed in lingerie.

"OMG." I dropped the pictures on the desk, jumping up and pacing back and forth.

Jennifer stood and hovered over the desk, grabbing the pictures.

"Who took these?" she asked.

Shaking my head, tears fell down my cheeks.

"I don't know."

"They didn't leave a note or anything. Do you have enemies?"

"I'm a senator. Enemies come with the territory."

"Maybe you should tell Mason." Jennifer picked up more

pictures, glancing up at me.

"I don't know."

Turning to look out the window, I saw Tony standing in front

of the limo, pointing at a photographer. They often came up to the capital to harass staff, and they knew him by name, which could lead me to feel that maybe he was behind this or Mason.

"What if this has Mason behind it?"

"You can't be serious. Mason loves you," Jennifer replied. A knock came at the door. Jennifer hurriedly put all the photos back in the envelope, passing them to me, and I slid them into my bottom cabinet.

"Come in!" I shouted, sitting at the desk and wiping tears away.

"Senator Hill, I think it's time we had a discussion about the bill you proposed," Congressman Kurt Jones said.

"Mr. Jones, we've debated, and you've made it clear where you stand."

"I'm inclined to change my mind."

"Why would you do that?"

He crossed his arms over his chest, his right brow lifted. "Let's say I have an idea that you'll need my help down the road."

"What is that supposed to mean?" I jumped out of the chair, agitated that he may know of the pictures I was hiding. He raised his hands in the air, smiling.

"You'll never get your agenda passed. It's better to play nice now."

"Jennifer, will you please escort Congressman Jones out of my office?"

"No need, I have another meeting with the speaker in a half hour. Remember, I can put a good word in for you." Kurt winked, walking out of my office.

"He's disgusting," Jennifer said, heading to the office door.

"Can you hold all my calls for the next two hours? I need to figure out what's going on."

"You going to call Mason?" Jennifer inquired.

"I just hope this doesn't come back to haunt me."

I pulled my cell phone from my purse and dialed Mason's

number. It went to voicemail, and I hung up and tried again. "Where is he?" I muttered to myself, then decided to call my

parents.

"Hey, Maya," Dad spoke.

"Hi, Dad. Where's Mom?"

Hearing something rustling on the other end, I pulled the

phone away for a brief second.

"What are you doing?"

"I'm out working on my car. Your mother's at the store." "Oh."

"What's wrong? Usually you don't call during this time of

day."

"Nothing. I just missed you two."

"We miss you, but you're only a forty-five-minute drive away."

I chuckled, knowing he was right. I always counted on my

dad to make me feel better about anything. Being an only child, it came with me as the apple of their eye. I was spoiled and treated like royalty growing up.

"Tell Mom I called, and I'll try to clear my schedule to have dinner later in the week."

"Are you sure everything is okay?"

"I'm fine, Dad. Call you later."

"All right. Love you, little girl," he said.

"Love you too, bye." We hung up at the same time. I sighed,

sitting back in the chair, holding my hands up to my face. Whoever was behind these pictures was trying to destroy my life, and I refused to let my parents be hurt.

Jennifer strolled into the office, holding bags of food.

"Lunch is here, but the speaker wants to talk with you." She placed soup and a sandwich down.

"When did you talk to him?"

"While you were on the phone," Jennifer said.

"I don't have time for this, and I'm not hungry."

"You need to eat. Do you want me to make up a lie?"

"Yes... No... wait." I groaned, lifting the phone to see if

Mason called or texted back.

"You know it's because of Jones that he wants to see you." Nodding in agreement, I stood and grabbed my cell to head to his office. I figured it was better to find out what he wanted before things got even crazier.

"Hold my calls for the rest of the day. I doubt I'll be up to having another meeting when I get back."

"Try not to get yourself too stressed," Jennifer replied.

Pursing my lips, I checked my appearance before leaving, and Jennifer followed by shutting the door. Walking through the busy hallways, I scanned the crowds and got a feeling like someone was watching me. Shaking off the reaction, I continued to the elevator and waited with another few members as the doors opened. Stepping on a few seconds later, I punched the top level for his floor. Arriving five minutes later, I treaded over to his secretary's desk, motioning toward his open door.

"He's waiting for you," she said.

"Thanks."

Knocking on the door, he waved me in, and I closed the door behind me, strolling to the chair in front of his desk. His office always creeped me out, with the pictures of just him hanging on the wall; there was nothing with his wife or son.

"I wanted to meet with you about this proposal of yours." Adam held the early draft of my bill in his hands.

"What would you like to talk about?"

"Jones thinks you should scrap this for now, and I'm inclined to agree."

I pushed down my honest thoughts. Adam's bushy brows furrowed, and I glared right back at him.

"My agenda is to support my community."

"You will, under my leadership."

"I won't be silenced, and Kurt has no right to go behind my

back."

"Do you know how laws get passed?" he asked.

"I'm not here to debate on my job, Mr. Speaker."

"Then you'll put this aside."

"Are you saying you won't bring it to the floor?"

"I'm saying I run things around here. Get with the program," he argued, throwing my bill in the trash can. I scoffed and stormed out of his office with a headache forming, smashing the down button to head back to my office. Stomping off the elevator toward my office, Jennifer waved a stack of messages in front of my face, and I snatched them out of her hand before pushing my door open and slamming it closed.

"Arghh!" I screamed, pacing back and forth.

"What happened?" Jennifer tapped on the door, pushing it open, not waiting to be called.

"Nothing."

"Maya, I can clearly see something happened."

"Kurt is what happened."

"Take the rest of the day off; you're not up to finishing any

meetings."

"You're right. I have the worst headache." I hugged her, grabbing my purse and coat before passing back the messages, and leaving the office. While going toward the elevator, I saw Kurt and Adam talking in a huddle together. They were up to something, and I just needed to be prepared.

❧ 3 ❧

MASON

Morris knocked on my office door, strolling in with a hard grimace on his face. He was a silent partner in Club Seek, and with him being a security agent, I was able to leverage a lot of his clients to join the club.

"She's pissing me off."

"Who?" I finished signing off on inventory for the club.

"Lisa." Morris unbuttoned his jacket, standing with his

hands on top of the chair in front of the desk. When Maya told me about her friend Lisa, I wasn't as forthcoming with inviting her in as she was. She was well known, and the lightest slip could hurt not only my business, but Maya's career. Her job in the media was a big no for me and my business. My clients trusted that I could keep their privacy from being revealed, which was the reason I had strict requirements on my contracts.

Leaning back in my seat with my hands clasped together in my lap, I could see the veins clearly in Morris' forehead.

13

"Tell me something new; it seems like every week you two are fighting."

"She refuses to take security when she comes and goes."

"Has something happened?" I needed to know if Maya was in jeopardy. Even though being a senator, she was equipped with her own security, I preferred to have my own people with her at all times.

"No, Lisa just thinks I'm overprotective."

I shrugged my shoulders, chuckling to myself.

"What's so funny?"

"I hear the same thing from Maya."

He came around and sat in the chair, propping his arm on

the desk.

"At least with Maya, you're able to get her to understand." "Lisa's headstrong. You might need to go easy on her."

"The last thing she needs is me going easy on her."

"Well, I have my own problems."

"Your dad or Maya this time?"

I shuffled the papers on my desk.

"He wants me to come work for him and quit this little frat

boy work," I scoffed, thinking over our last conversation in my head.

"He's still on that same argument?"

I nodded, sighing with a hand running down my face. "Doesn't matter that I have multiple businesses and am doing fine without using his connections."

"Sounds like you have just as many problems as me."

"Yeah, you want a drink?" I pointed, standing and strolling toward the bar in the corner of my office. Lifting the top from the brown scotch, I filled the cup halfway, passing it toward him and filling the second glass for myself.

"Thanks," he said.

Placing one hand in my pocket, I tilted my head back, gulping the drink down. Squeezing my eyes shut, I let the warm, subtle notes drain down my throat.

"I need another one."

"Keep drinking, you're never going to be ready for Maya."

"She's not coming tonight. We're supposed to meet for dinner," I replied.

Morris held his glass out for another shot, lowering his eyes toward his watch.

"I have to run. I called a meeting with my team before I came here." He stood, handing me the glass.

"Let me know if you're able to run point next week," I said. "Sure will."

"Try not to run yourself crazy over Lisa."

Morris waved me off, walking out of the office, and I finished off my second drink, sitting back down in my chair, looking over last-minute emails.

When my phone rang, I groaned at someone disturbing me during my downtime. I picked up the phone, hearing my father's secretary on the other end.

"Please hold for Mr. Norris," Sheila said.

A part of me wanted to hang up, but he would just have her call me right back.

"Mason," my father said.

"Sir."

Adam Norris was the type of person who only looked out for himself. Growing up, if I didn't follow the rules, I would basically be seen as the piranha of our family. All my cousins followed in the family business of politics, and I strayed toward business, then owning a few clubs that happened to cater to people's sexual needs. My father only told them I was the owner of a few restaurants, which was true, but he left the part of Club Seek from my resume.

"What do you need?"

Massaging my temples, I stayed silent, waiting to hear what new request he had for me.

"I'm having a little fundraiser at the house."

"I can't."

"You will. Your mother hasn't talked to you in a while."

"Why? Not like you're going to introduce me to anyone."

"Because I said to come. You don't think I have the power to end your little business?"

There's the Adam Norris I knew very well.

"Threatening your son?" My brow lifted in surprise.

He cleared his throat.

"Mason, this is important. Put our differences aside," he said.

"Send the details to me, and I'll see if I can make it," I said,

hanging up, not waiting for him to respond. Shaking my head, I sent off some more emails and decided it was time to end the day and meet up with Maya for dinner.

❧

I OPENED THE DOOR TO THE SPARTINE, AN ITALIAN restaurant not too far from my house, and the hostess seated me right away since I was a frequent guest.

"Two tonight, Mr. Norris?"

"Yes. She should be here soon."

Sara placed the menus down on the table, and I grabbed my

phone from my pocket to check my messages. I saw

Jameson and my mother texted me, but nothing from Maya.

Jameson: The order of liquor came in.

Catherine: Son, I'm glad you're coming.

Me: Where are you?

Me: Did you get my message about dinner?

"Well, look who stumbled into my little world."

I lifted my head up, smirking at Erica Brownstone, actress

and former fling of mine. Standing next to the empty chair, she bit her bottom lip.

"Erica."

"Mason, don't tell me you're eating alone." Erica leaned over the table, running her palm across my shoulder. I backed up so her hand would fall off and get the hint as the waitress came up to my table. Erica Brownstone never had a problem with showing off, and today was no different. Out of the many years we'd known each other, she always wanted more from me. The problem was that she was extremely self-absorbed and wanted all the attention on her.

"I'm actually waiting for someone."

"Really? Maybe I can keep you company until she gets here." Erica sat without me inviting her.

"Are you ready to order, sir?"

"I'd love a glass of white wine," Erica said.

Glancing at my phone again, I didn't see a response from

Maya.

"Anything for you, sir?"

"Um... I'll have the same thing." As I placed my phone in my

pocket, Erica smiled, tossing her hair back.

"So, are you seeing anyone?" Erica questioned.

"I saw a commercial for your latest movie. You looked good," I said, trying to change the subject. She laughed, taking a sip of water.

"Come on, Mason, we used to be able to talk and be friendly."

"True, but now you're a big star. I'd hate for any rumors to get out."

"Some rumors can be helpful." Erica extended her hand, rubbing across my palm. Removing my hand from her reach, Erica looked around the room, likely to see if anyone saw the rejection. Our waitress came back with our drinks, and I thanked her, letting Erica order a meal.

"Listen, it's good seeing you, Erica, but I have to go," I said, attempting to stand.

"Wait! It's just dinner, Mason," Erica pouted.

"Dinner that I was expecting to have with someone else." "Do you love her?"

"I'm not answering that."

"Well, she's a lucky girl."

"Have a good night," I said, treading out and stopping at the bar to tell the bartender to put her meal on my account. My next mission was finding out why Maya never showed up tonight.

SENATOR HILL

"**A**rghhhh!!!" My wrist tightened against the cuffs as the second strike came across my ass, clenching my teeth, and my body continued to be dominated by the flogger. I

ignored his calls yesterday, consumed with work, and we'd promised ourselves that would never happen. Even though I wanted to tell him what was going on, I wanted to let the night be about us only and leave work outside these walls.

He peppered kisses against my spine, leaning in behind with his chest to my back. I wanted to touch and taste him in my mouth.

"Maya, you drive me crazy," he murmured, running his hands all over my body.

"I want to taste you," I begged.

"Not tonight. You lost that luxury."

I gasped, pumping in, feeling him in my stomach. My breath caught in my throat.

"You understand what this is about?"

Nodding my head, I knew he was pushing my boundaries

and challenging me to disagree, but I wouldn't because this was both of us becoming as one. He couldn't deny me for too long, hearing his groans and grunts of satisfaction. Our mouths parted in whimpers, hearing his moans next to my ear. Grip- ping my hips, Mason pulled out and sucked on my pussy, sliding his one finger into my asshole.

"Mason!" I trembled under his touch. The entire bed was soaking wet from juices and combined sweat. I tensed up, feeling the tingling rise, wanting to beg for a release.

"Please, baby, can I come!" I screamed, yanking against the cuffs again.

All of a sudden, he drew back his finger and tongue, sliding his dick back in, pumping faster, leaving me on edge.

"Arghh... Fuck, Maya, come for me!" Mason shouted, reaching around and playing with my clit. I squirted on command, shaking beneath the restraints. All I wanted to do was fall asleep in his arms.

"Relax, I'm not going anywhere." I heard, a few seconds later, a warm towel wiping me clean.

"I love you," I mumbled slowly.

"I'm still upset with you."

He pulled me into his arms.

"I was upset after talking with your father," I confessed. Mason cupped my chin, staring into my eyes.

"What happened?" he asked.

I moved out of his hold and adjusted to sit up against the headboard.

"He won't move forward with the bill I co-wrote. Plus. I think he's working to destroy my career."

"Explain."

"I don't want to put you in the middle of my problems."

I started to get out of the bed, and Mason gripped me around the waist.

"Tell me, Maya."

"I need to get in line with what he wants, or I need to look for a career to end."

"Son of a bitch," Mason grunted, tossing the sheet off his body, reaching for his boxers and pants.

"Wait! What are you doing?" I crawled toward the end of the bed.

"I'm going to talk to him."

"No! Mason, this is my problem."

"He's my father, and no one threatens you," Mason demanded.

Shaking my head, I stepped off the bed, wrapping the sheet around my body. Capturing Mason's arm, I turned him toward me.

"I understand, but please let me handle him."

"Maya," Mason groaned, pulling me into his chest.

"Please, it will only make things worse."

"I'll let you handle it for now, but I can't promise."

"Thank you."

"I want you to come as my date."

"To what?"

Going out in public wasn't our thing. Seeing things change as we got closer caused an unexpected flutter in my heart.

"A fundraiser."

"Fundraiser?" I pried, watching him lean down and peck my lips.

"Nothing major."

"Ummm... huh."

"Are you coming to my place tonight?"

Reaching down to grab my dress and shoes, I went to the

bathroom to get redressed, leaving the door halfway open.

"I have so much work."

"Maya, you keep pushing me away, and you think I don't notice."

"Mason, you're overreacting," I said, running my hands through my hair.

"After last night when you stood me up. I decided this was moving forward." He pointed between him and me.

"Who made you in charge of deciding my life?"

He stood in the middle of the doorway of the bathroom, still shirtless with his muscles on display, begging for my tongue to taste every square corner of his broad chest.

"I did. Because we both know that you love everything I do to you." He stalked in slow toward me, reaching out to caress my cheek.

"May I suggest you be patient with me?"

"You can suggest, but we both know you like it when I take control." Mason smacked me on the butt, squeezing both cheeks, making me moan in anticipation of another round in bed together.

"I do love you, though."

"Show me."

"Another time. I have work to do," I said, standing on my

tiptoes, pressing a kiss to his lips.

"You can work at my place." Mason pulled back, letting me

out of the bathroom first, following after.

"Okay, and you can tell me more about this fundraiser."

FRIDAY AFTERNOON.

I sat with Jennifer at lunch, going over my schedule for the

week at Spartine, debating on what else I could do to handle Mason's father without causing a rift between them.

"I have you scheduled for back-to-back calls," Jennifer said. "Who are they with?"

"A few senators and small business owners."

"Try to make them all in one day."

"I got your dress for the fundraiser with Mason." "Did he finally send the information over?"

"That's what I wanted to confirm with you."

Lifting the fork, I pushed pasta around on my plate.

"What do you mean?"

"Adam Norris' fundraiser," Jennifer remarked.

I choked on my food, coughing as she passed the glass of

water over to me.

"Are you sure?"

"Yes." She passed her phone over to me. I looked at her

email exchange with Mason, seeing the time, date, and specifics.

"I told him I didn't want to deal with him."

"Do you want me to cancel?"

I started to answer when I saw a flash of light go off, and

the door opened as a woman walked inside with a crowd of people surrounding her.

"No, I already said I would go."

I went back to eating my food when I heard a voice call out my name.

"Maya Hill, right?" the woman amongst the entourage called my name. Wearing large shades, I figured she was someone important.

"Yes."

She held her hand out toward me. I reached over and gave her a shake.

"Erica Brownstone, we have something in common."

"I doubt we have anything in common."

"Oh... really... hmmm, I guess Mason didn't tell you about

our dinner date."

I yanked my hand back.

"No worries, he's mysterious like that," Erica said.

"How do you know Mason?"

"We go way back. Surprised he's never spoken about our relationship," Erica replied. "Yeah, really surprised."

"Well, I'll let you get back to your lunch. Tell Mason I'll call him soon." Erica winked, swishing her hips before heading to her friends. They sat in the booth giggling at the performance she had just put on, and I rolled my eyes. Jennifer snapped her fingers.

"That's Erica Brownstone; she's an actress."

"She needs more training because she's terribly dramatic." Jennifer laughed.

"I remember seeing a movie with her not too long ago."

"At least she dresses better than she acts."

"You think Mason's dating her too?

"I don't know, but I plan on finding out."

"In the meantime, try to focus on what you're going to do

about the speaker."

"Maybe going to dinner wouldn't be so bad," I muttered,

cupping my chin with my elbow on the table. I'd been playing things too easy with everyone, to the point they felt like I was a pushover.

"Seeing the gleam in your eyes, I can only imagine," Jennifer responded, taking a bite of her baked ziti.

"I need to gather more information, but I'm not letting them run me out of Congress."

❦

HE RAN A HAND DOWN MY CHEST, ACROSS MY STOMACH, and over my navel, dipping his middle finger in my warm canal. After work, he surprised me at my place and brought dinner. Before I could even talk with him about the fundraiser or Erica, I was tied up against the headboard with my legs spread open, with his tongue and fingers exploring. Feeling his smooth, warm palm move in and out at a slow pace drove me insane. It was all about his plan to tease me and push me to the cliff. As tired as I was at first, this brought new life into my blood.

"Are you ready?"

"Mmmmm..."

My hair was out of the normal ponytail, fanned around my

pillow. I looked up with wide eyes as he cupped the side of my face. He recaptured my lips, sliding his tongue inside. He pressed his hard body against my skin. I was panting, groaning, wanting to feel him take me again.

"Yesss..."

"You are so beautiful, baby."

Snaking his tongue to lick my nipple, it was intoxicating and frustrating, wanting to touch him but unable to wrap my arms around his neck. I arched my back a little, moving my hips and feeling aroused.

"I want to feel you." "You will, in time."

❊ 5 ❊

SENATOR HILL

The next day, it was finally Sunday. The bright sun was shining, and I wore my shades sitting in the backseat, looking over the text from Mason. Right now, he was texting to set another date, and I didn't know if I would be able to get time off with the upcoming schedule. Whenever we had our meetups and I left, I still craved his presence.

Mason: Are you still thinking about me?

Me: Always.

Mason: Come see me.

Me: I can't, meeting with my friends.

Mason: Afterwards, what are you doing?

The car stopped, and Tony opened the door and stepped

out to help escort me inside.

"Thanks, Tony. I can ride home with Lisa. Take the after-

noon off." "Senator—"

"I'll be fine, Tony, don't worry."

"I'll feel better if I stick around." Tony released a

breath, shutting the door and leading me in toward the backroom. The hostess nodded at me, and I smiled, never looking around at the other guests. We continued toward the private dining area, and Tony slid the doors open to reveal Lisa, Kyla, and Chelsey sitting and laughing.

"Tony!" all three blurted out excitedly, and Tony blushed. All my friends flirted with Tony whenever he came around them. I could admit he was tall, dark, handsome, protective, and loyal.

"Finally, the queen has made her presence known." Lisa giggled, holding up her glass of mimosa. We'd been friends since freshman year of college, and she was a TV anchor. Kyla, the youngest of our group, was a well-known actress filming a movie in town. So, it was extra special when she came to visit. Normally, she lived in New York. Our friendship came about from Lisa when she interviewed her at a movie premiere. Then Chelsey was new to our group, but I felt a connection from the first time I deposited money with her family's bank.

"Ladies," Tony said, shaking his head at them.

"Thanks, Tony." He pulled the chair out for me, and I sat, placing my phone and purse down on the table. My phone vibrated, and I quickly remembered Mason texting me.

"Oops, someone's in trouble," Lisa said.

"Ohhh." Kyla and Chelsey chuckled.

Mason: Will I see you later?

Me: Sorry, I was talking with the girls. I'll call you when I leave. Mason: Don't forget, Maya.

Me: I won't.

Mason: If you do, punishment of my tongue is coming.

I squeezed my legs together and bit my bottom lip, flashing

back to the last time I disobeyed him, and I was

deprived of his tongue, watching him come in front of me without letting me touch him.

Lisa snapped her fingers in front of my face.

"Tell Mason you're busy, and you'll ride his tongue later," Lisa joked, slapping hands with Kyla.

A crooked grin came across my face. I placed the phone down, searching all three of their eyes.

"Have you ordered yet?" I inquired. Right as the doors opened, trays of food were placed on the table. The restaurant served everything from Italian, soul food, breakfast items, to steak and seafood. Lisa's boyfriend knew the owner, so the atmosphere was casual but expensive. They catered to a lot of high-profile customers on the weekends.

"Yes, and I'm starving," Chelsey replied, picking up her fork and digging into her vegetable omelet. Today would be the best time to talk about the incident at the club since Mason and Xavier hadn't met officially.

"I hear you and Mason are together now," Kyla said, passing her empty glass over to the server.

"We just agreed a few days ago."

"So it's serious between you two?"

Lisa's black hair hung loosely out of her everyday updo she

wore on air, with her deep-set brown eyes standing out to her yellowish-brown skin tone. Each of us was different, and most people wondered how we became friends. Lisa was the most outgoing. Kyla was the strongest, ready to fight out battles. I was considered the mother of the bunch, and Chelsey was the quieter one.

"Too early to tell."

"Chelsey told us about Xavier and Mason," Kyla mentioned. I stared, trapped by her smoky, warm, bronze skin tone. Her mother was Haitian and Hispanic, and her father was Jamaican. Lisa nicknamed her Babydoll because she looked like a doll with her big, wide eyes, button nose, and high cheekbones.

"Xavier's just overprotective," Chelsey told us and I nodded, understanding having the type of guy who was overprotective of his woman.

"All men get like that at some point."

"I'm going to meet Morris there tonight," Lisa explained.

"Have you been invited yet, Kyla?" Chelsey questioned.

"No, doubt I have time with my schedule," Kyla answered, her dreadlocks lined against her oval-shaped face.

"Mason owns the place, Maya. You take Kyla," Lisa suggested, biting into her pancakes, revealing her devilish smile.

"I have to check my schedule. You know what I'm dealing with in Congress."

"How is everything at work?" Chelsey pushed loose strands of her bouncy hair behind her ear. The glossy lipstick covered her full lips.

"Stressful. I'm trying to push my agenda and get things going."

"Don't let it discourage you."

"Let's make a toast."

"To what?"

"Toast to us for being boss women." Lisa raised her glass up,

and we cheered, taking a sip.

❧

AN HOUR LATER, I PUT MY SHADES ON, HEADING OUT behind Lisa and Tony covering me as much as possible. People often stopped me to start a conversation on some issue they were dealing with. When I was dressed down, I liked to not be noticed if I didn't need to be. Tony pushed the doors open, and a swarm of photographers and reporters yelled, shoving microphones in my face.

"Senator Hill! Senator Hill!" reporters yelled.

"Back up. Back up!" Tony replied, pushing through the crowd, holding onto my hand. I usually didn't have a huge group surrounding me and wondered what the issue was this time. Reporters kept a distance sometimes, but this was insane with over twenty people surrounding my town car.

"We need to leave," Tony said.

"What happened?" I asked. He reached for the door, and I started to get inside when someone shoved a picture in front of my face.

"Is this you, Senator Hill?" a reporter asked. I pushed her hand away and jumped inside my car. Tony shut the door, not waiting to see if any of the girls were able to leave through the massive crowd.

"Check your phone," he replied, starting the car, honking his horn as the audience grew bigger with cell phones out, filming us.

"This is nuts," I muttered, opening my phone and seeing nonstop messages and missed calls.

"Senator, call me ASAP," Jennifer said, with an attached photo of me dressed in lingerie with Mason holding a flogger behind me.

"Oh My God!" I shouted.

SENATOR HILL

I shut the TV off from another reporter telling people how much of a disappointment I was, pacing back and forth in front of Mason, Jennifer, and Chelsey. I shook my head, feeling on the brink of breaking down in tears. My entire career was plastered online with people making comments about how I shouldn't be in public office. I loved my job and wanted to make a difference in the world. I never expected that what I did in private would cause so much backlash. I'd been at Mason's house since everything happened, taking calls and meetings over the phone. Even Jennifer got pulled into my problems with people hounding her family. Kyla and Lisa messaged me and wanted to come to check on me, but I declined, not wanting any more spotlight on me. Bad enough reporters were camped out down the street from Mason's house. It was so bad, Kyla had to take a few days off from the news station because they wanted her to report on the news, and she felt a conflict of interest.

"My life is ruined."

"Don't say that, Maya," Chelsey replied, walking over and

placing her hand on her back.

"I knew this was a mistake." I balled my fist up, wanting to scream.

"What did you say?" Mason called out.

I wasn't up for fighting with him.

"Mason, please let's not do this right now." I raised my hand,

stopping him from coming any closer.

"No, I think this is the time to get some things straight." He

reached for my hand, and I tried to turn away.

"Maybe we should grab some food," Jennifer spoke, standing up with her purse and keys.

"That won't be necessary," I said.

"Jennifer, take all the time you need," Mason remarked, making me roll my eyes at him trying to control everything.

"I know a great barbeque place," Chelsey said, hugging me. "All right, take Tony," I demanded, wanting to make sure

they were protected. Chelsey nodded, leaving with Jennifer. Pushing Mason away, I stomped off to the kitchen, needing fresh air.

"I can't believe you," I huffed, pointing at him.

"Listen to me, Maya."

"Mason, you don't understand what this means for my career." I threw my hands in the air.

"I get it, baby, but you're pushing the wrong person away." "Maybe coming here was a mistake."

He gripped my chin, forcing eye contact, pressing his chest

to mine.

"I don't give a damn what the newspaper or online says. This is not a mistake."

I jerked out of his hold.

"Because your father is Adam Norris, you never have to deal with anything!" I shouted, regretting the words when they left my mouth.

"I've heard that same thing over and over my entire life but never expected you of all people."

I extended a hand out to him.

"Mason..."

He shook me off.

"If this is too much, I won't fight you on leaving." Mason

marched out of the kitchen.

Standing alone, I felt the weight of the world falling in on

me. I heard the door open, then close, and I jumped up, running to see where he was going.

"Mason! Mason!"

Jumping in his car, he drove off and didn't look back. Before I ran toward his car backing out of the driveway, a swarm of reporters accosted me.

"Senator Hill! Is it true you're resigning?"

"Senator Hill! Are you a prostitute?"

"Senator Hill! Senator Hill!"

Nonstop questions and cameras hit me in my face, I pushed

through the crowd, running back inside. Upstairs in his bedroom, I hid under the covers, crying over the end of my relationship with Mason.

FOUR HOURS LATER, I FELT STRONG ARMS AROUND me lying in bed, sniffing from my earlier tears. I tried to turn around in bed, but he wouldn't let me.

"No."

"I'm sorry."

He sighed, kissing the back of my neck.

"I know."

"Please don't leave me."

"You're making it hard."

"What can I do?"

Squeezing me close, he loosened his hold, letting me adjust

so we were face to face. The back of his palm ran down my

cheek.

"Stop fighting me. My father is more than likely behind

this."

I tried to sit up, but he forced me back down, kissing me on

the lips.

"How do you know?"

"I went to see him."

"Wait, are you serious?"

Mason turned, lying on his back.

"Adam Norris is controlling. He would do anything to keep me under his thumb, and I refuse." "So he's trying to ruin my career."

"Pretty much."

"Bastard."

"The best way to get him to stop is to play fire with fire." "That's not me, Mason."

"Maya, do you trust me?" Mason questioned.

"Yes."

"Then let things play out. Let me handle this for you." Mason rolled over, wrapping his arm around my waist.

"What about Erica?"

A hard grimace crossed his face.

"She's more than likely getting paid."

"I agree."

I recalled her doing an interview about how Mason was only using me to get his business funded since I was a senator and had connections. Obviously, Adam wanted to make Mason seem weak in public so he could crawl to him and get a job.

"I forgot we bumped into her at the restaurant."

"Jennifer told me while you were asleep," Mason informed me.

"Did Tony take them home?" I asked. "No, they're still downstairs." "What?"

"They didn't want to leave you alone, so we let you sleep." "Let me go downstairs and tell them to head home."

He moved back, letting me out of bed. I pecked him on the

lips again, holding his hand while we strolled down the stairs to see them watching a movie together.

"You look a little better," Jennifer said.

"I needed rest."

"We left you some food in the microwave," Chelsey said. "Thank you, but I'm not hungry. I just want to thank you

both."

"You don't have to thank us," Jennifer replied.

Letting go of Mason's hand, I walked around the couch to

sit between them.

"I do. Everything is upside down, but you've been

supportive beyond words."

"Well, your friends are here no matter what." Chelsey reached over to grip my hand.

"What's the plan? Are we beating Erica's ass?" Jennifer blurted out, and all three of us burst into laughter.

"I have more than enough problems. Having friends in jail for fighting wouldn't work."

Jennifer's bottom lip poked out, crossing her arms over her chest.

"For now, Mason will handle things because his father is behind everything."

Chelsey and Jennifer's eyes rose wide in shock.

"Speaker Norris?" Jennifer said.

"Wow." Chelsey shook her head in disbelief.

"Maybe doing an interview would help," Jennifer suggested. "You don't think it would lead to more unnecessary harassment," Chelsey asked.

"Right now, I'm going to eat and head to bed."

"All right, keep me updated." Jennifer stood. I followed, walking her to the door along with Chelsey. Shutting the door, I stared out the window, watching them leave with Tony. Mason came in front of me, picking me up bridal style and carrying me back to his bedroom. He helped me out of my clothes and took me into the bathroom. Putting me on the counter, he turned the water on in the tub. He kissed the top of my forehead and left me alone.

"Relax, and I'll be out here."

Smiling back at him, I nodded, stepping down and getting in the tub. I leaned back, closed my eyes, and prayed things would go away.

❦ 7 ❦

MASON

Two days later.

I was standing at the door of my parents' home, with Maya on my arm. It was the night of the fundraiser for his campaign. Maya had been camping out at my place for the past few days because the reporters and photographers were constantly following her around when she went to work. Talking her into even coming tonight was an argument, but I promised we wouldn't stay long. I wanted to see how people were kissing my dad's ass just to get a leg up on any deals. Remembering the conversation we had the afternoon I stormed out on Maya played in my mind all night.

Flashback.

Arriving at my parents' house, I parked and jumped out of the car, not waiting for the butler to let my father know I was here. I slammed the door, stomping toward his office, the only room he stayed in most of the time. He was on a call, and I jerked it out of his hand and hung up.

"Mason, that was an important call."

"I don't know who you paid off but fix it now." I picked up the phone, holding it toward him.

"What are you talking about?" he questioned.

"Are we playing stupid now?"

"Listen, I'm your father, young man," he argued, pointing at me. "Old man, I let you get away with a lot of things, but this is where I draw the line." He glanced away.

"Who do you think you're talking to?" He rose out of his seat.

"A man I thought wasn't so fucking greedy to hurt his son." He chuckled.

"Her pussy must really be good for you to talk to me this way." I balled my fist up and punched him in the jaw. The door flew open, and my mother ran in, looking between us.

"Mason! What did you do?" She pushed me aside and went to my father.

"Get the hell out of my house!" he yelled.

"I know you paid somebody to take a photo of Maya."

"That little bitch is only after your money," he spat. Mother helped him up off the floor, and I tried to hit him again. She stood between us.

"Mason, stop it! What is this all about?" she asked.

My mother was naive to the dealings of my father and stayed more focused on her image and keeping up appearances.

"Your husband can explain."

"Adam, what is he talking about?" she said.

"Catherine, stay out of this," he said.

"I'm telling you right now, either you fix this, or I'll make your life a living hell."

"You will not speak to your father that way," she responded.

"Tell Mother how you paid a photographer to stalk Maya." My nostrils flared, and my chest heaved up and down. I was ready to beat his ass and go to jail if need be.

"Adam, please, whatever you've done, end it now," Mother pleaded.

"She's a liability, Mason," Dad remarked, sitting back down in his chair.

"Why? Because you can't have her under your thumb like a puppet?" I hissed.

"Damage our family name with those clubs and now sleeping with a woman who has no morals," he said, grabbing the napkin from my mother's hand and wiping the remnants of the blood off. I bent down, staring him in the eye.

"Fix this now, or you'll never see me again," I demanded, walking away as my father called my name.

❧

PRESENT.

Running my palm across Maya's lower back, I kissed her shoulder blade as people stared at us. I held her hand, heading into the ballroom of the massive twenty-thousand-square-foot home I grew up in. Adam Norris was the son of Jimmy Norris, my grandfather and a politician who forced all of his kids to follow in his footsteps. I wanted normalcy, so I did my best not to go to a private school like my friends and be a normal kid. Now looking like the black sheep of the family, I had to deal with every judgment.

"Are you okay?" Maya asked, stopping us from walking further into the room.

"Just hard coming back here." I looked around the room, reminiscing on all the parties I had to attend when I was younger.

"I can just imagine with a father like Adam."

"Did I tell you how beautiful you looked?"

I tugged her into my arms, staring at her red lips that I wanted to taste. We hadn't been back to the club, let alone had sex with everything going on. I understood because we'd been distracted by having to deal with the public opinions every- where we went. The other day, I tried to take her to dinner, and Tony had to keep her in the limo and turn around to head back home from all of the reporters camping outside the restaurant. I had no clue they knew we'd be there, other than someone at the restaurant calling the media.

"No, you haven't."

"I like this dress. Did Jennifer pick this out?"

She glanced down at the off-white, single-strapped dress that wrapped around her neck. Her curves poked out in the right places, causing my dick to strain in my pants. "Yes, I told her you'd be very happy with the choices," Maya said, fixing my bow tie.

"Maybe we can cut out now," I joked.

Maya giggled, shaking her head.

"Son, I'm glad you came," Dad said, glaring at Maya.

I pulled Maya in tighter on my side.

"I came here for one reason," I responded.

"Mason, please, we're having a party, son. All of that fool-ishness can wait." Mother waved at a few friends.

"Can we get a photo of the family together?" A photogra-pher approached.

Maya started to walk away, and I pulled her in front of me. "Immediate family," Dad told me.

"She's my family," I replied through clenched teeth.

"Mason, it's okay," Maya said.

"See, even she knows," Mom remarked, keeping a fake smile on her face.

"As of right now, I'm no longer family." I leaned over and pecked my mother's cheek, turning to leave the party.

"Adam, fix this right now!" Mother shouted.

"Catherine, be quiet," he fussed.

We strolled out of the ballroom through the hallway, grip-

ping Maya's hand. I wanted to go back and punch my father in the face again but thought against it with so much media here tonight.

"Mason!" Erica yelled.

My head glanced to the left at my name being called, and I groaned, seeing Erica coming from the bathroom.

"Great," Maya grimaced, dropping my hand and trying to leave. I pulled her back to my side, kissing the side of her face.

"Why haven't you returned any of my calls?" Erica interro- gated me, ignoring Maya.

"Why would I do that?" I quizzed, not up for her manipu- lating the situation. She knew what Maya was dealing with and probably worked with my father to destroy her career.

"We both know this won't last," Erica muttered.

"Girl!" Maya started to charge at Erica, and I tightened my hold, pushing her behind me.

"Not here," I whispered in her ear.

"Let me go," Maya demanded.

"Promise you won't hit her," I mumbled so she would only hear me. She nodded in understanding. I released her and looked back at Erica.

"Erica, our time was over a long time ago. Move on."

"You don't mean that." Erica closed the space between us. "Step one more foot toward him and find out what happens," Maya spoke.

"Adam Norris probably paid you a lot of money, but he can't save you from her," I told her.

Erica pursued her lips, glaring at Maya and taking a step back.

"He promised to finance my film project if I helped break

you up," Erica confessed.

"What!" Maya gasped, covering her mouth in shock. "Mason, please come back into the party." Mother came from around the corner with my father. My body heated up, and I charged toward him and punched him in the face, hearing loud gasps and screams of surprise. His security came over and pulled me off. I jerked away, pulling Maya with me.

"I'm done with you." I marched out of their home and helped Maya into the limo, then Tony sped away.

❧ 8 ❧

SENATOR HILL

Sitting with my legs wide open, laying on the couch, I felt the tip of his dick against my lips, wanting entrance. I ran one hand down my torso, dipping my index finger between my folds, using my left hand to grip him in place. Licking from under the base of his balls, I pressed a kiss on the tip twice, fully taking him down my throat.

"Damn it, Maya!" His eyes narrowed.

"I believe you."

Seeing the way I had him almost ready to come undone, I removed my hand from my pussy and pushed toward his lips. He sucked my finger at the same time as I felt him thrust up in my mouth. Our moans grew louder and louder.

"Baby, make love to me," I whispered, popping him out of my mouth.

"Turn over."

Nodding in answer, I maneuvered on the couch with my back to his chest and felt his hands roam around my body.

"Stop teasing me."

Feeling his chest against my back, he grabbed my waist tight, placing kisses across my back, up to my neck and ear.

Gripping both breasts, I felt him thrusting inside, taking me off guard, and pushing through my walls.

"Ahhh..."

"Never doubt my love for you," Mason demanded, pulling my arms behind my back and pumping faster. Panting from the sensations of his touch, his gasps came in short spurts. Feeling his delicious thick member caused a tingling all over my body.

"Please..." I cried out.

My head spun as he released my arms, and I fell over the couch as his body fell on top of mine. Surrounding my clit with his finger, he tightened his right hand around my neck, biting my ear.

"I'm here, baby," he said, making me feel warm as the orgasms rolled around.

I whimpered, feeling heat wash over my face. Trembling in his hold, Mason slid out of me, turning around and making me straddle him.

"You're mine." He thrust up, never taking his eyes off me. I leaned back, caressing his balls and rotating my hips. Smacking my ass, I rode Mason until we were on the edge of a cliff.

"Fuck, you're sexy like this, baby," Mason said.

"Ohh... Yes..." I gasped.

"Sweetheart, I'm about to come."

"Come in me," I whimpered, tightening my thighs around

his dick. He growled, stroking faster, playing with my clit, with sweat seeping down our bodies.

"Ughh... Fuck! Maya," he cried out, pulling me into his chest, demanding my tongue.

I moaned into his mouth, pulling back and resting on top of

his chest, exhausted and hot. Rubbing my butt slowly, he kissed the top of my head, and I drifted off to sleep.

TWO HOURS LATER, I woke up in bed alone in the dark. I yawned, stretching my arms. I pulled the covers back and stepped out of bed. Taking the robe off the back of the door, I slid my feet in slippers and headed downstairs, looking around for Mason. I checked the kitchen, then his office without a trace. Sauntering out back toward the pool, I saw him sitting with a glass in his hand. I slid the door open and stepped outside, keeping the robe closed tight, wondering how long he had been out here.

"Hey," I said, sitting across from him on the chair.

"Sorry, I didn't mean to wake you."

"You know I only sleep if you're near me."

I stood from the chair and straddled his lap, taking the glass

out of his hand and guzzling it down.

"Eww ..." He patted my chest from tasting the sour scotch he loved so much. He chuckled, lifting his hands on my hips. "Can't handle scotch." Mason pressed a kiss on my chest. "Gross."

"I didn't want to wake you up."

"You talked to your parents?" I wondered.

Mason looked off.

"My mother tried calling, but I didn't answer."

"Maybe Jennifer's idea of me doing an interview would help."

"No." He tried to lift me off his lap.

"Wait! Just listen."

"Nothing to discuss."

"Baby, I hear you, but I would control the questions." "Things will blow over."

"It's been almost a week."

"Fine, but I'm going with you," Mason said.

"I never doubted you wouldn't." I laughed. He picked me up

with my legs wrapped around him.

"What are you doing? Mason, put me down."

He grinned, walking toward the pool. I tried to get down, and he tightened his grip.

"No, Mason!" He dropped in the pool with me in his arms. I came up for air pissed off, trying to catch my breath.

"Ughh! You asshole!" I splashed the water at him.

Mason chuckled, swimming toward me, pulling me into his chest.

"I love you," Mason said.

I pulled my hair into a bun, pushing him away.

"Asshole." I kissed him on the lips.

We decided to order food and watch a movie. I showered,

dried my hair, and emailed Jennifer to set up an interview with Lisa. The public would hear the truth and hopefully cut Adam Norris off at the knees.

❧

THE NEXT DAY, I KNOCKED ON THE DOOR OF Chelsey's office. I waited for her permission to come in when I heard whispering. A few seconds later, the door opened with a stern glare on Xavier's face.

"Did I interrupt something?" I tried to hold in my laugh, but it was hard with his eyes staring a hole in

Chelsey's direction. Obviously, they were doing something they shouldn't have been or probably often got away with, like Mason and me in his office.

"No, you didn't interrupt anything." Chelsey came around her desk and reached out for a hug.

"Hi, Xavier."

"Argh," he grunted, pecking Chelsey on the forehead, leaving her office.

"I hope he doesn't hate me for interrupting you guys."

"He'll get over it, and the man can't go one day without seeing or touching me." Chelsey plopped down in her chair.

"I understand. Mason's the same way."

"So what brings you by today?"

"I had to make a deposit, so I asked if you were working today."

"Being the manager, I end up working all hours of the day,"

Chelsey replied, fixing her top.

"Have you been to the club lately?" I asked.

"Xavier took me a week before everything happened, but

lately, no."

"I plan on going back."

"You should, as an adult. Owning our pleasure is no one's

business," Chelsey ranted.

"I needed to hear that."

"Are you ready for the interview with Lisa?"

"Yes, I plan on telling the truth. Whatever happens after

that, who knows."

She extended a hand, gripping my right palm.

"No matter what, you have our support."

"Thanks but let me get out of here. I doubt Xavier has

left." "He gets grumpy from time to time, now that he's running

multiple gyms."

"How's that going?"

"Amazing. Everyone wants to invest in his company. I hardly see him because of our schedules."

"As a girl in love, take the time to connect with your man." "You're right. Maybe I can go to lunch with him now,"

Chelsey mumbled, checking her watch.

Standing, we hugged once again, and she walked me out of

her office. We noticed Xavier talking to the security guard.

"He never left." I chuckled.

"Keep me updated, and I'll talk soon." Chelsey waved good-

bye, and I nodded, walking past Xavier. "She's all yours," I whispered to him. "I know," Xavier answered, smirking.

SENATOR HILL

A *week later.*

I sat in the chair at Lisa's news station, preparing to give an interview and discuss where things stood with my career. Some fellow Congressmen tried to get me to resign, but I refused and sent out a statement in the press that I would only do this interview one time and explain how this came to be. Mason still hadn't spoken with his family, but Erica did come out and apologize for getting involved after she tried to defame my name on social media. A grown woman stooped to high school bullying.

"How are you feeling?" Jennifer inquired, standing next to me in the makeup chair.

"Nervous."

"Kyla knows the questions; you should be fine."

"I hope so."

"Just remember to speak from the heart."

A knock at the door interrupted us.

"We're ready for you, Senator Hill," a crew member informed me.

"Okay, thank you," I replied.

"Is Mason here yet?" Jennifer asked.

I checked my phone, sliding off the chair. Smoothing my jacket down, I decided to wear a pantsuit for today in my favorite grey color. Something subtle and not over the top to give any critics a chance to overanalyze what I wore. Jennifer and I walked out of the room, heading to the set as I checked my message thread.

"Sorry I'm late." I looked up, hearing Mason speak.

He bent down to give me a hug.

"I thought you weren't coming," I said.

"Traffic," Mason responded, kissing my forehead.

"You'll sit right here, ma'am," the assistant told us.

"Okay. Is Lisa ready?" I questioned, and they looked over at

the other crew people.

"Senator Hill, I'm so glad to finally meet you." Barbara Mitchell reached her hand out for a shake.

"Where's Lisa?" I asked.

Barbara was notorious for being a gossip queen and trying to break people down on live TV. I expected Lisa, as my friend, to handle this situation delicately.

"I'm sorry, Lisa's been assigned to another story," Barbara answered, and the director motioned for me to sit down.

"Wait..."

"Action!" the director yelled out.

"Thank you for being with me today. I have Senator Hill joining us," Barbara said.

Barbara turned in her seat, holding up her note cards. I felt my throat close up.

"Senator Hill, please tell me and the audience why you deserve to be in this role?" Barbara questioned. "Excuse me?"

"Isn't it true you've been frolicking with a married man?" "That's a lie!"

"According to public opinion, you've been seen at some sex dungeon," Barbara continued, spouting out lies.

"I... I..."

"Please be honest; we as taxpayers want the truth of where our money goes."″

I fiddled with my hands, feeling like I was on the verge of throwing up.

"Barbara, I'm a single woman," I answered.

"But Erica Brownstone says you've been messing with her fiancé?" Barbara held up a notecard.

"I'm not sure where she got that idea, but Mason Norris is single," I scoffed, crossing my legs.

"Well, some people are saying you're with him for money. I mean his father is the speaker of the house," Barbara brought up.

"I have my own money." I ran my hand through my hair, feeling the lights bearing down on me.

"So the story in the *Daily News* of money being added onto the bill you're proposing is fake?"

A light bulb went off in my head at the mention of the bill I helped sponsor. The only person besides Adam Norris was Congressman Jones. They'd stepped into a different level of sabotage by making it seem like I was stealing money and dating a married man. Clearing my throat, I sat up straight, deepening my stare into her eyes.

"Barbara, my record speaks for itself. What I do in my private life is my business."

"Not if that hinders your job like dating the son of the speaker."

"Not a crime. Yes, it's abnormal, possibly, but he's single, and I'm single."

"Shouldn't you try to present a wholesome image and not some sex fiend?" Barbara said.

"Again, my private life is my business."

"What about these images that are circulating of you being tied up?" Barbara pointed at the screen, showing me in lingerie with a blindfold and Mason behind me.

"Something that shouldn't be shown without my permis- sion. I suggest you take this down right now because I'm done with this interview." I ripped off my microphone and stormed offset. I heard her call my name, but I didn't care to listen to a full-on setup trying to embar- rass me.

"Let's go," I told Jennifer, grabbing my purse and jacket with Mason next to me.

"Senator Hill! Wait, please," Barbara shouted, stopping me at the door.

"I was only doing my job," Barbara said.

"That was bullshit, and you know it."

"People like you think once you get into politics, it's all cookies and rainbows."

"You're right. I thought another woman would understand

what I'm going through."

She shrugged her shoulders.

"If you'd stop slutting yourself out, then..."

I punched her in the face, interrupting her last words. "Shit," Mason said.

"I think we need to go," Jennifer remarked, pulling me by

my arm out of the news station. I pulled my phone out of my pocket, dialing Lisa's number.

❧❦❧

LISA FLEW BACK INTO TOWN, AND I CALLED THE girls meeting at my house to discuss the events that happened since the interview.

"I promise I didn't know anything about this," Lisa pleaded. "Who made the change?"

"My producer called and said an important story came in,

and they needed me out of town," Lisa replied. "Sounds like Mason's father probably set you up," Chelsey explained.

"I'm starting to think that as well."

"What can I do?" Kyla said.

"Honestly, nothing."

"Maybe we can do another interview," Lisa mentioned, lifting the wine glass.

"I'm done with interviews."

"What did Mason say about everything?" Kyla queried.

"He's working with his lawyers to get the pictures removed from the internet." I flopped down in my seat, exhausted from having to deal with more drama of the recurring video of me punching Barbara.

"I have to say, you hit Barbara good. She hasn't spoken your name once," Lisa said.

"That's not funny, Lisa."

"You're right, but she deserved that punch." Lisa raised her hands in the air, surrendering.

"Maybe I should just resign."

"No!" everybody answered at the same time.

"Mason will fix this," Jennifer said.

"He's probably thinking of ways he can distance himself from me."

"Are you still staying with him?" Chelsey wondered.

"Yeah, I just came here today because I wanted to meet with

you guys."

"Things will blow over; give it time," Lisa stated.

"Turn that up," Jennifer called out, pointing at the TV screen with breaking news.

"We have breaking news coming from the Capitol," Barbara

spoke into the camera.

"Isn't that Adam Norris?" Lisa pointed at the screen. I nodded.

"Today, I'd like to show my support for Senator Hill and state that she's been nothing but a professional at all levels," Adam stated.

My mouth dropped in surprise at the complete change in his tone for me.

"The investigation concluded that Senator Hill did nothing wrong, and her private life is that... private," Adam said, reading from a piece of paper.

"What about the bill, sir?" a reporter called out.

"It's come to my attention that some things were mishan- dled by my staff. Senator Hill did nothing wrong," Adam replied.

I smirked, knowing Mason probably had something to do with his father throwing his support around me.

"Again, Senator Hill is a fine congresswoman and deserves the support from the rest of her colleagues and me."

Jennifer turned the TV down, raising a glass toward me and passing one to Chelsey and Lisa.

"Time to celebrate! To Senator Hill." Jennifer popped the bottle of red wine open, pouring in each of our glasses. I was ready to sulk away with alcohol all night, but now things were looking up for me.

$\maltese$ 10 $\maltese$

MASON

hree hours earlier

My father glared at me as I stood in his chambers with an envelope in my hand, ready to bring his entire career down. I tried to always stay out of his way, and he stayed out of mine, but coming for the woman I loved was something I couldn't stand for any longer.

"I'm not going to ask you again." He dropped the envelope on his desk.

"What's this?" He picked it up, turning it around removing the documents.

"Something you'd prefer to not get out."

Adam Norris was stealing not only from his charity but taking bribes from the businesses he approved to get government contracts. I had my private investigator dig into his back- ground who brought me something I could use as a final negotiating tactic. I didn't want to stoop to this level with my own father, but he left me no choice. Congressman Jones co-sponsored some of these bills, and the one Maya proposed would have put a spotlight on what they were doing. So it was easy to make her seem like some homewrecker and have Erica pretend in the media like we were engaged.

"Where did you get this?"

"I have my sources."

"Do you understand what you're doing, Mason?"

"Yeah, protecting my woman."

"This would hurt your mother and our family!" he shouted. "Then I suggest you do the right thing."

"It wasn't my idea."

"Money was always more important to you."

"You're selfish."

He slammed the papers on his desk, jumping up and pointing in my face.

"I'm your father! She's—"

"Say it! I dare you." I glared at him.

"Get out of my office."

"Gladly, and I suggest you make a statement publicly, or this

will go viral."

"Mason, think about this before you make a bigger problem."

"All my life, you've tried to control me, and now it stops." "We're family!" he argued.

"No, you want me to follow like the rest of your minions

and make you look good while robbing people blind." I pointed to the documents on his desk.

"Silly fool."

"Does Mom know?" I questioned.

"No," he muttered, running a hand down his face.

"What happened to you?"

"It's called politics. You have to play with the big boys."

"Sell your soul for money."

He snarled, coming around his desk and pushing his finger
in my face.

"Go ahead, judge me, but this lifestyle helped you get to where you are now."

"There you go once again, always trying to act as if I owe you something."

"Get out of my office." He pointed toward the door. "Just remember, I have copies of everything."

⚜

THE NEXT DAY, FINALLY MAKING IT HOME, I WAS exhausted after working overtime to make sure Maya didn't have any more issues with my father and his team. I had planned on going to the club to finish paperwork after closing the deal to open more clubs in Chicago and New York. My stomach growled as I locked my door and headed into the kitchen to grab a bottle of water. I gulped it down, standing at the counter, letting tiredness peak. Feeling my phone vibrate, I groaned, not wanting to talk to anyone. I pulled it out and opened the messages, seeing Maya's name pop up.

My World: Come upstairs.

I was intrigued by her being here since we rarely stayed at my place or the club. I finished off the bottle and tossed it in the trash. Turning the phone on Do Not Disturb, I jogged upstairs and pushed the bedroom door open, smirking at the display before me.

"This is a surprise." Maya was completely naked, lying in my bed with only her red heels on.

"I hoped for a good surprise." She crawled off the bed, stalking over to me with determination in her eyes.

Grasping my hand, she walked me over to the bed and pushed me down.

"What do I owe for this surprise?"

Maya stood in front of me with her hands on both sides of my face, bent down to peck my lips.

"Thank you for supporting me with your family."

"I'd do anything for you," I assured, running a hand up her thigh.

"I believe you, Mason."

"So does this mean..." I helped her to straddle my lap. Clasping my hand behind her neck, I pulled her in close, forcing my tongue inside and exploring her fully. Rubbing against her engorged clit, I snarled, wanting to eat her pussy and listening to her cry out in pleasure. Tossing her on the bed, I removed my shirt and pants, and stared into her eyes. Tweaking her brown nipple, I squeezed, taking my favorite pillows into my mouth at the same time.

"Mason... Oh God—"

"Let me hear you, baby."

Feeling her leaking down her thighs, I watched her fall back

into the pillows in a daze. Wanting to tease her some more, I pinched her nipple, hearing her moans get louder.

"Baby, you're so wet," I murmured, watching her juices cover my fingers.

She shuddered against me, dipping one, two, then three fingers into her folds.

"I'm going to fuck the shit out of you." My breath brushed against her ear.

"Yesss!" she panted, opening her legs wider. Sucking on her neck, I slid my dick in and paused, feeling her tight, warm core surrounding me. I bent down, sucking one plump breast in my mouth, watching her squirm in my arms as I slowly moved in and out.

"Uhhhh... fuck." She dug her nails in my back.

"I'm drowning here, baby; you feel so good."

Kissing on her lips, our eyes locked, and my chest swelled with love knowing she was the one for me. Squeezing her thighs, I pulled back, thrusting faster as I felt her getting close to her climax.

"Come for me, Maya," I demanded.

Gripping the sheets, there was a look of rawness, longing for this to never end, and I'd make it my mission to always give her body pleasure.

"Oh my God! I'm coming," she screamed, running a hand down my chest, brushing against my balls.

"Aghhh, shit!" I released, falling over on the bed beside her, out of breath. She leaned over, running her tongue over my nipple. I grasped the back of her head, cupping her sex.

"Mmmmm..." She opened her legs wider.

Wrapping a hand around her throat, I said, "Next time I have to use the flogger with you." I smacked her ass.

"Promise?" I grinned. "Keep teasing me like this..." Rubbing her back, I crawled between her legs. "How are you feeling about things?"

"Did you talk to your father?"

"You don't need to worry about that."

Maya smiled, caressing my cheek.

"I'm hungry."

"What are you hungry for?" Gliding my tongue down her stomach, I noticed her breathing heightened as her eyes rolled in the back of her head.

"What would you suggest?"

"Maybe I could cook your favorite lasagna with red wine and Italian bread." She sucked in her breath when I slid a finger across her bud.

"That sounds good." Maya reached down, placing her hands on my shoulders.

"Perfect."

I placed another kiss on her lips, moving off her and reaching for my robe. Maya wrapped the cover around her naked body.

"When are we going back to Club Seek?" She placed her arm up on the bed, cupping the side of her face.

"I didn't think you'd want to go back so soon." Pulling her robe off the back of the door, I helped her out of bed to follow me to the kitchen. Maya stepped in front of me, cupping my face and staring into my eyes.

"What we do isn't wrong, and I won't let anyone dictate our relationship." She bit my bottom lip, moaning and sucking on my lips, snaking her tongue around mine. Wrapping my arms around her waist, I groaned, wanting to go for another round but hearing my stomach growl at the same time.

"More of that later. I'm starving." I pulled back from the kiss.

"Yes, sir. I love you," she said. "I love you more."

EPILOGUE: SENATOR HILL

Two Years Later.

I turned the TV off from the endless cycle of reporters talking about my life choices, and what I'd done in the past and how my life with Mason started in not the most realistic of ways. People didn't know me but claimed to speak with sources that could verify every little detail of when I first lost my tooth as a baby. Chuckling at the thought, I finished typing out emails and sending text messages. I rose from my seat, walking out of my office after finishing another meeting with Jennifer. Today's debate was about funding for our schools. I forced the speaker to finally listen to what I had to say after he found out Mason and I eloped. I wasn't trying to hide what we had and how we started, but I wanted to keep my personal life private. After the storm that almost brought me down, my goal was to be attuned with the people I knew and aware that it may seem friendly, but the beast of politics was very much real.

"You ready to go to lunch?" I turned around at the voice

that kept me weak in the knees every night in our bedroom. He

still had that devilish smile and sexy full lips that I missed kissing when I got out of bed this morning.

"I didn't expect you for another ten minutes," I spoke, standing from my desk, and headed into his open arms.

He kissed me on the cheek, lifted my chin, and bit my bottom lip. He slid a hand around my waist to pull me in close.

"Daddy!" our daughter called out, trying to push my face away. I chuckled at her movements. She was so spoiled and only wanted to be the number one girl in his eyes. Malia reminded me of Mason's cocky demeanor in the early days of our courtship. He was determined to make me fall in love, and I tried to push him away, but love broke through the walls, and I more than made up for our time, learning to balance my career and family life. Mason held my hand while holding Malia in his arms, escorting us over to the conference room. I was making an announcement on the launch of a new program for women in business after negotiating enough votes for a year to pass the bill.

"You two look so cute together." Jennifer walked up next to me, carrying my notes.

I smiled. "Thanks. Is everybody here?"

Tony stood in his usual spot, holding the door open for us, and the reality of winning re-election for another term was the most important thing to me. I was grateful for all the support. Since the events of the past still ran through social media, I had to be careful with how I responded at times.

"Senator Hill, are you planning to run again?" a reporter in the back yelled out. The room went completely quiet, and the stares focused on me. Today's announcement was about the outstanding accomplishments we'd made, but it seemed gossip and drama might cloud the subject. I glanced at Mason and Malia. He kissed her on the cheek, winked at me, and I smiled, knowing he supported me in my decision.

"I was waiting to do this at another time. But I can announce that—"

"OMG!" Another reporter from CBG News shoved their phone to the reporter next to them.

I cleared my throat, about to respond.

"Is that Lisa Reyes?" Hearing Lisa's name caused me to tense. I covered the microphone with my hand, stepping over to Jennifer.

"You need to call Lisa," Jennifer whispered, passing me her phone. I saw a broadcast video of the news station where she worked with a breaking news story with Lisa and Morris in a video clip at Club Seek.

"This can't be happening," I mumbled under my breath. "Senator Hill, what do you have to say about the video?" "Senator Hill, do you think Lisa did this on purpose?" Everyone threw questions at me, and all I wanted to do was call Lisa and see how she was doing.

"Lisa Reyes is a close friend, and I ask that everyone respect her privacy." Mason reached for my hand as we walked out of the room together. Keeping my head high, I shook inside, feeling sick to my stomach that someone was doing the same thing to Lisa they did to me.

"Senator Hill! Senator Hill!" Photographers continued shouting my name for attention, heading toward our town car. Tony opened the door, and I slid inside, with Mason next to me. I unbuttoned my jacket, reaching into my pocket to grab my cell. Pulling up the video again showed her in a red lingerie set. Morris was behind her, gripping her hair in his hands. Closing the video, I went to social media, and there was non- stop coverage of the video being replayed and calls for her to step down.

"I can't believe this is happening."

"Mommy, what's wrong?" Malia asked, laying her head on my shoulder. I lifted her in my arms and placed her in my lap.

"Just remember, no matter what happens in life, Malia, seek out what makes you happy."

Tony clicked on the turn signal to pull into traffic, Jennifer turned her phone off from the constant alerts, and Mason grasped my hand and brought it up to his lips.

"Are you having regrets?" Mason wondered.

"I only regret never putting this first." I motioned my hand between the three of us, and a smile tugged at the corner of his lips.

🕸

I HOPE YOU ENJOYED MAYA AND MASON'S STORY. Please also check out **"Seeking To Touch Book 2"** next.

Lisa, a TV news anchor, is used to pressure at the job, but when she learns that someone is about to leak a video of her at a sex club, the pressure could make her life implode. If she doesn't do something to stop it, she'll lose her job, her family will disown her, and that's only the beginning.

Enlisting the help of her best friend's husband's business partner and security agent to help her may be her only hope. If they can find out who is behind the scheme, her worries are over... she hopes.

Can they figure out who is out to ruin her before it's too late?

❧ II ❧

LISA

It was ten at night, and a cool breeze flowed in Tennessee as my heels hit the gravel of the sidewalk in my new Stuart Weitzman custom shoes. I ordered them a week ago specifically for tonight. The black Andria strap heel paired perfectly with my off-the-shoulder short dress and side split. I had my hair pulled back in a bun with minimum makeup at his request. It wasn't like this was my first time; watching as Tony turned the lights off in the car parked down the street from my destination gave me comfort. He was Maya's security and driver, but she'd ask him if he'd accompany me whenever I made a trip over here. Looking from right to left, I raised my hand and knocked on the door, waiting to be let in like any other time. The place was mysterious, forbidden, and exotic to a regular person, but to me, it brought out a feeling of belonging. When Maya introduced this world, I hadn't looked back since. Once the door opened, I smiled to see my favorite bodyguard on duty tonight.

"Stephen."

"He's been waiting for you." Stephen helped to pull off my coat, and he whistled.

"Behave." I shook my index finger in front of his face.

"Never." He chuckled, and I giggled, shaking my head as I walked off down the long hallway of the entrance. I was grateful Maya had introduced me to Mason and allowed my entry into Club Seek. I was going on the fourth visit. I hadn't planned to stay too long since I needed to work early in the morning. As a reporter, our schedules changed if a breaking story popped up. As the head anchor, I had a duty to be ready and willing to get the correct information to the audience. Moving through the crowds, I took note of the new paintings Mason had hanging on the walls. The place still had the same old feel of a nightclub but an upscale adult lounge. Approaching the bar, I smiled at Sharon, who already had my drink ready for me before I even ordered. I was becoming a regular by now, or it probably had something to do with the person I was here to see.

"One apple martini." Sharon placed a fresh napkin next to the glass.

"How did you know this was the drink for the night?"

She winked, pointing over my shoulder.

"He wanted to make sure you were comfortable."

I lifted the glass and scanned the room when I noticed him standing near the crowd of couples huddled together in the corner. His watching me as I stared back gave me chills about what my night would entail.

"Don't keep him waiting too long."

Taking a sip turned into me gulping the entire martini down in one take. I nodded in response and placed it back on the counter.

"Thanks, Sharon."

Strolling through the crowd, a guy bumped into me, spilling a little of his drink on my dress.

"Shit, sorry about that." He tried to wipe the stain off.

"It's okay."

"No, let me buy you a new drink."

I felt a touch on my lower back, glanced behind me, and knew things would only get worse.

"The lady doesn't need you to buy her anything."

"My bad, Morris," the guy muttered, stepping back.

"She's with me."

I rolled my eyes; he always needed to be in control.

"It was an accident."

"Sorry again."

"Yeah." Morris grasped my hand and pulled me away, stalking down the hall to his office. Opening the door, he pulled me inside and pushed me up against the wall.

"Are you trying to drive me crazy?"

He reached out, gripping my left thigh.

"Depends."

"On what?"

"How many orgasms I get tonight?"

He growled, gripped the bottom of my chin tight, and bit my lip.

"Is that what you're seeking tonight?"

"For your touch. Yes."

"All you had to do was ask."

Morris leaned down, capturing my lips. I raised both arms up, locked them around his neck, and pulled him in close. Lifting me in his arms, sucking and nibbling on my bottom lip, he carried me over to his desk and pushed everything to the floor. I worked fast to unbuckle his pants, helping to remove his jacket and remove my dress.

"Let's... go... to my room." He trailed kisses down my neck.

I shook my head no.

"Here is fine." I squeezed his thick wood through his pants.

His tongue ran across my shoulder, up to my neck. Our eyes never left each other when he extended his hand, releasing my breasts. I thumbed my nipple, squeezing. He bent down, sucking it into his mouth.

"You want this, Lisa." He caught my chin with his index finger.

I planted both hands on his shoulders, holding him in place, squirming. I was so wet and ready to feel him.

"Mmmmm... Morris." I panted as he eased in my opening.

"Hmmm..."

Clenching my thighs around his waist, he thrust and kissed me hungrily, gripping the back of my neck. My eyes closed as he dragged his lips to the curve of my neck, making me shiver in place. I gasped, feeling his girth move faster and faster as our bodies crashed together, tightening my muscles around him.

"Stop... you playing games." A growl spilled out.

"Morris! Yessss... I'm coming."

He pulled out of me and turned me around, forcing me to lie on my stomach. I grasped the edge of the desk, and he slipped back into me.

"Uhhhh... All I ever need." I made an inaudible noise.

"Fuckk!" he groaned behind me, pushing one more time and feeling the condom fill up. I leaned up, fixed my dress, cupped his face, and sucked on his tongue. Morris gripped my ass and held me close in his arms.

"Let's go to your place," he said.

"Maybe another time," I replied, grabbed my purse, and checked my makeup.

"Where are you going?" He gripped me by the elbow.

"Home. I need to work early in the morning."

"So, this was a hit and run?" he questioned.

"Morris, stop thinking like that." I kissed him again on the lips, patted him on the chest, and walked out.

⁂

THE NEXT DAY, I WOKE UP BRIGHT AND EARLY TO MEET my contact at a local coffee shop for a story I wanted to tell. Being a reporter, sometimes people looked at me as a threat. Sometimes there were reporters who only looked to exploit people. I prided myself on being the person who rooted out the bad guy and worked for the people without a voice. When everything went down with Maya, I did everything in my power to turn the story around, having them do a new interview with me as a couple—diving into her accomplishments as senator and more. When she decided to run for re-election, the numbers increased for most likely to vote. Then I felt a duty to always tell the truth and be honest above everything else. I put the car in park and took the keys out, making sure I had my recorder and notepad. I got out of the car and headed inside; the young woman was already sitting down. I slid into the booth across from her and smiled.

"How are you, Marisal?"

She scanned the room.

"Nervous."

I reached a hand across the table and patted hers.

"I promise it won't be as bad as you think."

"Are you sure you weren't followed?"

"I wasn't followed; I can make it anonymous."

"I think that's best."

"Sure, let's get started." I removed the recorder from my pocket and put it on the table as the waitress approached.

"Hello, can I get you something to drink?" the short older woman with auburn hair asked.

"Can I get an iced latte and anything she wants?"

"Water is fine," Marisal said.

"Okay, I'll be right back with that," the waitress replied.

I took out my notepad and pen, ready to get the goods on Rhett and his business.

"All right, so tell me exactly what you know about Rhett."

Marisal looked around the shop nervously, and I reached out to comfort her.

"No one knows I'm here, and you're safe."

"He's paying people to push us out," Marisol explained.

"Do you have any evidence?"

"I overheard some guys roughing up a few tenants."

"I will need more evidence before I can go to my boss."

"I'm not getting more involved than I already have."

The waitress came back to the table, dropping our drinks on the table.

"Thank you."

"If he finds out it was me..." Marisal whispered.

"Nothing will happen to you, I promise."

"You don't have a family to worry about."

I sighed, turned the recorder off, and put it back in my coat.

"Look, I can't force you to talk to me. What I'm doing can be dangerous, but it's not just about you and me. We need to get this guy."

"Let me think about it."

"I understand. Here, take my cell phone number and call me if you change your mind." I pulled a business card out and wrote my cell on the back of the card. I hurried out of the booth, removed twenty dollars, and tossed it on the table to pay for our drinks.

"Call me if you change your mind," I called out, and she smiled.

I strolled out of the café and felt around my pocket for my phone, seeing a voice message I missed from my mom. Tommy and Erin were old school and wanted their daughter to go to medical school or become a lawyer. They felt being a reporter wouldn't be real work with too much inconsistency. I took after my mom with my long, wavy, black hair, short, curvy figure, and small button nose. From my dad, I got my attitude and work ethic to always strive for what I wanted even if he disagreed with my career choice.

"Hey, Mommy."

"Why have I not heard from my child?" Mom questioned.

I rolled my eyes, popped the door open, and dropped my bag before putting my seatbelt on.

"Mommy, you know I have to work."

"Work, work, work."

"I promise I will have lunch with you soon."

"Your father is the same way."

"Where's your husband anyway?"

"Your father is playing with his fishing rod."

I chuckled, knowing it pissed her off when she felt ignored by us whenever she wanted attention.

"Leave Daddy alone."

"Get over here soon."

"I will."

"Love you."

"Love you, old lady."

"Bye, child." She ended the call, and I chuckled at her childishness.

I started the car and drove off, heading back to pull an all-nighter on this story.

❦ 12 ❦

LISA

A week later.

Kyla opened the door, and I stepped inside, holding a bottle of wine for our girls' night celebration. Removing my jean jacket, I placed it on the coatrack, kicked off my black ankle boots, and passed her the bottle of wine to open.

"How is filming going?"

I rolled up my sleeves, following her to the kitchen.

"Do you need help with anything?"

"Nope, you're my guest. Have a seat." Kyla grabbed the wine cork out of the drawer, as I reached up for four wine glasses.

"Where's Chelsey and Maya?"

"Should be arriving soon. Maya is at work, and Chelsey is leaving the bank."

"That reminds me... I need to ask Chelsey about opening an account for my goddaughter."

"Which one, Cailey or Amber?"

"Cailey is finally heading to college, and I wanted to get her a gift. As the best godmother in the world, I planned on giving her a bank account with a thousand dollars to start."

"I don't know what's worse, them being older or us getting old," she joked, pouring the red wine in the glasses.

"Both." The doorbell rang, and I hopped out of my seat in the kitchen and ran toward the door.

"Coming! Hold your horses."

I opened the door, stepped to the side, and gave Maya and Chelsey a hug.

"You both look like you need this more than me."

"I need the whole bottle," Maya replied and took the glass out of my hand.

"Well, okay then."

Chelsey plopped down on the couch and closed her eyes, not saying a word.

"What's up with her?" I whispered to Maya.

"Not sure, she was quiet on the way here," Maya answered.

"Ummm... Chelsey, you okay, sweetie?"

Chelsey popped one eye open.

"Men," Chelsey muttered.

"Kyla, grab another bottle; it's going to be a long night," I called out.

Maya removed her coat and took a seat on the opposite side of the couch from me.

"What do you have to eat, Kyla?" Maya questioned.

Kyla came out of the kitchen with two more glasses of wine on a tray with snacks.

"I have all of your favorites. It's been awhile since we've been together," Kyla said.

"Good, cause I'm ready to pig out." Maya gulped the wine down, stood, and went toward the kitchen.

"Chelsey, spill the beans. What's going on?" Kyla asked.

"Work. My father is trying to bring in another manager at the bank."

"I thought you ran the bank." I tucked my feet under my leg, sitting sideways.

"I do, but he still can have a say in things."

"How is your brother doing?" I asked.

"Fine. He's married and a father now," Chelsey answered, picking a cracker and cheese off the tray.

"Tonight is about us unwinding, so no talk about work," Kyla said.

"Wait... did you get the film role?" Maya asked.

Kyla nodded, and their eyes met.

"I did. I'm super excited to be in a meaty role finally and not the sexy girlfriend."

"What about you, Lisa? How are things at the news station?" Maya inquired.

"Good, until I have to curse Ryan out."

"What did he do now?"

"Same old thing, but I have a story I'm working on that could get me in a good position for morning news."

"Okay, now get to the good stuff. I haven't been back to Club Seek, because work is piling up," Chelsey questioned.

"I was there a week ago with Mason," Maya responded, turning music on the radio.

"I have plans to go back sometime this month," Kyla said.

All eyes scanned toward me. I shifted in my seat, not wanting to give myself away at how much I loved being at the club with Morris.

"Someone must have gone recently to be so quiet now," Kyla teased.

"Like last night," I mumbled under my breath and covered my face with my hands.

"I was waiting for you to say something. I overheard

Morris talking to Mason about you."

"That man drives me up a wall." Folding my arms across my chest, I sighed in annoyance.

"I bet money you won't say that to his face," Chelsey joked.

"Girl, no, and risk not getting any. I think not." I laughed, high-fiving Maya.

Kyla jumped up and strolled to the kitchen.

"I'm still surprised you've lasted this long. Lisa, you know relationships aren't your thing," Maya said.

"We're both surprised. I didn't think I would be able to hold out." Kyla brought out another tray of food: wings, pizza, and sushi.

"This all looks good," Chelsey said.

"It's still early, but I have hope he won't give me a reason to dump him."

All three of them burst out in laughter.

"What's so funny?"

"I think we're more worried about Morris than you," Maya responded.

"Morris knows how I feel."

We all looked around, hearing a phone ring. I rose off the couch and grabbed my coat to see it was my phone.

"Hello... Hello."

Not receiving an answer, I hung up.

"Who was that?" Chelsey asked.

"Probably the wrong number."

"Where's Morris anyway tonight?" Kyla asked.

"With my brother and Mason, playing cards."

"Xavier had to work at the gym, and my brother had the baby tonight," Chelsey said.

"Tonight is about hanging out with my girls, and I will do a couple things another day."

"So, tell us about this news story," Maya insisted.

I ROSE OUT OF BED THE NEXT DAY WITH A LIGHT hangover. The girls filled me in on everything that was happening. I was so happy to hear that Kyla received the part she'd been wanting for so long. Chelsey was still dealing with her family's annoyance, and Maya was in the early stages of wanting to run for office again. Today, I had a meeting with Rhett Fuller and wanted to see if he'd admit to the accusations of criminal activity with forcing people out. I strolled out of the bathroom and grabbed my vibrating phone. Seeing Morris' name across the screen, I didn't have time to call him back.

Morris: Why didn't you come over?

Me: Sorry, I lost track of time.

Morris: What are you doing today?

Me: I have work and meetings.

Morris: We can do lunch.

Me: I have a huge story; I can't do lunch.

I dropped the phone on the bed and went to my closet to pick out a comfortable dress suit for my meeting. My phone rang, and I grunted in frustration. I looked back at my phone to see Morris was calling. I hit decline and turned the phone off.

"I'll call him later," I muttered, finished finding something to wear.

An hour later, I arrived at the Fuller Industries office building, showing my ID to security.

"Hello. Do you have an appointment?" She moved the clipboard in front of me, and I looked down, seeing it was for appointments only. I signed my name and nodded.

"Yes, I have an appointment with Rhett Fuller."

"Lisa Reyes."

"That's me."

She typed my information in the computer, and a visitor badge printed out. I attached it to my suit jacket.

"You can have a seat, and someone will be out to escort you back."

"Thank you."

I scanned the front office; it wasn't much to look at compared to other millionaire slimeballs who tried to take advantage of the little people. His taste was more homely style of brown and black colors, with pictures hanging on the wall of him and his staff.

"Lisa Reyes." I heard my name called and glanced up.

"Yes." I stood and followed the young girl through the employee entrance.

"Mr. Fuller is finishing up with a call. You have to go right in and have a seat." She pointed to his open office door, and I thanked her, heading inside. His back was to me, and I stood near the entrance, peering around the room. His office was way different from the front lobby. Everything was marble and silver in color. A table held photos of himself and awards, and a wide window faced the front of the building.

"Miss Reyes, sorry to keep you waiting."

"Huh." I zoned out, not hearing his comment.

"I apologize for leaving you waiting."

"No worries."

"Please have a seat." He motioned toward the seat in front of his desk.

"Thank you, Mr. Fuller."

"Call me Rhett."

"Well, you may not like that after this conversation."

"Oh, what is this about?" He sat up straight in his chair.

"It's about you pushing people out of their homes."

"Who are you with?"

"I'm a reporter."

He jumped up out of his seat.

"Leave."

"Mr. Fuller, I'd think you would want to make it known if you're doing things legally or not."

"Miss Reyes, I wouldn't go down this road if I were you."

He leaned over his desk and pointed his finger in my face. I stood, staring into his eyes.

"I don't intimidate easily, Mr. Fuller."

"My business dealings have nothing to do with you."

"It's about the people you're hurting and leaving homeless."

Rhett hit the call button on his desk.

"Yes, Mr. Fuller?" the receptionist asked.

"Send security up here and escort Miss Reyes out of here."

"No need for security. I'll see my way out."

His nostrils flared, turning bright red with his fists clenched together.

"Right away, sir," the receptionist replied.

A second later, two security guards opened the door, waiting. I grinned, took a business card out of my purse, and placed it on his desk.

"Hopefully, you'll change your mind."

I turned and headed out of his office, with security following. Once out of the building, I looked back at the building, glanced over to the office window, and waved. I slid in my car and drove off feeling excited that I rattled his cage. Peering at the clock on the radio, I saw it was still early and could meet with Morris before I needed to be at the station. I called Kyla while enroute to Morris.

"Hello..." Kyla drew out.

"Are you sitting down?" I asked.

"Uhhh... no."

"What are you doing?"

"At the gym."

"Well, I couldn't wait to tell someone. I just came from Rhett's office."

"Who?"

"Rhett Fuller, the guy I'm doing the story on."

"The millionaire real estate guy?" Kyla questioned.

I stopped at the red light, when all of a sudden, I heard a loud horn behind me, and a car sped past me, with someone cursing me out.

"That was weird."

"What's all that noise?"

"Somebody just drove through a red light."

"Crazy people everywhere. It's Tennessee." Kyla chuckled.

"You're right. I'm almost at the club."

"Kind of early to be at the club."

I bit my bottom lip.

"My energy is on high right now; I need to release some tension."

"Hmm... huh."

I pulled in around the VIP parking area and turned the car off.

"How long are you going to be at the gym?"

"Probably another hour, then I need to run home and study my lines."

I checked my makeup in the mirror, pushed the door open, and glanced around to make sure no one was out.

"Okay, we should have dinner one day this week."

"That's fine. Call me with the details."

"Will do." I ended the call, knocked on the door, and heard the camera moving in the upper-right corner, scanning down on me. Finally, the door opened, and I went back to Morris' office to look for him.

❦ 13 ❦

MORRIS

I blew out the candles, tossing the matches on the table, arching a brow, and staring at my beautiful creation. Lisa was held up in a three-sixty spinning swing set, with her legs open, wearing a red bra and thong. We hadn't talked in a few days since our last encounter in my office, and I needed to make things clear before we moved further. My little devil liked to play hard and pretend what we were doing wasn't a full-blown relation- ship. After declining my calls earlier and not showing up at my place the other night, today, she was mine, and I was hers. Her eyes were covered as I approached the bed, ran a hand across her tight ass. To find a woman who loved to be fucked aggressively and worshipped was a breath of fresh air. How she committed to Club Seek and all aspects heightened my desire for her. Hearing her sharp breaths at the lightest touch of my hand, caused my dick to twitch in my boxers. I gripped the head, easing the ache to be inside her to calm down.

"You have me ready to fuck before we talk."

"We can talk afterwards..." She moaned when my finger slid between her thong.

"What did I tell you about trying to run things in here?" I removed my hand and tapped her lightly on the right butt cheek.

"Sorry, sir."

"Good girl." I bent my left knee and climbed up on the bed with my chest to her back.

"Please touch me," she rasped.

"I will in time. First, I want to hear you beg."

I dropped to my knees, turned her around, slid the thong to the side, and brushed my lips against her inner thigh. Moving from the left to the right and pressing kisses, I skimmed my hands up and down her stomach, to her feet as I slid my tongue along her slit.

"Oohh... God." She trembled in my hold.

"I've been waiting all day for this."

"She's ready for you, baby."

Her wetness seeped through and down my chin, nothing like pleasing and hearing her cry out for me to stop torturing with my tongue. The need and want in her voice only encouraged me more. When Maya and Mason first introduced her to me, I didn't want anything to do with this woman. We were both considered dominant, not only in life, but in the bedroom. After our second time together, I made it known that I was in charge by betting I could give her four orgasms in one night. I drove my tongue from her sweet lips to her butt, nipping at each cheek.

"Morris, please!" she yelped.

Pushing my finger in her back door, she gasped at the sensation as my tongue continued sucking her sex.

"She is so wet, baby. Ready for me to own her," I said, removing my finger and letting her have a moment to cool down. I reached over to the chest and grabbed some wipes to clean my hands. Throwing them in the trash and removing my boxers, I picked up a condom and slid him against her lips up to taste. She stuck her tongue out, wanting to taste.

"Will get to that later, baby."

Lining my shaft to her entrance, I eased in slow, nibbling on my bottom lip. She was warm and so tight, I was ready to burst.

"Fuck!" I needed to think of something else before I came too early.

Gripping her by the hips, I moved in slow, gradually keeping my pace so we were both coming undone. Taking my right hand, I grasped her covered right breasts, sucking on her stiff chocolate nipple that I loved to fall asleep against at night.

"Shit, you feel good."

"Ahhh... Sir!"

"You want me to fuck you, baby?"

Nodding her head, I grinned, knowing I was about to wear her out. Biting and licking the pain away, I went to the left breast, holding her in place by the shoulder. I thrust upwards faster. Her breasts bounced up and down, watching them call for another round of my tongue to envelop.

"Damn, you're everything to me, Lisa," I grunted, feeling her juices cover my dick.

"I'm... coming!" she yelled.

"You know better." I yanked out of her, dipped my tongue back inside, closed my eyes, and gripped both her ass cheeks.

WE FINISHED TWO HOURS LATER AFTER GOING FOR A third round on the floor, and I promised to have her again when I got back in town in three days. She reached her wrist out for me to tighten the clasp on her bracelet that fell off.

"Where are you going again?" she questioned.

"It's a new account with a client looking for security at their mall," I said, sliding my navy-blue suit jacket on.

"Why do you have to be gone for three days?" She poked her lips out and frowned.

"We're not together, so why are you questioning me?" Her brow hiked in surprise.

"Morris, don't start." She waved off the conversation and went to grab her shoes from the floor.

"Either we're a couple or not, but you don't get to question me."

She was flushed at my statement.

"I have to get home and work on a story."

"There you go, running out of here before it gets too heated."

"When have I ever run from anything?" She stepped in front of me, and I grabbed her around the waist, pulling her close to my chest.

"You keep the same attitude, see what happens." I kissed her forehead and let her go, and I went back to my office.

KNOCK! KNOCK!

"Yeah."

"I was going through these figures and wanted to get your opinion." Mason stepped in, holding some documents. Being a silent partner, I didn't get involved as much with the day-to-day things about the club. My security company was my primary focus, and I was expanding to Vegas, possibly moving if things worked out in my favor.

"You know I hate looking at numbers."

"Well, too bad. You're part owner." He dumped them on my desk, and I groaned.

"Asshole."

"You packed for Vegas?" he asked.

"Yep."

"I saw Lisa here earlier. Everything good?"

"Fine."

"Something tells me you're not exactly happy with being fine."

I sighed, pushing the forms away from me.

"She's pissed that I'm going out of town."

"It's for work."

"I know that, and I told her, but she's freaked out."

"Headstrong like Maya, and only wants us on their time."

"What did you do to get her as your wife?" I inquired.

"I told her."

I laughed at his words and ran a hand down my face.

"I'll try to remember that."

"Go home or finish working. Take your mind off Lisa and let her come to you," Mason explained.

"I don't know."

"Either you set boundaries now, or you'll be second guessing always." Mason shrugged his shoulders, slid his hands in his pockets, and walked out of my office.

I went through the numbers again, signed off, and made notes on what I would change to make it run smoothly.

Knock! Knock!

"Come in."

"You've been hiding back here all this time," Claire said.

She was a waitress at the club and one time a lover of mine. It was never anything serious, but we became friends. She worked here to put herself through college.

"Guilty," I chortled, sending out an email.

Claire held up a tray with a glass filled.

"Here, I thought you could use this."

"How'd you know?"

"All day, you've been snapping at people." She grinned and sat at the edge of the desk.

"Work stuff."

"You look annoyed."

"I wanted to apolo—" I was surprised at Lisa standing at my office door.

I jumped out of my seat and put the glass down on the desk.

"I see you're busy right now. Have a good flight, Morris," Lisa said as she left.

"Wait!" I yelled, jogging to catch up to her.

"No worries. We can talk when you're back."

"Lisa, stop running." I grasped her arm and nudged her against the car door.

"Go back inside. Your girlfriend is probably mad you're out here with me." She rolled her eyes and looked around, not giving me eye contact.

I smirked. "You're jealous."

"Jealous! Morris, leave me alone." She tried to push me back.

"Claire is a waitress and friend."

"Morris, I'm not stupid."

I gripped her jaw and forced her to face me.

"Claire is nothing to me."

"Then why was she sitting on your desk?"

"So, we question each other now."

"We do when—" she started to say but caught herself.

"What was that?"

"When you're dating someone, and you want a commitment."

"So, is that a yes?"

Lisa looked around the parking lot, bit her bottom lip, and pulled my hand toward her pussy.

"This is a yes."

I cupped her sex, rubbing slowly and kissing along her jawline, as her head fell back on the car door.

"Come with me."

"I can't. I have work on a major story."

"What's the story on?" I lowered my head to her chest, pressed kisses, and moved my left hand up to grab her breast.

"Baby, we can't. People will see."

"Let people watch me touch you and please you."

"Morris! Morris!" We stopped and looked back at Mason who shot daggers at us.

"He started this." Lisa tried to point the blame, and I smacked her on the ass.

"Go home and call me when you make it, so I know you're safe."

"All right, how long are you going to be here?"

"Probably another twenty minutes, then I need to pack before the trip."

"Try to not have too much fun in Vegas."

"Never." I pecked her on the cheek, opened the door to help her slide inside, and watched as she reversed, and headed toward the main street.

"Sorry, bro."

"At least do it away from the cameras," Mason complained, and I laughed. He and I were the only ones with access to the cameras, so he more than likely saw us almost fuck outside. Mason led the way back in the building, went past the bathroom, and saw Claire on the phone. She seemed to be arguing with somebody. She turned away from me and I left it alone, finishing up paperwork.

⟐

THE NEXT MORNING, WHEN I ARRIVED IN VEGAS AT MGM Hotel, I showered and met with potential clients. Barry Lindale owned a chain of smaller casinos, and he was interested in hiring my company to provide security for twenty-four hours. This would lead me to possibly opening an office and moving here.

"Mr. Fields, thank you for coming." Barry extended a hand for a shake. I sat in a chair opposite him.

"When business is called, I run."

"It was nice meeting you at Club Seek."

The waitress poured coffee and left a menu.

"Thank you."

"Order whatever you want. All on me."

"In that case, give me pancakes, scrambled eggs, home fries, and sausage."

"Coming right up," she replied, taking the menu back.

"When did your flight arrive?"

"Around six this morning."

It just turned nine, and my team was waiting for me to brief them on the details.

"After breakfast, we can go over to my casinos."

"How many do you have?"

"Like we talked about, I have about ten casinos, but other businesses as well."

"You want security for just the casinos or everything?"

"To start out, the contract is exclusive for the casinos."

"To cover that amount, I would need to hire more men."

"I saw your background and your experience from the military."

"Most, if not all, of my team is either ex-military, police, or trained by the best."

"Great." Our waitress came over and placed the food down, leaving extra napkins.

"I think you'll like it in Vegas," Barry stated, wiping his mouth, while I sipped on the coffee and started to eat, listening to him work out the details of a contract. A few hours after eating breakfast, we headed to his first casino and did a walk through with my men. I had Warren Kingston tag along to help me scope out any potential details I might miss. Barry talked about the layout of the casino, and I stared over the entire first floor, watching as guests interacted at tables. The place stood on four floors with a stage and entertainment for events on the west side of the building. When high-profile clients came to perform, we'd have to do extra planning for big events.

"He has ten of these casinos?" Warren asked.

"What are you thinking?"

He rubbed his chin in thought.

"Are you planning on moving here permanently?"

I blew out a breath.

"I don't know yet."

"Why? Not like you have anything holding you back home."

I looked at him with a scrunched face. He laughed and slapped me on the shoulder. Warren was like a brother to me; we were both over six feet in height, loved to work out, had large families, and were the oldest among our siblings. The only difference was he has light brown skin, with a low-cut short fade, from New York, whereas I was more athletic in tone. He was muscular and with broad shoulders.

"That look must mean your girl pissed you off."

"It's complicated."

"See, that's why I don't do love."

"The time will come."

"Not too soon, but I like this place. If you want me to help get it off the ground," Warren suggested, pointing to the specs on the blueprints.

"Are you sure?"

"I know you have the club to worry about. Until you make a foolish decision, I can help."

"Thanks, brother." I reached out and gave him a hug and felt my cell phone vibrate in my pocket.

Barry approached us, and I motioned to my phone. Warren took over the tour.

"Hey, Mason."

"Calling to check in and see how things went," Mason asked.

I looked over my shoulder at Barry and Warren talking.

"Things are good. We might have a deal."

"Nice. Just don't forget about the club business once you become a billionaire," he joked.

"My first priority is the club, don't worry."

"That's what I like to hear. We just got approval for another building to expand."

"Email me the information, and I'll look it over."

"Sounds good. See you when you're back," Mason said, and we both hung up at the same time. I finished the rest of the visit with Warren and Barry before we spent the night out on the town. I made a note to call Lisa tomorrow.

❧ 14 ❧

LISA

Two days later.

Tonight was my debut story I'd been working on for a few months about a local businessman who was trying to push residents out of their homes to build condos. I'd spent almost a year getting information from residents. Some didn't want to be named, while others were fine with it. I wore my favorite light-blue and cream dress, red heels, and my grandmother's good luck charm bracelet. I ran over the video coverage last night to make sure I had every angle covered. Rhett was doing everything from harassing more tenants, to sending me threats online, and having people call the station to get me fired. Tonight would be the big reveal and hopefully, he'd run scared and get locked up for his crimes. I couldn't be intimated. By the time I was done with him, I could predict I'd end up getting my own show and probably an award for bringing him down.

"Okay, Lisa, you're ready." Frida, my makeup artist, removed the cape.

"Once again, Frida, you've outdone yourself." I stood and checked myself one more time in the mirror.

"Thanks, lady. Good luck."

Production staff stood at the entrance.

"Lisa, five minutes," he said, holding the walkie-talkie in his hand.

"I'm ready." At the beginning, when I found out how the news station played the photos of Maya and Mason, I was ready to give the station management a piece of my mind, but Maya wanted me to stay out of it and not jeopardize my job. If this promotion didn't go my way, then I'd know for sure they were never planning to promote me to my own show. I stepped up on the news desk and let the audio attach a mic to my dress, while I read over my cards.

"Lisa, I'm surprised you're here," Ryan said.

"I'm the cohost of the six o'clock news. Where else would I be?"

"Probably sucking some rich guy dry," Ryan muttered. Our relationship at work was a contest of who could top who in getting the coveted nightly morning news solo spot. When the cameras were rolling, we put on the best friendly atmosphere. Behind the scenes, we couldn't stand each other. Ryan Latchman was a yes man, only out to kiss the boss' ass to get ahead.

"Ready to roll," the director announced in my earpiece. I sat up straight, looked right at the camera, smiled as the light turned red, and the director yelled action.

"Welcome everyone to Nightly CBG News. We have a special report," Ryan said.

"We do indeed, Ryan, and everything has been vetted and approved for air."

"I agree with Lisa, so tonight, our story deals with the latest details on Rhett Fuller."

"They do, Ryan. I personally have worked on this story

for the past few months."

"Do we have the tape?" Ryan asked.

"*Mmmmm... Morris.*" My mouth dropped in surprise.

"*Shit... Lisa, baby.*"

"Wait, is that you, Lisa?" Ryan questioned.

"I...I... This is not."

The video turned off, and I jumped up and ran away to my dressing room. My breath was ragged, my hands shaking, and my eyes watered. I felt nauseous. I covered my face, not understanding how someone was out to get me and switched the tapes. I didn't know anyone was following me, but thinking back over the past few weeks, Rhett was the only person behind sabotaging me.

"Lisa, it's me Frida."

"Go away."

I grabbed my purse, searching for my phone to call Morris. I hadn't talked to him since our little blow up at the club before he went out of town. It was childish to not call him, but I needed time to figure out this mess with Rhett. Now, my head was spinning, and I couldn't believe they'd done the same thing Maya went through. I dialed his number, and the voicemail popped on.

"Lisa, please open the door."

I wouldn't let them see me weak. I wiped the tears away, stood with my shoulders back, and yanked the door open. Frida stood alone with a bottle of water at my door.

"The manager is on his way down now," Frida said, extending the water toward me. I waved it off.

"I'm suing this station."

"First, you need to breathe and take a moment."

She opened the bottled water and forced me to drink.

"I bet this was Ryan."

"He seemed pretty shocked. Most of the team was surprised."

"Somebody knows something."

"What the hell is going on around here!" Taylor, the station manager, barked, stalking into my dressing room.

"That's what I would like to know," I shouted, pointing at the set stage from my room.

"We're getting multiple calls about showing porn on air."

"My privacy was violated!"

"You did it in a public place. I doubt you were looking for privacy," he said sarcastically.

"I want a public apology."

"All of our sponsors are thinking of dropping us, and the station owner wants you to take some time off."

"What!"

"Lisa, you've put me in a bad position."

"My life was just blasted across the world. This has Rhett Fuller all over it."

"Are you still on that story?"

"You don't believe me... typical," I huffed, crossing my arms.

"What I believe is that you need to go and let me try to salvage this station."

"I'm not leaving."

"Then you're suspended. It's not just about you; we have other people who could lose their jobs."

At the mention of other people, I glanced over at Frida and felt a tightness in my chest. I cared about her and the other people who worked at the station. If I put anyone else in a bad spot to lose their job, I'd hate myself.

"I'll leave, but I want an investigation into who did this to me."

"We will let you know. Go home and don't talk to any other media outlets."

"Fine, Taylor." I scooped up my bag and phone, trying

to dial Morris again. I stomped out of the station and kept my head down, not making eye contact when Ryan ran up to me.

"Lisa! Hold up."

"Ryan, you won. I'm on suspension."

"I don't want the position on a technicality."

"How do I know you didn't set me up?"

"You know if I stab you, it's from the front, not behind your back," he said.

I peered at him for a long while, thinking about his words. He was right... Ryan was evil, but he didn't do anything sketchy behind your back if he was coming for you.

"Well, hopefully, Taylor can find out what happened. Sorry about everything," Ryan said.

"Thanks."

৩৫৩

IT WAS GOING ON SEVEN AT NIGHT, AND I WAS IN BED with a bottle of wine, lying in the dark with the covers over my head. My phone was on silent, while I searched my name online, saw comments about me being a slut, whore, and slept my way to the top. I went to journalism school and had always been independent. Morris still hadn't responded to my calls earlier, and I wondered if he was pissed off that his business was getting bombarded now.

Bang! Bang!

"Go away!"

"Open this door." I heard Kyla talking to someone on the other side of the door.

"No."

"Lisa, it's Maya. No one more than I can understand what you're going through."

I groaned, threw the cover off me, crawled out of bed, and went to unlock the door. Kyla's face held a harsh glare. Lying back on the bed, I moved the blanket back over my head, and Kyla yanked it out of my hand. A few seconds later Chelsey approached and waved her hand in her face, avoiding the smell.

"Stop hiding and get up." Kyla dropped the comforter on the loveseat in the corner.

"My career is over; my life is over." I reached to the night table to gulp more wine, and Maya snatched it out of my hands.

"Drinking won't help." Maya walked toward the bathroom, and I heard the faucet turn on.

"Okay, so Chelsey, what are you going to do to me?"

She looked around the room, turned the light on, and then opened the blinds.

"Let some fresh air come in. It helps to think clearer," Chelsey replied.

"I don't need an intervention."

"But you need friends," Kyla reminded me and took a seat on the bed.

"It will take a little time for this to go away," Maya explained.

"At least you had Mason to work through the shambles."

"Where's Morris?" Chelsey questioned, and I shrugged my shoulders.

"He hasn't called?" Kyla asked.

"No, and I've blown his phone up for the last few hours," I fussed and checked my messages again.

"Maybe he's still in Vegas," Maya said, which I felt was an excuse she would give since her husband and Morris work together.

"I don't care."

"Yes, you do."

"Shut up, Kyla."

"Get up. We're going out," Kyla said.

"Nope. I'd rather suffer in my room alone."

"This isn't the Lisa Reyes I know," Kyla said.

"Yeah, that Lisa is out of order," I responded and pulled another bottle of wine from under my bed.

"Lisa, give me that!" Maya reached out for the bottle, and I shook my head and ran across the other side of the bed.

"Stop!" Maya screamed and ran to the closet door to hide, and I locked myself in the bathroom.

"Lisa, sweetie, drinking won't help you." Chelsey tried to talk me down.

"Tell that to someone who's not dealing with the world seeing you getting fingered."

"All of us have things we regret," Maya said.

I closed my eyes, took in her words, scanned the bottle of wine, and nodded my head. I went to turn the lock, and they busted in, pulling me in a group hug.

"Where's the fighter who threatened to kick everybody's ass on my behalf?" Maya asked.

"That's different. When it's my family or friends, I become someone else."

"Well, you need that same mentality for yourself. It's not over," Kyla explained.

"Great, you tramps have me tearing up in here, and I hate to cry." I chortled, and they laughed.

"Do you know who has it out for you?" Maya questioned.

"Ohh yeah, Rhett Fuller."

"Who is that?" Kyla asked.

"I've heard of him. A big-time real estate agent," Chelsey answered.

"I was doing a story on him, and I received a few scam

calls but didn't think anything." The girls followed me to my bedroom, and I went into my walk-in closet to grab something to wear for dinner.

"That's how it starts," Kyla said.

"I had one tenant... Marisal."

"Have you spoken to her lately?" Maya typed in her cell phone.

"No, I'll call her tomorrow."

"Just be careful." Chelsey shook her head at me when I held a one-piece jumpsuit up to my chest.

"Let me freshen up." I tossed a short skirt and crop top on the bed, with fresh underwear. I planned on going to find Morris after dinner, to find out why he was ignoring me.

"Maya, do you know anyone who could help me investigate the leak?"

The atmosphere at the restaurant was chilly while we waited for our food to come. At first, I wanted to wear dark shades and hide, but the girls nicked that idea and told me not to hide myself. If Maya could still walk around with her head held high, I knew I could do the same. Tony was still her security, and he sat a few tables away to keep an eye out for anything crazy.

"I can ask Mason, but I think Morris would know better." Maya sipped on her red wine.

"Call Mason," I suggested. Hopefully, he could tell me if Morris was back in town.

"Lisa, I'm not getting in the middle of you two."

"I'm not putting you in the middle," I replied, holding my hands up in surrender.

"Her face looks like she's up to something," Kyla joked.

I flipped her off.

"Please... I just need to confirm something."

She groaned, picked her phone up, and dialed on

speaker.

"Having a good time with your friends?" Mason's deep voice blasted through the phone. Maya's face lit up like a high school girl.

"Hey, babe. Is Malia asleep?" she asked.

"We're still watching *Soul* and painting toenails." Mason grunted, and we heard Malia in the background.

Maya snickered, and I laughed. Mason spoiled Malia rotten, and Maya was more of the disciplinarian when she messed up.

"She needs to go to bed, but we'll talk about it later. Have you spoken to Morris?" she asked.

I shifted in my seat, leaning forward over the table to hear.

"I talked to him earlier today," Mason said.

"Hmmmm..." Maya replied.

"Thanks, Mason," I blurted out and ended the call.

"Lisa! He's going to kill me for hanging up on him," Maya whined.

"Mason's the least of my problems," I remarked, tapped my fingers on the table, leg shaking in nervousness at Morris' behavior.

"You look scared," Kyla said.

"More nervous and curious why he hasn't called me."

"You want to go see him?" Kyla suggested.

"You think they'll let us dress like this?" I inquired, looking down at my outfit.

"All of us showing up wouldn't be good. Maybe just you," Chelsey answered.

"Yeah, I need to go home and make sure my husband isn't pissed," Maya said.

"Or you just want to get home to get some rest while Malia's asleep?" Kyla replied, and they all burst into laughter.

❧ 15 ❧

LISA

I bumped into a hard chest and almost fell on the floor, but strong hands caught me.

"Sorry about that." I glanced up at the smooth, deep, raspy voice.

The man in front of me was extremely cute, with a wide smile, dimples on both cheeks, and talked like Morris. His light-brown skin matched perfectly with his brown eyes and bushy brows.

"No problem. Ummm... do you know if Morris is here?" I asked.

"He's not here today. I can take a message for you."

"Yeah, can you tell him Lisa was here?"

"You're Lisa... nice," he said.

My eyes dipped in curiosity.

"What does that mean?" I crossed my arms over my chest.

He extended a hand.

"I'm Warren. I work with Morris in his security business."

"Ohh... Well, Warren, it's nice to meet you."

"You too." He winked, turned, and left the lobby. I sighed, wondering where Morris was hiding out and why he hadn't returned my call. Feeling more and more concerned, I went to the bar and got a drink to settle my nerves. I hung out for a few hours before going home and sleeping off the day.

Ring! Ring!

"Hello."

"You should have known not to mess with things you know nothing about," the voice said.

"Hello! Who is this!" I shouted and checked the number, but it came through anonymously.

"Another one for the road?" the bartender asked.

"No, I've had enough for the day." I sighed, placed money on the bar, and left the club.

I got in my car and drove home but made a turn to head to my parents' house to catch up since I missed having lunch.

"The ghost has brought my child home," Dad taunted, holding his arms open.

"Dad, don't start." I reached up and kissed him on the cheek.

"We were worried you left town or something."

I kicked my shoes off and plopped down on the couch. Mother walked up from the hallway.

"She finally remembers who her parents are."

"Hey, old lady," I teased, and she slapped me on the thigh.

"What are you doing here?"

"I just wanted to see you both before I head home."

"Ohhh Lord... it must have something to do with a boy," Dad said.

"Let's not go there."

"Have you met someone?" Mom asked.

"What did you cook for dinner?" I questioned.

"Don't change the subject."

"Mommmm..." I groaned and rose off the couch.

"He must be important for you to be this annoyed." Dad chuckled, leaned over, and picked peanuts out of the candy jar on the table.

"Leave her alone, Tommy."

"Thank you!" I called out from the kitchen, opened the fridge, and picked up a bottle of water.

"Tell me the truth." Mom approached me in the kitchen.

"He's somebody."

"Somebody."

"This is why I don't come here... for the third degree."

"Keep yourself protected."

"No babies coming this way."

"Not just from babies," Mom explained.

"Okay, Momma." I looked over her shoulder at the pot of chili she prepared.

"Are you staying for dinner?" she asked.

"Yeah." I checked my phone again, and there were no messages.

Maybe this was his way of breaking up with me. I chuckled; it was kind of funny since I refused to be in a relationship with anybody. Here's a perfect example of what happened in relationships that weren't anything but headaches. I wasn't the type of girl who got cheated on or lied to; something about being with one person forever felt stifling.

***

The following morning, I felt something off as I slept. Like someone was watching me sleep. I had experience with self-defense, but someone to get in my place without me knowing caught me off guard. I lowered the covers, opened my eyes, glanced from the door to the closet, and felt relief. I was surprised to see Morris sitting in the corner loveseat. He wore a blue blazer, blue slacks, double-breasted suit showing his thick muscles almost bursting at the seams, and his hair was freshly cut. I didn't know if I wanted him to strip out of his clothes or take me out on a date with the way he looked so dapper.

"How did you get in here?" I asked.

"I have my ways."

"No reason for you to be here."

"We won't start the pushing me away a bit."

He stood and stalked toward the bed.

"You can't just stroll in here unannounced."

"I can, and I did."

"Probably was off with your girlfriend."

Morris grabbed my feet, tossed them over his lap, and massaged them.

"How are you doing?" he asked.

"Pissed at you and the world." I shrugged.

"I talked to Maya to get more details."

"Details."

"The video clip of us."

"Are you ashamed?"

"Are you?" He went to massage my thigh, gripping my hand.

"No," I mumbled.

Morris lifted my chin, made eye contact, and kissed me on the lips.

"Don't worry."

"What does that mean?"

"It means Rhett Fuller won't be bothering you."

"Wait, what did you do?"

He stood and walked out of my bedroom. I ran to catch up to him in the kitchen and saw a table filled with food.

"You cooked breakfast?"

"Sit and eat; you're losing what I love about you over stress."

"What do you love about me?"

"Everything." He pecked my lips and poured orange juice in my glass.

"I met Warren last night." I picked up the fork and picked up a strawberry.

"He told me."

"He's cute."

I looked over at his reaction. He stopped drinking his coffee, and I smirked.

"Get your ass spanked."

"Maybe I want to be spanked today."

"Focus on your job first, and that can come later," he explained.

"I'm suspended."

"Do you know who leaked the footage?"

"No, I thought it was Ryan, but I looked into his eyes."

"Hummm..."

"What about someone at the club?" I asked.

"Only people with access are me and Mason."

"Can we just stay home in bed today?"

"No, I have work, and you need to focus on your story."

"Not sure working the story will benefit me anymore."

"That would mean Rhett Fuller wins."

"Maybe he should."

"What happened to the strong, opinionated, feisty woman who takes no bullshit."

I laughed at him.

"I love you."

He stopped eating, stared at me, and leaned forward to slide his tongue inside, and I moaned, feeling tingling at my lower lips. It wasn't time for sex at the moment. He was right, we needed to figure out who's behind getting me pushed out.

❧

WEARING BLACK SHADES, I FOLLOWED MORRIS INTO HIS office at his security firm. I never came here because he was always at the club, working alongside Mason. I was shocked at the massive ten-story building and the amount of people who all looked like they were able to bench press a thousand pounds. I licked my lips; the amount of sexiness in the room gave me naughty thoughts I knew Morris would never share.

"Oh, sorry." I bumped into Morris' back.

"That's what happens when you're so busy looking at other people," he growled, grabbing me around the neck to capture my lips in a kiss. I moaned in his mouth and gripped him around the waist.

"How did—" He shushed me with another peck on my lips.

"I know you," I said to the guy sitting at Morris' desk with his feet kicked up.

"You're thinking about me already," Warren joked, winking at me. Morris smacked him on the back of the head, and he stood and chuckled.

"Warren, this is Lisa, my woman," Morris announced.

"Nice to finally meet you formally, Lisa," Warren replied.

"You as well."

"Now that introductions are over, Warren is caught up on your situation."

Warren stood next to my chair.

"I looked into Rhett, and the guy is nothing but a money-hungry leech," Warren explained.

"I know that already."

"Yeah, but he's connected through some nasty people."

"So, what are you saying?"

"We've scoped out his business, and the only way to get him to back off is to play dirty."

"Are you saying kill him?" I whispered, and they looked at each other, then burst into laughter.

"If we told you, we'd have to kill you," Warren replied.

"I don't understand."

"Relax, everything will be fine," Morris answered.

"I trust you."

16

MORRIS

A week later.

Every last news channel played the story of Lisa being a member of Club Seek. They talked about her not being respectable and not belonging as a news anchor. I had our tech guy trace the calls that kept hanging up on her, and I found out he worked for Rhett. What I hadn't told her was the person behind the video leak; I needed to brace her for that revelation. Normally, I had men do the following and investigate to get information on criminals, but this was personal. Rhett fucked with the wrong woman this time—my woman. The only thing I could guarantee her was my promise to protect her. Nothing would stand in my way, not even if it meant going to jail. Warren and I laughed at her comment on killing Rhett, but deep down, if he needed to disappear, I could make that happen without batting an eye.

With my connections in security, anyone I loved that was hurt would have my full protection and the problem eliminated. I decided to camp outside his office building alone. Warren was taking my place at the club tonight. I apologized to Lisa for not calling her right when everything happened. I dropped everything when Claire called me about seeing pictures on the news and looked into what happened. Lisa didn't know that I had talked to Ryan and her news station manager, plus other coworkers. Soon as I finished here with making sure Rhett put a stop to all the bullshit, I would show my girl a good time with dinner and a movie. I headed in and saw the secretary talking with another person at the desk. One of my men distracted her as I slipped through the employee door to his office. It was obvious Rhett didn't have too many loyal people since it was easy to pay a few security guards off to give me the layout and hours of him coming and going. I twisted the knob on his office door and pushed it wide open. He jumped up, still holding the phone.

"Who the hell are you?!"

"End the call."

"I'm calling security."

"You probably shouldn't do that if you want to live."

He hesitated for a moment, then finished the call.

"What do you want?"

"You're going to fix the mess you made with Lisa Reyes."

"That bitch!"

I charged at him and pushed him up against the wall.

"Say that again and watch me push my fist down your throat."

"Sorry, sorry. I didn't mean it."

I let him go, smoothing out his suit.

"Here's the problem, Rhett, your underhanded greed is hurting many people."

"I'm a legit businessman."

"No, you're a slimeball."

His eyes rose in shock.

"No need to be shocked. I've done my research."

"You can't prove I had anything to do with her losing her job."

"Do I look stupid to you?"

"Maybe I cut a few strings in business dealings."

"Make it right or find out what I'm capable of doing."

Hours later, I stacked the weights up and stood in front of the mirror, working off the stress from Rhett. Warren invited me to the gym that he and Mason frequented. Come to find out, it was owned by Chelsey's boyfriend Xavier. Lisa ended up going on interviews for other news stations and promised to make up missing dinner plans.

"What happened with Rhett?" Warren marched over to the weight room area.

"He's going to call off his dogs." I raised the fifty-pound weight up to my chest.

"You need me to check in on him." Warren grabbed the towel off his shoulder and wiped the sweat off his face.

"For now, but Vegas is a go. I need you to look into office space."

"I'll handle Vegas and Rhett."

I dropped the weights, bent down, and took a sip from the water bottle.

"Is Xavier here?"

"I guess he's at the other location."

I nodded and gulped the rest of the water down. Hearing my phone go off, I patted my shorts and grabbed my phone to see Lisa on FaceTime.

"You good?" I answered, smiling at her beautiful face.

"Where are you?" she asked.

"At the gym with Warren."

"How long will you be there?"

"Somebody must be missing me?"

She rolled her eyes.

"You're so cocky."

"You home?"

"Yes."

"Meet me at the club in twenty minutes."

"Too stressed."

"I have something that can relieve that stress."

"Is it something that'll put me to sleep?" She lay across the bed, propped her hand under her chin.

"Come find out."

She grinned, and I licked my lips, thinking of what I could do to ease the stress.

"I'll be there in twenty minutes. Don't keep me waiting."

"I promise the wait will be worth it." I bit my bottom lip, ended the call, and turned to see Warren wearing his headphones in the corner, lifting weights. I laughed, slid the phone back in my pocket, and went to let him know I was leaving for the day.

17

LISA

I pushed the door open, still reeling over getting suspended from work. Being a reporter was the only thing I'd ever wanted to do, and now my career was about to be taken away from me. Maya was helpful, letting me vent to her, but I needed something else to take the pain away. Calling Morris to see if he was here was the only thing on my mind. Normally, you wouldn't catch me out of the house without being dressed up, but today, I only wore a large shirt, tights, and drove fast to get here. Stephen saw how upset I was and allowed me entry even though the rules were not to allow guests unless in all black, upscale attire.

"You've been crying," he stated, standing up from the bed, strolling toward me.

"Terrible day at work."

He wiped the tear away from my cheek and pressed his lips toward mine.

"How did the interview go?" he questioned, running a hand through my loose hair.

"It doesn't matter. I need you."

"Undress."

"I need to feel you, have your arms wrapped around me until I fall asleep."

Morris stood back and watched me undress in front of him. He grasped my hand, closed the space between us, and kissed my lips. It was the sexist thing I'd ever seen. He was so mesmerized or in awe of me. His top lip turned up in a devilish grin.

"What's that look for?"

"I ran you a bath."

"That was sweet."

"Go relax and come back. I have plans for you to take some of the stress away."

Thirty minutes after soaking in the tub, I came out in only a pink silk robe. Morris had a massage table and food laid out for me.

"What's all this?"

"I'm going to help you relax."

"I get a massage."

"Yep, hop on."

Excited, I dropped the robe and climbed on top of the massage table facedown, but he stopped me.

"I want you face up first."

"What type of massage are you giving me?"

"One that will satisfy both of us."

He nudged me on my back, reached over, and picked up a bottle of oil.

"What type of oil is that? It smells good."

"Edible honey cream."

Morris poured a little amount on my stomach, and I felt a cold chill before his warm palm rubbed across my stomach.

"That feels good."

Morris took a small amount and pushed to my lips, and I sucked his finger in my mouth.

"Mmmm... I like the taste."

"Keep sounding like that, we won't get through this massage."

"I'm okay with that."

"In time."

Some of the oil drizzled around my breasts. He bent down and sucked a right nipple in his mouth, and I arched my back off the table. While he made my breast his current meal, I rubbed his back, moved toward his eight-pack chest to a large girth, and reached in his pants to squeeze.

"You relaxed."

"Yes, I need more."

"Your breathing is labored, breasts full, and pussy wet."

"Morris! Ahhh... baby."

As I felt his tongue plunge into my sex, I opened up more for him, and gripped the back of his head. I tossed my head back and forth in pleasure, drenched in my own messiness.

"I'm about to come."

"Hold on."

A few minutes later, I humped his face, and I needed to release and let off my first orgasm as tears pooled in my eyes.

"Let it go," he demanded, pushed both legs back to my chest, and thrust his tongue in my butt.

"Ughhh. Ohhhh... Morris."

Feeling lightheaded and unable to feel my legs, I was ready to sleep from that little bit of pleasure.

"Not so fast." Morris picked me up and turned me around to stand. He kicked my legs apart and slid in my pussy. Part of me tried to scoot away since it was awhile since we last had sex. He knew how large he was, and his slow strokes were just as powerful as his fast ones.

"Oh... yes, Morris," I wailed, gripping the massage table.

He pushed down on my back to right his position, and I felt him slide in deeper.

"You're feeling relaxed!" he taunted, smacking my ass cheeks.

"Yess! Yess. Oh God."

"That's what I wanted to know." He kissed the back of my neck, trailed down my back, and fucked me until we both passed out on the floor, never finishing the food.

☙❧

"What did you do last night?" Kyla dipped her sushi in the sauce and took a bite.

"Hung out with Morris." I kept it simple.

She called me to meet up for lunch after she finished with a dress rehearsal. Maya was in DC about some bills, and Chelsey had to work at the bank.

"Hung out or slid in?" she remarked.

"I'll say he helped me relax."

"That glow on your face tells me he did a good job."

I blushed and covered my face with a napkin.

"Anyway, how are things with the job hunt?"

"Slow. I went to some interviews, but I'm still waiting to hear from the station."

"You think they'll fire you for real?"

"Honestly I don't know."

"That's like some HR rule. Maybe get a lawyer."

"I don't plan on giving up so easily."

"That's the Lisa Reyes I know."

"Anything new with your love life?" I asked.

"No, unless you call my favorite toy keeping me warm."

"You ever go to Club Seek like I told you?"

"I don't know if that will be a good idea."

"You can't hold back because of what Maya and I went through."

"Maybe I will, but for now, I'm fine with my toy."

Raising my glass of water, she picked up hers for a toast.

"To our toys." We clinked glasses and laughed in sync.

❦ 18 ❦

MORRIS

A month later.

I scowled at the guy who thought he was in control of any decisions being made. Mason was able to work his magic and spoke with his father to get the legal ball rolling on his properties. Lisa put me in touch with Marisal, and she confirmed with photos and signed notices from residents about the living conditions. A lawsuit was imminent, and criminal charges were filed. The phone calls stopped as soon as we found out they were coming from his own phone with a fake app he had installed. If you're going to be a criminal, at least be a good one and hire out the work. A few blogs still reported on the scandal, but most were removed from their pages, and we were able to get a public apology from some of them for running with the story. She'd been in the business for too long to have her name run through the mud. Rhett, on the other hand, wouldn't back down and tried to run a smear campaign at her station to not hire her back. So, I made a stop today to let him know that his plan wouldn't work. I didn't plan on putting my hands on him, but I knew patience wasn't my friend, so Warren tagged along with me.

I held the yellow envelope in my hand and slid it across the desk toward him.

"What's this?" Rhett asked, picked up the envelope, and held it up in the air.

"Something you don't want out in public."

Warren did what he did best and found photos of Rhett with another woman who wasn't his wife and a small child. I'd bet his wife had no clue he was cheating on her with Frida, the makeup woman at Lisa's network.

"That doesn't prove anything."

"Keep looking."

The smoking gun, a photo of him in bed with her and a tape of them together in bed, and he didn't need any medical care.

"How did you get this?"

"Same way you tried to come for what's mine. I have certain connections as well."

"I did what you said and put a stop to the calls."

"But you're still trying to ruin Lisa's name at work."

"She got in the way!" he shouted.

"No, your ass is just plain fucked up for having people live in terrible conditions."

He started to cry, and I didn't feel sorry for him.

"You have twenty-four hours, or I'm showing your wife and the media."

"Listen, I can pay you whatever you want."

"I don't want your money. Turn yourself in and send an apology to Lisa."

"I can't go to jail!" he shrieked.

"Whose problem is that?"

"Okay, wait... maybe we can negotiate," Rhett pleaded, dropped to his knees in front of me.

"You may want to save the begging for your wife." I turned and left the office, while he continued to call my name.

⚮

I SMELLED HER BEFORE SHE EVEN WALKED IN THE kitchen; her floral and lavender scent flowed in the air. It was my favorite shower gel on her that I continued to buy whenever she stayed overnight.

"What are you cooking?" She dropped her bag on the counter and hugged me around the waist. I stirred the spicy, tangy sauce for the hot wings and fries I was making for dinner tonight; it was one of her favorites. Living in a three-bedroom house alone without someone to come home and cook for left me empty. The way Mason embraced being a husband and father was something I admired. Now, after everything Lisa and I went through, I needed to know we were on the same page with what we wanted out of this relationship.

"Taste this sauce." I held the wooden spoon up, and she pulled her hair to the side, to keep it from getting in the sauce.

"Hot and spicy like you," she said, leaning into a kiss.

"I have your favorite wine, if you want to wash your hands for dinner."

"Something must be serious for you to have my wine ready."

"I'd rather have you drunk before I spill this news."

"You're scaring me now."

"First wash up." I turned the oven off and removed the apron before turning to kiss her on the forehead. She was hesitant but finally left the kitchen to clean up. I fixed our plates, opened her wine, and set everything on the table, along with the photos. Warren sent a message that he tracked Rhett meeting with his attorney, then heading to the police station. Only a matter of time before Frida quit and skipped town.

"I'm back, so tell me."

"Sit first and have a glass of wine."

"Morris, I'm not a child. I can handle whatever you have to say."

"Are you sure?"

"Yes. Now what is going on? Are you breaking up with me?" She jumped out of her seat.

"No, sit and eat, so I can explain."

Her slanted eyes watched as I picked up my glass and drank.

"I signed a deal to do work in Vegas."

She gasped in shock.

"You're moving."

"No, not yet anyway. Possibly in a few months."

"Then why did you declare this love and want to make a commitment?"

"I haven't decided if I'm moving, and I have people who can handle my company."

"I knew this was a setup." She gulped her wine down and slammed the glass on the table.

"Stop thinking the what-ifs. I wouldn't just up and leave without consulting with you." She sucked her teeth. "Anyway, that's not what I want to talk about; it's not that important."

"You moving is important."

"Woman, shut up!" I shouted, and she froze and rolled her eyes.

"Not your woman," she murmured slowly.

"Keep pouting, and you'll have something other than this to eat on tonight."

She smiled at my statement, and I chuckled. She was spoiled and entitled, but it was all my fault.

"Rhett is having an affair with Frida, and she leaked the footage," I blurted out, and her mouth dropped open in surprise.

"Frida who?"

"Frida, the makeup artist you work with, babe."

"Morris, I need you to back up and explain."

"Warren did some digging for me on Rhett Fuller, and he was the one doing the phone calls from a fake app, and he had Frida get the fake tape on air," I explained.

Lisa dropped her head in her hands, and I scooted the chair back and went to lift her out to sit on my lap.

"That bitch," Lisa yelled. She tried to get out of my hold, and I tightened my grip.

"Lisa, you're not fighting."

"Like hell I'm not. Let me go."

"Baby, let me handle things. I promised, and I delivered on my promises."

Lisa stopped fighting me and dropped to the ground. I picked her up and carried her to the bedroom upstairs.

"She's been smiling in my face and pretending to have my back."

"Rhett probably promised that he would marry her and leave his wife."

"Wait, she has a kid?" she questioned.

I kicked my bedroom door open and placed her down, moving the pillows off the bed.

"Relax and get some rest. We can talk more after you've had some time to yourself." I tried to get up and leave, but she gripped my arm.

"Please stay and hold me."

Her pouty lips begged to be kissed, but now wasn't the time for sex.

"I'll stay until you fall asleep."

"You keep me protected," she said.

"You keep clear."

❦ 19 ❦

LISA

Three days later.

After ending a call with Marisal, I watched the news talk about Rhett Fuller being indicted on charges and his attorney trying to get him out on bail. I was still suspended, but I decided to come up to the station and cause a fit. My attorney had the papers drawn up and ready to file a lawsuit. I decided to not sit and dwell on what I couldn't control, so I jumped in my car and drove here to the station. Morris had no clue. We'd spent time at his house for the past three days, and I even had clothes in his closet. He had to fly back to Vegas two days ago and came back today. We'd be together for dinner tonight.

I waved my badge, and security allowed me in even though I wasn't supposed to be on the premises. I caught Frida leaving work and kicked her ass for helping Rhett. Taylor threatened to call the police on me. Frida tried to apologize, but she made her bed with the devil. Her money train was cut off; the wife knew about the affair and made sure to cut Rhett off from everything. Frida got fired, and I didn't feel bad at all for her child. The devil was in the details.

"What are you doing here?" Ryan asked.

I looked around the station, and the crew was moving cameras and dollies around, getting set up for the next segment.

"I came to see Taylor."

"Does he know that?"

"Ryan, either you're friend or foe."

"Not my business." He stood to the side, and I swished down the hall toward Taylor's office. I just happened to see the door open and saw two other men in his office, looking just as upset. One was Dimitri, the owner, and the other was his assistant, I believe.

"Lisa, what are you doing here?" Taylor questioned. My head cocked slightly to the side. Keeping my life on hold wasn't a high priority for him. Everyone in this station knew I was the fan favorite with the audience, and the ratings had dropped over the past few days.

"I'm here to find out when I'm back on air."

"It's not a good time."

"Why? I think now is the perfect time. I mean you've allowed my reputation to be destroyed and continued to allow Frida to work here even after finding out what she did."

"Lisa." Taylor's breath hitched.

"Here's what I'm going to do. You can either put me on for Friday, with a raise and two-week vacation, or a ten-million lawsuit will be at your door before I leave this building."

Taylor and I stared at each other.

"Lisa, we understand what has gone on and owe you an apology," Dimitri Carruthers explained.

"Mr. Carruthers," Taylor spoke.

"No, Taylor, you've done enough. Give her whatever she wants," Dimitri ordered.

"Thank you, Mr. Carruthers." I smirked, extending a hand to him, then Taylor. I couldn't blame him for being upset, but he messed with the wrong woman.

⚜

I SPOTTED FRIDA WITH TWO BAGS OF GROCERIES, arguing with someone on the phone, and I bet it was Rhett. I jumped out of the car, removed my shades, glanced at the car door still open, and walked over to see a baby boy in the back, playing with a teddy bear.

"Are you here to fight again?" Frida asked.

She reached in the car and grabbed her son, heading to her front door.

"Why?"

Frida looked at the ground.

"I thought we were friends."

"Look, Lisa, I didn't mean for this to happen."

"But you knew how much my career meant to me."

"I had to do what's best for my child."

"I guess you can't find loyalty anywhere."

"You got what you wanted. You're more famous now," she snapped back.

"Frida, you're lucky your child is here right now." I clenched my fist at my sides at her nonchalant attitude.

"Rhett's in jail. I'm broke and about to move in with my family," Frida informed me, and I didn't care. She brought this on herself.

"Too bad, so sad." I gritted my teeth, left to go home to my man and grab another session if he was at the club.

Driving, I called the girls on the way through Bluetooth.

"What happened?" Kyla asked right away.

"Did you get your job back?" Chelsey questioned.

"Yes, they didn't want a lawsuit on their asses." I slowed at the red light.

"Same hour slot?"

"Yeah, then I went to see Frida again."

"You didn't fight her again, did you, Lisa?" Kyla questioned.

I giggled and pulled off when the light turned, heading on the freeway toward downtown.

"No. Her son was there."

"Thank God," Chelsey muttered.

"Since that's over, did you talk with Morris about Vegas?" Kyla brought up, and I didn't know how to answer that question.

"Not yet."

"Has he made a decision?" Kyla inquired.

"Right now, Warren is handling everything."

❧

Fifteen minutes later, I arrived at the club and parked around back in the VIP reserved area.

"I'm about to see him now. Let me call you tomorrow."

"You're at the club?" Kyla questioned.

"Maybe."

"Have fun," Kyla joked.

I ended the call, checked my makeup in the mirror, and sprayed some perfume on my wrist and neck. As I hopped out of the car, I checked my outfit over, sauntered to the door, and released a breath before I knocked.

❦ 20 ❦

LISA

"**K**eep your eyes forward." He lifted the remote and clicked a button. The wall slid open to a TV screen. I sat butt naked on the bed with my legs cocked open.

"Morris..." My breathing was desperate at seeing him between my legs, eating me out. One of my favorite things I liked was to watch us together, making little movies of our escapades brought me excitement and joy.

"I want you to watch us on the screen, while I eat you out."

Whap!

He spanked me on the ass, flipped me on all fours, and spread my legs wide.

"You're not allowed to touch me or come until I say so," he demanded.

"Awwww!!!!" I panted and reached back to grip Morris by the back of his head.

"Don't take your eyes off the screen," he said.

The clip showed Morris with a flogger going across my breasts. I licked my lips, thinking of that night together.

Listening to my cries and pants of how much I busted in his mouth when he double penetrated me with the vibrator and his dick.

"Please..." I gasped, rocking back and forth.

"You want to come."

"Aghhh..." I yelled and felt my heart pounding. I would miss having these moments if he left for Vegas full time. His fingers pushed through my walls, pistoned in and out, repeatedly.

"Shhh..." Morris trailed kisses up my back, yanked my head back by my hair, and rushed to thrust back in with his large girth. "Fuck!" he croaked, moving in long strokes, and pushed me flat on the bed, holding my hands tight behind me.

A strangled cry was on the tip of my tongue as sweat dripped down on the sheets and makeup smeared all over.

"Ughhh... Shit."

There was nothing simple about this sex session beyond him defining what we meant to each other. I trusted him without a doubt. We'd be together forever.

"Ahhhh... I'm about to come."

"Let it go," he replied, speeding up his pace as slid his hand underneath, playing with my clit.

"Fuckkk!" I screamed. I felt his hands release my arms and grip the sides of my waist to catch his orgasm.

He fell on the side of the bed with his hand over his eyes. I moved my hair behind my ear, scooted over, and planted a kiss on his chest up to his lips. He wrapped a hand around my waist and snuggled his face in my neck.

"That was amazing."

"Glad you're satisfied," he replied.

I grinned, lifting my hand to run a finger on his pink, full, bottom lip.

"Have you decided about Vegas?" I didn't want to make

this awkward, but I needed to know where we would stand in a few weeks.

"Warren and I will rotate and fly back and forth to Vegas."

"A new business needs a manager at all times."

"We have someone who'll be there at all times, but I'll need to check in on them."

We gazed into each other's eyes, and I thought about the first time we met. I was having lunch with Maya, and he was with Mason. Our first meeting wasn't the best, and I thought he was an asshole. Life had a way of showing you the love of your life could be in the form of the most challenging man.

"Come with me to Vegas," he suggested, moving to grab the remote and turn the TV off.

I sat up and wrapped the sheets around my body.

"I can't. I have to work this week."

"You have your job back?" he questioned, and I nodded. "After you finish work, we can fly out for the weekend."

"What are we going to do in Vegas besides gambling?"

"Anything you want, love." I chuckled at his response. "I like hearing that from you."

"Spoiled ass." He smirked, rubbed my ass, lifted me out of the bed, and I dropped the sheets on the floor.

"Tonight, you're all mine." He growled, sucked my bottom lip, and carried me to the bathroom.

THE WEEKEND IN VEGAS.

"How much are you going to put on her, Morris?" Kyla asked, laughing at Morris. My girl came out with me to Vegas so I could have company while he worked with Warren. We've already gone shopping and gambling, so we ended up at the pool in our bikinis, lying under the sun. Chelsey and Maya had to work and FaceTimed us earlier. Next time they were free, we would all fly out together.

"As much as I think she needs." Morris grunted, and I chuckled as they went back and forth like brother and sister. He was a perfect gentleman and didn't allow me to pay for anything when we arrived and had us in the suite for the entire weekend.

"He hasn't taken his hands off you since we've been out here," Kyla said, grabbing her margarita to sip.

"Kyla, leave him alone." I laughed at the scowl on his face.

"Oh, calm down, crazy man. You've run all the guys away," Kyla fussed, and he kissed my forehead.

"Good," he said.

"Morris, I got Barry on the phone wanting to talk to you." I glanced up as Warren approached us.

"Hi, Warren," I said.

"What's up, brat?" he teased, nudging me playfully.

Morris took the phone from Warren's hand and stepped near the empty cabana for privacy.

"Kyla, you remember Warren, right?" I introduced them, and they stared at each other.

"Ummm... hey," Kyla said.

"What's up?" Warren responded and went to walk toward Morris.

"What was that?" I asked.

"Huh."

"You two just eye-fucked each other," I whispered.

"Lisa, please," Kyla chortled.

"I'm just saying we're here for the weekend—nothing wrong with a one-night stand."

"No, thank you. Men and relationships aren't on my agenda," Kyla explained.

I raised a glass, Kyla picked up hers, and we toasted.

"Then maybe you should try out Club Seek when we get back."

"Hmmm..."

"The best place to be." I laughed, took a sip of my drink, and watched my man talk with his friend. I thought of all the fun we would have later tonight.

EPILOGUE MORRIS

One year later.

I stood in the corner as Lisa sat at the anchor desk of the CGN Morning News, doing a segment on the latest oil industry. Our relationship had grown deeper and more intense as we balanced our lives together. Recently, her parents came out to Vegas to stay at the casino where I worked security, and they fell in love with the place. We had dinner the other night to celebrate her new gig as solo anchor. Our nights at the club had slowed down because our work schedules increased. I still went back and forth between Vegas and Tennessee every other month, so I built our very own sex club in my house. She finished her segment and when the camera was off, we clapped as balloons and a cake came out. Her growth only inspired me more, and I opened another security business location in Chicago and worked with Mason on opening a club out there. Warren stood next to me and stared at Lisa hugging her friends.

"I'm assuming you're only looking at Kyla."

"What?"

"She's the only single one left."

"I'm not looking at her."

"Uhhh."

"Unlike you and Mason, I'm not into love and answering to somebody."

"Welp, you're missing out." I laughed. Lisa placed her hand on my chest.

"Hey, handsome," Lisa purred, pursing her lips for a kiss.

"Congrats again, Lisa," Warren said.

"Thanks, Warren."

"Are you ready for lunch?"

"Can we make it a big lunch? I invited the girls."

"Sure."

"Great. I want a huge glass of red wine."

"Sure, babe."

"Warren, are you coming to lunch?" Lisa asked.

He raised his wrist and looked at his watch.

"Not this time, brat. I have to get to the office," Warren responded, reaching over to hug her.

"Shut up, Warren." She rolled her eyes.

He chuckled and walked off.

"Can we go to my office?" Lisa whispered in my ear.

"No."

"Why not?" She pouted.

"Because I'll be here all day."

"Lisa, we're not about to wait on you so you can get some dick," Maya murmured, and Kyla laughed.

"With friends like you three, I'd never get away with anything." Lisa huffed. I held the door open for the women to head toward the parking lot.

"Good," I responded, kissing her on the forehead.

I hope you enjoyed Lisa and Morris story. Check out Kyla and Warren next.

SEEK TO BARE: BOOK 3

Kyla worked hard to make her Hollywood dreams come true. She wanted the roles and the opportunity to do what she loves. What she never expected was how quickly she would lose her right to privacy and safety. Unfortunately, she learns that lesson in a frightening way when a delusional stalker sets his sights on her.

It was the man she couldn't forget after a one-night stand in Vegas who came to her rescue in more ways than one. She will need Warren to help her, but will she be held back by her past? Neither could've anticipated it would blow up in their faces.

PROLOGUE

The Weekend in Vegas.

"How much are you going to put on her, Morris?" Kyla asked, laughing at Morris. My girl came out with me to Vegas so I could have company while he worked with Warren. We'd already gone shopping and then gambling, so we ended up at the pool in our bikinis, laying under the sun. Chelsey and Maya had to work and FaceTimed us earlier. Next time they're free, we'd all fly out together.

"As much as I think she needs," Morris grunted, and I chuckled as they went back and forth like brother and sister. He was a perfect gentleman and didn't allow me to pay for anything when we arrived, and he had us in the suite for the entire weekend.

"He hasn't taken his hands off you since we've been out here," Kyla said, sipping her margarita.

"Kyla, leave him alone." I laughed at the scowl on his face.

"Oh, calm down, crazy man. You've run all the guys away," Kyla fussed, and he kissed my forehead.

"Good," he said.

"Morris, I got Barry on the phone wanting to talk to you." I glanced up as Warren approached us.

"Hi, Warren," I said.

"What's up, brat?" he teased, nudging me playfully.

Morris stood, took the phone out of Warren's hand, and stepped near the empty cabana for privacy.

"Kyla, you remember Warren, right?" I introduced them as they stared at each other.

"Ummm... Hey," Kyla said.

"What's up?" Warren responded and went to walk toward Morris.

"What was that?" I asked.

"Huh."

"You two just eye fucked each other," I whispered.

"Lisa, please," Kyla chortled.

"I'm just saying we're here for the weekend—nothing wrong with a one-night stand."

"No thank you. Men and relationships are not on my agenda," Kyla explained.

I raised a glass, Kyla picked up hers, and we toasted.

"Then maybe you should try out Club Seek when we get back."

"Hmmm..."

"The best place to be." I laughed, took a sip of my drink, and watched my man talk with his friend. I thought of all the fun we would have later that night.

KYLA

*F*lashback: Vegas

I bit down on my bottom lip as the rope tightened around my wrists; I couldn't explain why I agreed to this besides showing him I wouldn't flake on him, that I could go with the flow. All we'd done this whole time in Vegas was stare at each other throughout the night; something about him intrigued me. The only problem was making sure nothing leaked out, and we promised each other this was a one-time thing. Soon as it was over, we would act like strangers once again and ignore each other. I noticed the thick muscles of his arms and couldn't wait to have them wrapped around my body. The suitcase on the floor held different intricacies, and I got to pick which one to use. Lisa told me this weekend was about being spontaneous, and taking her up on the offer would come in many rewards.

"*Kyla.*"

"*Huh.*"

"*Shit, you're already leaking, baby.*"

"*Warren...*" *I felt the push of his finger entering my awaiting canal. He moved the flogger across my thigh gently.*

"*Who made you drip like this, baby?*"

"You did... Ahhhh!"

He picked the whip up next and went across my inner thigh. The growl he muttered beside me somehow made the scene more intense. Was I really doing this? Kyla Stevens, actress and daughter of Abigail Stevens, the well-known baker in my hometown was about to indulge in a one-night stand with a man while he performed a BDSM scene with me.

⚜

I RELEASED THE LAST BREATH I HELD AND FELT THE bright lights against my left cheek, as the director called action on set. Today was a quick scene of me doing the opening act of my character finding out she needed to get closer with her mother. I'd been wanting this role for a while and as an established actress, getting the meaty type of film parts where you were stripped of all the glitz and glamour came sparingly. Lately, my mind had been distracted by the little situation I had in Vegas. Living in Tennessee for a limited time to complete the project kept me busy and stressed at times. For today, it would be me and one other actor on set, but in two days, I would need to do press, try to film two more long scenes, and clean my rental place before my cousin came to visit. I'd dreamt of this life, but the only way to ease the tension at times and the demand was to join Club Seek. Lisa told me how she was introduced to the club as a place where she could go without any judgement, to escape the day-to-day life choices.

"Kyla, let's try that again. I need more emotions," the director ranted, making me want to throw in the towel and call it a day.

"Can I have a minute?" I asked.

He shot me a look. "Five minutes."

"Thanks." I tightened my robe, went over to the actor's chair, and sat, closing my eyes and running a hand across the back of my neck.

"Guess who." Two hands covered my eyes, and I cuffed both wrists, shaking my head.

"Not sure. Is this my best friend who I forgot to call back yesterday?"

"Correct." Lisa dropped her hands and stepped in front of my chair.

"You look cute today."

"I had a good night's sleep," she teased, biting on her index finger. I grinned, tapping her on the butt.

"I bet you did."

"Kyla, we're ready for you." The assistant director approached me.

"Thanks, Brandon. Lisa, you don't mind waiting, do you?"

"No, go be the star that you are."

"Great, it's a small scene." I hugged her, heading back to set. I sat on the couch, lifting the photo in my hands.

"Quiet on set please. Kyla, make sure you remember what I said," Tevin said, stepping behind the monitor to watch the scene. I cleared my throat, focusing on the photo and concentrating on the goal of the character in the moment.

"Action!" he yelled.

"All I ever wanted was your love. Why did you do this to me!" I slammed the photo down on the table and covered my face as I cried.

"Cut! That's it for today," Tevin informed me.

I jumped up and strolled over to the monitor, looking at the playback of myself.

"Keep pulling those types of emotions, and we're good." Tevin pushed the headphones toward me to listen.

"Thanks, Tevin."

An hour later, I drove over to meet up with my friends. I stopped at the stop sign and swiped up on my cell to see a new email notification. My agent was working on trying to get another sit-down for a huge film with me as the lead.

"Please be the one," I mumbled underneath my breath, clicked into my email, and my lip twisted up in disgust.

Unknown: We know about Vegas.

"What the fuck."

Bark! Bark!

A car horn went off behind me, and I ignored it, trying to respond, and closed out to pull back on the road. Ten minutes later I arrived at the restaurant a little frazzled.

I was sitting with Lisa and Chelsey at London's restaurant and bar, wearing black shades, sitting in the back near the inside of the booth. I took every precaution when going out to avoid being harassed by photographers.

"What have you been up to, Chelsey?" Lisa questioned.

"Working at the bank as usual, focused on family." Chelsey placed her fork down and wiped the residue of the mustard from the corner of her mouth.

"Did you tell her about Vegas?" Lisa asked.

"No, and I thought we promised not to speak on that."

"What happened?" Chelsey questioned, her face squinted in concern.

"Can I tell her?"

I waved her off; nobody could stop her from talking. Not even Morris. She smirked, sipping her wine.

"Fine, she hooked up with Warren in Vegas."

"Warren... Morris' business partner?" Chelsey asked.

"A one-time thing, not a big deal."

"Only because you're on this career path, forget your personal life," Lisa blasted me in front of Chelsey.

"You have your career, same as Maya and Chelsey. Why is it a problem for me?"

"Because that's all you think about." Lisa rolled her eyes. It's been over a year since I met the rest of the women after Lisa introduced us. We'd met because of an interview she did with me, and our friendship blossomed from there. Sometimes she could be a little overbearing with trying to boss everybody around.

"Not true, but the men I've seen aren't used to my lifestyle."

"Have you gone to Club Seek yet?"

"No."

"You need an escape; you've done the Vegas thing. Now try something that will get your inhibitions going," Lisa teased, bumping me on the shoulder.

"Unlike you and Maya, my public persona would get run through the mud."

"Stop worrying about what people think about you."

"Can we change the subject?" I dropped my fork on the table.

Lisa lifted the bottle of wine and filled our glasses.

"One night, and then I'll shut up about it." Lisa held her hand up.

"Why do I have a feeling this is going to backfire?"

Chelsey sat back and crossed her arms over her chest, pushing her breasts up and revealing her silk blouse. I was surprised Xavier didn't say anything about her walking out of the house with one.

"One night, Lisa, and nothing more."

❊ 22 ❊

KYLA

I decided on a nude silk dress that showed just enough cleavage, with a small gold necklace and black heels with a key shape on the back. The crowd was packed inside, and I shouldn't have been surprised since Lisa told me the weekends were the most popular. I followed behind Lisa as her plus one since Maya and Chelsey had other plans tonight. I'd wrapped up filming and went straight to Lisa's place to get changed, and Morris had a car waiting to bring us to the club. Mason had the place secluded and mysterious with it being away from other businesses and sitting as a stand-alone location.

"Did I tell you every man in here is watching you?" Lisa turned with a huge smile and passed a martini toward me. The bartender didn't charge her for the drinks and said everything was on the house, according to Mason.

"Thanks. I didn't know what to expect, so I wanted to be classy, but sexy at the same time."

"No worries, babe. You're making a huge impact on all the guys tonight."

"They have shows up front, but if you like to watch privately, it can be arranged."

"I'm fine right here." I took another sip of my drink.

Right as I started to speak, my mouth shut, and my body tingled at seeing him again so soon without warning. I would hope Lisa didn't set me up, but something told me it wasn't an afterthought he'd be here. This man knew what he did to women, the small curve of his upper lip as his tongue grazed his teeth. Remembering how well he kept his dreads neat, sides freshly shaved as I pushed my hands through them, I gulped down the rest of the drink, cursing myself for thinking about the way he had me calling out his name over and over again, while he hovered over my back. Soon as I went to order a second drink, I smelled his cologne getting stronger, which meant he was getting closer.

"Warren, I didn't know you'd be here," Lisa said, a slight smirk spread over her face.

"What's going on, Lisa? Your boy didn't tell you I was coming?" Warren replied, never taking his eyes off me.

"I must have forgotten. You remember my friend Kyla," Lisa responded, taking the drink out of my hand.

"I was still drinking that." I pouted, placing my hands on my hips.

"Warren can order you another one. I need to see Morris." Lisa waved goodbye, and I felt duped for even thinking she'd be my wingman.

"You look disappointed?"

"I have no reason to be disappointed."

"Glad to hear that." He pulled on his beard.

"What is that supposed to mean?" My eyes narrowed in a glare.

Warren's eyebrows hiked up, and he grinned.

"Lil mamma, that feisty attitude won't work on me."

"Warren, please, you're not God's gift to every woman."

"I don't need to be. Only one woman will get this gift." He walked up on me and closed the space between us. I tried to take a step back, but he closed both hands against the bar on either side of me.

"Warren, you want a drink?" the bartender interrupted our stare off.

"I'm good. You want anything?" he responded, stepped back, and put a space between us. A part of me liked the closeness and protectiveness he provided.

"Uh... No... No," I muttered low under my breath.

"Great, because tonight I want you fully open to what I'm going to do your body."

"Huh."

"Did you enjoy what we did in Vegas?"

"Yeah..."

"Do you want to explore those moments again, Miss Stevens?"

"Okay."

"Then come with me." He took my hand and led the way out of the club's main entrance and through the private section. My thoughts ran all over the place at what he'd be doing to my body tonight. A part of my brain said to just turn around and act like this never happened, but I wanted to be Kyla and not the superstar actress everyone looked at as simple and cute. I could be bold, daring, and outgoing with my choices in life, but I always thought that would lead me to a path that would hinder my career. Warren went to the front of a private door that held a sign in gold plate labeled Restricted.

"Are we supposed to be in this room?" I asked.

He slid a key in, turned the knob, escorted me inside, and shut the door behind me.

"For high-priority guests," Warren said, removing his

jacket and laying it on the back of the door. Warren turned the lights down low from the wall, picked up a remote from the side table, and I scanned the room in surprise. The palace was huge and unexpected for a club, but Mason was well known and rich. The colors were fire red, and the bed was raised off the floor with long drapes hanging; it was more of a Victorian or Greek style. I saw a door in the corner that more than likely led to a bathroom, so I walked off to gather my bearings.

"I'm doing this," I whispered to myself. I looked in the mirror and felt my face to make sure I wouldn't pass out or anything.

"It's just sex."

"Kyla?" I heard his raspy voice.

"Coming right out."

I shook off my nerves. The last time I was this nervous, I was losing my virginity at seventeen and believed I was in love with my high school boyfriend. Blowing out a long breath, I left the bathroom and stopped in my tracks. Warren stood completely naked, and I wasn't sure if his dick grew even more since Vegas, or I was that gone off his sex that I let something that big inside me.

"Uhm."

"Strip." He held up a pair of handcuffs in his hand.

"Warren."

"I can fulfill your needs, Kyla, but you have to let me, baby."

"Have you always been that big?" I extended my hand, dramatically forming what I thought was his size, and he laughed, causing his dick to jump.

"Come over here."

I followed him toward the bed and dropped my dress, only wearing a red thong set, and kicked my heels off.

Warren lay on the bed and locked his right hand in the handcuffs to the side of the headboard.

"What are you doing?"

"I want you to take the lead. Go at your speed."

"So, like you're my sex toy?" I giggled, not believing him.

"Just for the start, and then I run the show." He motioned for me to come closer, and I noticed the piercing on his shaft. I scanned from the top of his head to his beautiful brown skin against the bright red colors in the room. My mouth was ready to take him down my throat and show him how much I could please him. I wasn't just a timid lover.

WARREN

I watched as she crawled to me on the bed, wearing the sexy red thong set she wore under her dress. Our first adventure in Vegas sparked a fire in me to want to be around her all the time. She probably thought the first time we met was in Vegas, but I'd seen her with Lisa when Morris had to stop over to see her. The Vegas trip was the first time we actually spoke, and I thought she'd be some uptight bougie actress that would think I was beneath her or something. Watching her come up to my chest, she planted a trail of kisses and ran her tongue over my pierced nipple.

"Show me what you can do, Miss Stevens."

My right hand caressed her arm, moved to the back of her head, and yanked her closer to me, deepening our kiss. Out of all the women I'd been with, they never had me moaning, but Kyla brought the best upfront. Kyla leaned back and pushed her chest in my face. I slipped my tongue across her breasts, gripping her ass, and buried my face in her chest. Cuffing myself to the bed was a good idea at first, but not being able to fully hold her pissed me off. Kyla sat over my lap, stretched her hand back, squeezed, and grazed her fingernail gently over the tip.

"Warren... Warren... can I taste you?"

My breathing increased, and my eyes twitched when she scooted back and took him down her throat in one swift motion.

"Fuck!"

I jerked my hand, forgetting I was wearing handcuffs, trying to touch her while she watched me. She was teasing me, sticking her tongue out, then spat on my tip, and sucked me back in her mouth.

"Ssshhhittt." I gritted my teeth.

Her head went up and down quickly, then stopped and moaned.

"That's enough," I grumbled, reaching for the key from the table.

Kyla smiled and released me before I came. I pushed her on her back, swiped my tongue over her sex, still covered in her thong. Palming her breasts, I lifted her legs up, removed her bra and underwear, and nuzzled my nose in her sweet honey. I nibbled on her inner thigh and plunged a finger in her core.

"Awww!" she gasped, closing her eyes. I flicked my tongue over her warm sex, feeling her juices pour down my throat. Kyla would be thinking of me only from here on out.

Not to let her relax at her next release, I entered her as her legs trembled and wrapped around my waist. Leaning in and covering her mouth, I sucked her lip for a few minutes and clasped our hands together. Moving slowly at a pace to keep her on edge just a little without going over the cliff, her eyes fluttered open, and she humped me back. My head fell back to hold some type of composure.

"Kyla." I let her hand go and lifted her left leg up for a

deeper angle. I slid down further and felt my chest tighten at the connection.

"I know," she whimpered.

A few more pumps, I adjusted us with her back on top, and I watched her slim finger bounce up and down, staring in my eyes and sucking on my finger at the same time.

"I'm about to come!" she screamed, arching her back.

"Yeah, come for me, baby."

"Yessss! Warren."

⚜

I HADN'T SEEN KYLA SINCE THE NIGHT IN THE CLUB, partially on both our parts. I was in and out for work with Morris. Managing the Vegas opening of the security firm, plus training new team members for the organization left me with limited time for dating anyone. I thanked Esmee and gave her the signed papers for the hiring of new accounts for the Vegas building.

"Anything else before I go?' Esmee asked, standing at the office door. Morris mainly worked out of the club with Mason, and I kept things running here with calls and meetings. He'd built a business that was known around the world as the best security company. No major issues had ever happened on our watch.

Esmee was the office receptionist and annoying little sister that I was glad I never had. She was always trying to tell me what I should be doing with my dating life.

"Nope, you're free to go on your little date."

"Ohh, poor you. Don't be jealous." Esmee chuckled, leaning against the door.

"Nothing to be jealous about." I shrugged, sitting back with my hand behind my head.

Esmee's eyes lowered to slits as she waved her finger in my direction.

"What's going on here? You seem relaxed."

"I'm always relaxed."

"Uhm... I think not." She popped her tongue against her lips.

"Esmee, my life is not your concern."

"Ohh, she must have made an impression."

She started to come back to my office, and I held my hand up.

"I'm not your girlfriend. Gossip somewhere else." I shooed her away.

"Stop being a dork. Who is she?" Esmee shut the door behind her and walked back to sit on top of my desk.

"Nobody." I jumped up, smoothed my tie down, reached for the files on my desk, and headed to my door. I opened the door, jerked back in surprise to see Kyla.

"Sorry, am I interrupting something?" she questioned, looking behind me at Esmee. I looked over my shoulder, and she smirked, trying to reach around me to greet Kyla.

"You're Kyla Stevens! I'm a huge—"

"Esmee, didn't you have some papers to file?"

"No," Esmee responded, reaching out her hand.

Kyla smiled and shook her hand.

"Nice to meet you and thank you," Kyla replied.

"How do you know Mr. Grumpy Pants here?" Esmee pointed at me, and I shoved her out of the office. Kyla giggled as I shut the door in her face.

"Warren!"

"You're fired, Esmee."

"Yeah, yeah... you say that every day," Esmee answered. Kyla burst into laughter.

"What's so funny?" My right brow lifted.

"I like her."

"I don't." I shook my head, motioning for her to take a seat on the couch. I stood against the door as she placed her purse down and crossed her leg.

"I wanted to talk to you about something."

"What's wrong?"

Kyla reached in her purse, and I approached. She opened her email and showed me the email chain of someone talking about how much they love her. They threatened that if she sees me again, they'll expose her with photos from inside Club Seek, plus the time we spent in Vegas together. They had photos of her out shopping, gambling, and even at dinner.

❄ 24 ❄

KYLA

Ever since I came home from Vegas, I thought I could brush off these emails and social media DMs. At first, they were of me out at some industry events, but then it became more of me with my friends and now with Warren. Whoever was stalking me knew my entire day and what time I went to set for filming or out to dinner. I was apprehensive about getting protection, but now the threats were getting too intense.

"How long has this been going on?" Warren went to his desk and picked up his phone. I rushed over and ripped it out of his hands.

"You can't tell anybody."

"Kyla, whoever is doing this is serious."

I held the phone behind my back.

"I only want you to help me."

"What about Morris?"

"Morris is fine, but nobody else."

"I can't promise."

"Warren, this is my life. If this leaks, I'll end up losing my role."

"You can't worry about your career."

"That's easy for you. My career can go away like that." I snapped a finger.

"They know your every move and probably watched you come in here!"

Warren snatched the phone back.

"I knew this was a mistake."

"Let me break it down for you."

He pushed the phone in my face, scrolling over the emails.

kylastevens@gmail.com: Either you leave him alone or find your career gone.

Kylastevens@gmail.com: You think I won't hurt you.

Kylastevens@gmail.com: I loved your scene today.

"My life is going to be over," I groaned, pacing in front of his desk.

He sighed and came around to hug me with his chest to my back.

"Listen to me, I won't let anyone hurt you."

"Warren..."

"Sshhh."

"How can you be so sure?"

"I've trained all my life for this type of work. If having a military background has taught me anything, it's to be diligent at all times."

"Okay."

"I want you to go about your day, and I'll put someone with you."

"Wait... I... I don't want anyone but you." I shuddered.

"Kyla, I can't promise to be with you around the clock."

"Then I don't want security."

"No debate, you're getting security."

"Asshole," I mumbled, moving out of his grip, and started to leave.

"Ah…"

"What?"

"I like this little attitude, princess."

"Shut up."

"All right, I'll do a few shifts, but I can't be with you all the time."

"Fine, it's a deal."

"Where do you need to go now?"

"I wanted to go shopping and then home to study my lines."

"You have girlfriends to do shopping duties."

"Nope, I want you." I gripped his arm, pulled him out of his office, and strolled past his receptionist.

"Bye, Kyla!" she yelled, waving.

"Get back to work!" Warren shouted, holding the door open for me.

"Sure boss," Esmee responded.

❧

TWO HOURS LATER, I HELD THE CANDLE UP TO MY NOSE and held it out for Warren to smell. He held a thumbs up.

"I love candles and the fresh aroma in place."

"How much more shopping are you planning to do?"

"Not much longer, a few stores then we can leave."

"You said that about the last five stores."

Warren continued to text while I checked out more candles in Bed, Bath and Beyond. I needed to cleanse my condo after dealing with a stalker for the past few days. Before all of this, I was an open book with my fans and let them hug me, take pictures, and get close. But now, everybody was a suspect unless I knew you personally. I picked up a lavender candle set when my cell rang. I answered to hear my mom fussing in the background.

"Hi, Daddy."

"Hey, baby."

"What's wrong with Momma?"

"The neighborhood boys messed up her flowers."

"Tell her to calm down, otherwise she'll have a heart attack." I chuckled.

"I tried, but you know your mother."

Wendell and Kaitlyn Stevens never lost that charm as a couple and as parents, they always encouraged me to be the best no matter what I wanted to do in life. Even though they would have loved me being a doctor or a lawyer, like any parent, becoming an actress and letting them meet their favorite actors was a bonus for them.

"We wanted to check in with you."

"I'm fine, Daddy."

"Are you sure?"

"Yeah, why?"

"Well, your mother always talks about having these visions or feelings."

I laughed at his statement.

"Daddy, please don't indulge your wife in the crazy."

"Normally I don't."

"But."

"She said she had a feeling you were feeling down."

I looked up at Warren, and we made eye contact. I cleared my throat to figure out the best way to answer my father's words.

"Everything is fine now."

"What does that mean? Is somebody messing with you?"

"Don't freak out."

"Let me determine that."

"I have a stalker," I mumbled lowly.

"A what?"

"Daddy, don't make me say it."

"Mr. Stevens, this is Warren Combs."

I gasped in shock when Warren took the phone.

"Who is this?"

"Kyla's boyfriend."

My mouth gaped open.

"We've just recently made things official, but I can promise that you have nothing to worry about."

"Do I need to come out there?" Dad questioned.

"No, sir. Kyla's in good hands."

"Let me talk to Kyla again."

Warren handed the phone back to me.

"Daddy."

"Who is that guy?"

"Uhm...Warren, he's my boyfriend."

"You make sure you send a picture of him and his driver's license."

I chortled and nodded my head.

"Okay, Daddy. Tell Momma I love her."

"Everything good?" Warren said, wrapping his arm around my shoulder.

"He wants a picture of your face and your driver's license."

"I wouldn't expect anything less."

"I'm hungry now."

"Come on, dinner's on me."

"Can we order in at my place?"

"Sure, lil mama." Warren kissed the side of my face and grabbed my bags.

⊗⅏⊗

THIRTY MINUTES LATER, WE MADE IT TO MY HOME. I PUT my things away, ordered seafood takeout, and popped a bottle of wine. I changed into comfy shorts and a t-shirt, and lounged on the couch with *Pink Panther* playing on the screen.

"What made you tell my Dad we're a couple?" I asked.

I had this urge to leave the conversation alone, but the girls would annoy me to no end if they found out before I told them that a one-night stand ended with a relationship.

"Is something wrong with that equation?"

"No, just surprised." I ran a finger around the rim of the glass.

"We're both adults, and I know what I like."

"So, you like me to be your girlfriend."

"I don't make it a habit, but this pull between us won't go away."

"I agree with that, but what about your other women?"

"Probably surprising, but you're the only girl I've had sex with in the last four months."

"Very surprising."

"I'm not some guy who goes around sleeping with people."

"Even being into the club thing?" I gulped the rest of the wine.

"The club doesn't make my dick hard if that's your question."

"What does?"

"You."

We stared at each other for a few minutes.

❧ 25 ❧

KYLA

He fisted my hair, pulled it into a tight ponytail, and stared at me for a moment. He then ran a hand slowly down my chest, and I moaned out. I was so responsive to his touch, the arousal I felt as he bent down and took my left nipple in his mouth ignited my soul on fire.

"Yess... right there." I writhed in his hold, he left my left nipple and twisted my right one.

"You're so beautiful. I could watch you all day."

I gasped at the feel of his warm breath behind my ear. Thinking over how we meshed the other night and then in Vegas, I wondered if this feeling would always be here. Maybe Warren was the person I was missing in my life. Hopefully he knew after his touches, and kisses, it would be tough to leave him alone.

"What do you want to happen tonight?"

Warren turned the video off, helped me out of the shorts, spread my legs wide, and kissed the back of my ankle.

"I should ask you the same thing."

"We can test out how many orgasms you can hold."

"Mmmm..."

"Make it memorable and if you can hold them, I'll reward you."

"With what?" I was in a daze as he sucked on each toe one by one.

My head fell back as I reached down to play with my clit.

"Let me work with her tonight." Warren bent down, spread my lips open, and stuck his tongue inside.

"Warren... oooh."

"I can make you orgasm in one minute."

"It... it's... a bet."

He stuck a finger inside, flicked his tongue across, and lapped up my juices. Then he grabbed the bottle of wine and poured it on my sex and sucked it back up.

"Ahhh!" I cried out.

"That's one."

My leg wrapped around his shoulder, and I gripped his head, humping his face slowly and forgetting about my problems.

"She's sweet, succulent, tight."

Warren raised the bottle to my lips and watched as I took a sip.

"Ughh... please fuck me."

"You can't handle the bet?"

I shook my head no.

"I just want you to fuck me."

He chuckled, rotated his finger, and nibbled along my neck.

"Who fucks you?" he asked.

"You."

"Who am I?"

"My boyfriend!" I screamed, finally understanding his

dominance and command of my body when we were in this position. Warren had a way of awakening certain sexual points I never opened.

"Good. Come with me." Warren extended a hand for me to take.

"Wait... where are we going?"

He picked me up in a bridal style and carried me to my bedroom.

"To fuck."

"But—"

He pushed the first door open and placed me on the bed. After taking off his shirt and pants, he pushed my legs together, held them to the side, and thrusted forward. We both gasped in surprise.

"This belongs to me."

Warren grunted, backed out, and pushed back in, lifting his leg on top of the bed. The position gave me so much more, and I felt the room spinning. His large muscles flexed, and I watched him concentrate so hard, he gritted his teeth.

"Fuck! Baby."

"Yesss... Ughh."

"I promise to keep you safe."

"I know." I teared up, pushing my face in the pillow at his words.

"You need to relax and take this dick," he said, removing the pillows, as he pulled out, turned me on all fours, and slammed back in my entrance.

"Shit!"

"Kyla! Kyla!"

"Huh."

"Did you not hear me?"

"No. What did you say?"

"We're talking about throwing a dinner party for couples," Lisa said.

"Ummm."

Lisa invited us over to her place for lunch and since I didn't need to be on set until later, I agreed. She looked at me funny with a perplexed expression, and I felt like she already knew that Warren and I made things official.

"Couples."

"Yes, Chelsey and Xavier. Maya and Mason, maybe. Me and Morris."

"Just spill."

"What?"

"You know, don't you?"

Lisa held both hands up.

"I hate you."

"You're walking funny, and the off look says your mind is somewhere else."

"I'm dating."

"Someone I know?"

I pushed her, and she cackled.

"Chelsey, I won." Lisa ran in the living room. I followed and watched Chelsey pull out money to pass to Lisa.

"You bet on me."

"She bet you would date him in six months. I bet less than three months." Chelsey laughed and put her purse down on the table.

"I'm going back to California."

"Aww, you know you'll miss us."

"Not likely." I sat next to Chelsey on the couch and crossed my arms.

"She was acting the same way Kyla did when we caught on to her and Morris," Maya said.

"I remember."

"Let's keep my business out of this please," Lisa replied.

"So how is everything going with filming?" Maya questioned.

"Good, besides having a stalker."

The entire room went silent.

"A what?"

"Stalker."

"When did this happen? Did you call the police?" Maya asked.

"Warren is handling things."

"Yep, he spoke with Morris the other day," Lisa said, popping a chip in her mouth.

"You guys tell each other everything," I said.

"The best way to be in a relationship," Lisa answered, grabbing the dip and chips again.

"What type of messages are you getting?" Maya inquired.

"Basically saying I should leave him alone, and they'll expose me if I don't."

"Why are we constantly dealing with crazy people as successful women?" Lisa stated.

"Because people are crazy," Maya answered.

I nodded in agreement.

"Hopefully, it'll get squared away soon."

"If Warren is on the case, you'll be fine," Lisa said.

"Well, let me get out of here. I have call time and need to get going." I rose off the couch, gave each girl a hug, and grabbed my things to leave. Lisa followed and opened the door. I saw my bodyguard waiting at the car that Warren set for me today.

"He's cute at least," Lisa said.

"Don't let Warren hear you say that."

"You know we love those possessive men," Lisa replied.

"So, I shouldn't be crazy that I feel possessive over him?"

"No, girl. Obviously, he's just as interested to already be claiming and making sure you're safe."

"Thanks. I'll call you later."

"Not too late. I might be stuffed." Lisa winked, closing the door in my face, and I rolled my eyes at her craziness.

❧ 26 ❧

KYLA

*F*lashback.

His shirt fell on the floor before he unbuckled his pants and dropped his boxers on the floor. My mouth flew open, seeing something new that wasn't there the first time we had sex.

"I got him pierced," Warren said, walked up on me and grabbed me around the waist, lunging for my lips. The hunger and despair in our movements could be seen by the outside world as two people who had been apart from each other for years instead of a few weeks.

"Can I have you tonight?" he asked.

I nodded.

"I need to hear the words, Miss Stevens."

"Yes."

"Remove your clothes slowly."

He stood back and watched as I kicked my heels off, dragged the skin-tight red cocktail dress off, and dropped it on the floor. Warren walked around me in a circle, scanning my entire body when he gripped me around the waist and pulled my back to his chest. His thick shaft poked at my opening, waiting to enter. He sucked on my neck, and my head fell back as I felt one hand grasp my breast and another cup my sex.

"Once we fuck, you're mine. Do you understand?"

"Uhh..."

"This big motherfucker is going to slide into home."

"Okay."

"So deep, you won't be able to walk afterwards."

"Warren... shit."

His fingers deepened, and the wetness dripped down my legs.

"Let me feel you, Warren."

"At your request."

All of a sudden, I felt empty as he pulled away, until I saw that he grabbed a condom from his wallet.

"Bend over."

He pointed to the couch, and I obeyed and watched him sheath himself as he kicked my legs wider, and pressed his girth at my opening. We both moaned at him being buried so deep. Warren rocked forward, and I gripped the top of the couch and felt the piercing push against my bud.

"Ahhh... This feels good." My tits brushed against the coach, as I bit my bottom lip and ran a hand between my legs to reach his balls as they smacked against my ass.

"Yeah, take control, baby," he said.

"Jesus," I gasped. He moved me away from the couch and had me facing the wall. He told me to touch my toes.

"Tonight, it's just me giving you this good dick," he boasted, smacking me on the ass.

Warren had my pussy leaking and me lightheaded at the same time.

"Don't pass out on me now." He pulled out suddenly, turned me around, and took the condom off before he gripped my hair and pushed his dick in my mouth.

"Shit, Kyla!" he groaned. I masterly fondled his balls as my *tongue swirled around the head. I spat and sucked alongside the vein of his dick.*

Present.

"They're ready for you on set," the hairstylist said as she put the brush down and removed the cape. I stood and thanked her, checking myself out in the mirror. The production assistant knocked on the door again.

"I'm coming!"

"One minute, Kyla."

"Time to transport to another world."

"You feeling all right?"

"Why do you ask?"

"You drifted off."

"Long day." I grabbed my script, sauntered out of the trailer, and sat on the cart, while he drove to the sound stage. Today was a night shoot with me and Lee on some intense scenes. Truthfully, I wasn't into working tonight. I wanted to be curled up against Warren again, watching an old 80s film or something while he rubbed my feet. My mother left a voice message to call her when I got a chance. I doubt it'll be tonight.

"Thanks, Cedric."

"No problem, Kyla."

"Quiet on set!" the director shouted. I strolled to the right of him with the camera guy and sound talking over a scene.

"I'm here."

"Hey Kyla, are you ready?" the director questioned.

"Never have to question."

"Tonight, we're going for the jugular," he replied.

"I hear you."

I hugged Lee, dropped my script on the table, stood next to him, and listened as he talked through the scene with me.

"We're ready to film," the director said.

"Places, everybody!" the coordinator told me.

The lights shined on us, and I felt the world outside escape while I looked into Lee's eyes and became my character again.

"Action."

"I want a divorce," Lee spoke, turning his back to me.

"Divorce! How dare you."

"We've known this has been over and moved on."

"Who? Who have you moved on with?"

"Not that it matters."

"Cut. I want a little closer to Kyla's face," the director said to the camera operator.

❧

FILMING FINISHED FIFTEEN MINUTES AGO, AND I STARTED to walk out of the building to the parking lot, when a guy wearing blue jeans and a leather jacket approached me, holding flowers.

"Kyla." He held the flowers out to me.

"I'm sorry, do I know you?"

"These are for you."

"Who are they from?"

"A secret admirer."

"Sorry, I can't take them."

"Why not?"

"Because I don't know you. How did you get inside here?"

"Don't worry about that."

I tried to walk around him, but he gripped my arm.

"It's flowers. What's the big deal?"

"Let my arm go."

"Bitch," he spat and threw the flowers on the ground

and stomped away mad. I ran to the car and saw the body-guard asleep at the wheel. I banged on the window, and he woke up startled.

"That's him!" I pointed to the guy driving off in his car.

"What? Who?"

"The stalker. Go follow him."

"Let me call Warren."

"He's getting away!" I yelled, reaching in my purse to dial Warren.

"Calm down. I'll handle things." He turned the car on and drove off, but the guy was long gone by the time we left the parking lot. Twenty minutes later, we ended up at Warren's place, and I fired the guy and told him to leave. Warren stood at the door with a harsh glare on his face. I made it to the door, and he pulled me inside and roamed over my body to check for any wounds.

"Warren."

"Did he touch you?"

"No, I promise. I'm fine."

"Okay, come here." He hugged me close, tight in his grip.

"I can't breathe."

"Sorry, come sit."

"Did you fire him?"

"Yeah. Did you get a good look at the guy?"

"He was young looking, beady eyes, thin lips, freckled face."

"I don't think he's the guy."

"What do you mean?"

"He wouldn't have approached you so soon."

"Why do you say that?"

"The guy tonight was probably a regular fan, but your stalker was too familiar with me."

"So."

"I think it's about me."

"Someone is trying to get to you through me?"

He walked me to the couch, then went over to the bar and poured a drink for me. I gulped the whiskey down and it burned my throat, then held the glass out for another shot.

"Slow down on those now."

"After tonight, I can handle a bottle."

"Tonight, you'll sleep here."

"Sounds good."

❧ 27 ❧

WARREN

Two days later, I sat with the guys at the bar to grab some drinks after a long day of work, while guarding Kyla at her film shoot. Morris ordered a round of drinks, and I finished off my second before ordering a third.

"Lisa said Kyla's been with you lately at your place."

"We split between my place and hers."

"Any clues on the stalker?"

"Not really."

"You need more people on her?"

"At the moment, no, but if I go out of town, I'll let you know."

"Gentlemen, who wants to lose to me in a round of pool?" Mason asked.

"Rack them up," Morris said. I watched them place money on the table to bet.

"Xavier, how's the fitness business coming along?" I asked.

He popped the top on the beer bottle and chugged it down.

"Busy, which makes me think we might need to get security," Xavier said.

"Let Morris know, and we'll set up a meeting."

"Chelsey insists I hire a manager and spend more time with her."

"How long have you two been together?"

"A year," he replied, waving for the waitress to bring another round. Mason cursed when Morris made a score.

"No kids?"

"Not yet. Still in the honeymoon stage."

"I feel you on that. Kyla and I are the same."

"We've known each other all our lives."

I chuckled.

"I guess Chelsey waited for you to make a move."

"Actually, she made the first move."

"She's a boss."

"Yeah, Peanut keeps me on my toes."

"Peanut?"

"She hates that name, so don't tell her."

"No worries."

"Chelsey told me about some stalker."

"Kyla has a stalker, but I think it's a scare tactic."

"For what?"

"To get to me."

"Be careful."

"I plan to."

"Let's play teams!" Morris shouted.

"He's already wasted; you have him on your team," I said.

"He's the worst player. I'll pay you to be his partner."

We both laughed, and Morris flipped us both off. I grabbed a stick and played three rounds before ordering more beer. My phone vibrated, and I pulled it out to see Kyla messaged me.

"Miss you."

"Miss you more."

"Enough to come here and suck my pussy?"

"Don't tempt me."

"Tease, tempt, whatever works."

"Get off your phone!" Morris barked.

"Drink some water and sober up," I fussed back and leaned against the pool table. "I have a surprise for you," she texted.

"Let me see."

"You have to come and get it."

"On my way to you."

"I'm at your place."

"I thought... On my way."

"Stop wussing out and play," Morris said.

"Gotta go. My baby is waiting on me," I said.

❧

I DROPPED MY POOL STICK ON THE TABLE, TOOK MONEY out of my wallet, and grabbed the bottle of water to sober up enough to drive. Thirty minutes later, I arrived home, slid the key in the door, and called out for Kyla. The living room was dark with candles lit around the room, and I smiled, thinking about our time at the mall when she bought up all the candles.

I took off my jacket, kicked my shoes off and went to my bedroom. When I pushed the door open, I saw the last person I would expect lying on my bed.

"Hey, baby."

"Esmee." I shut the door behind me and walked further in the room.

"Come to bed." She held her hand out for me.

"You've been sending those messages."

"What messages?" She sat up on her knees, wearing only a robe and bra set.

"Have you been emailing Kyla?"

Her facial expression went sour.

"I don't want to talk about her."

"Why not?" I approached her and touched her cheek. I ran a finger across her lips, down to her throat, and gripped her around the neck.

"I... I... can't breathe."

"Why?"

"Please, Warren."

"Tell me the truth." I lightened my grip around her neck.

"She doesn't love you like I do," Esmee whimpered, wiping the tears from her cheek.

"Cut the shit."

"Please, Warren, I've loved you since the day you hired me two years ago."

"Too bad. I don't want you. Get dressed."

"No, that bitch has money, looks, and a career. Let her find her own man."

"You sound stupid right now."

"We are meant to be together."

Bang! Bang!

"Get dressed."

"Is that your little whore?" Esmee got out of bed and started to walk to the front door. I pushed her back and pointed to her clothes.

"Get dressed, or I'm calling the police," I said, left the room, and jogged to the door. I looked out the window to see Morris and Xavier.

"You forgot your money." Morris held out a hundred bucks.

"Glad you're here."

"Warren, we need to talk about this." Esmee came out of my room, causing Morris and Xavier to glare at me.

"She's the stalker," I said.

"What!" Morris and Xavier said at the same time.

"He's lying." Esmee tried to wiggle out of my arms, and I grasped her arm harder.

"Check her phone in her purse, Xavier."

I took it out of her hands and threw it to him, watching her fidget around nervously.

"She has an app downloaded to block out her number." Xavier held her cell up with pictures and text threads of Kyla coming and going around the city and to work.

"You don't understand." Esmee reached over to place her hand on my chest, and I smacked it down.

"Why?" Morris demanded, taking out his phone. I heard him calling the police.

"I love you, Warren, and she doesn't deserve you."

"We work together, nothing more or less."

"That's not true! We have the same interests, and I know you want me," Esmee explained. My thoughts ran around in my head. Many times, we'd work late together, or I'd have her fly with me back and forth to Vegas, but it was never any type of dating in my mind. I always thought of her as a friend.

"The police are on the way," Morris said.

"How did you know about the club?"

"I followed her," Esmee mentioned lowly.

"Did you send that guy to deliver the flowers?" I needed to find out as many details as possible before the police arrested her.

She nodded and wiped her tears.

"But we can be together, Warren. I know you better than she will ever know you," Esmee declared. Morris moved out of the way when two officers approached my door.

"Call Kyla," Morris said.

The officers talked with Xavier, taking notes. Another officer took Esmee off my hands.

"No! I love you, Warren. Why are you doing this!" she screamed.

"How long has this been going on?" the officer asked me.

I ran a hand down my face, sighed in disgust at the person I'd been working alongside in my presence. I remembered Kyla meeting Esmee, and she seemed cool and starstruck, but all along, she was envious and wanted to ruin her career and life over me.

"She's been stalking my girlfriend."

"All right, you'll need to come down to the station, and your girlfriend, for a statement."

"Please, Warren! I'll leave her alone if you promise to love me," Esmee cried, fighting to get out of the handcuffs.

"This is crazy." I slid my hands in my pants pockets, watching them push Esmee in the police car.

"Glad it ended with Kyla not getting hurt," Morris said.

"I need to call her."

❦ 28 ❦

WARREN

A week later.

Kyla placed her hands on my chest and straddled me, showing her tight, sexy lips that I couldn't wait to suck, and fuck until we both passed out. I let her move at her own pace instead of controlling tonight. I knew she'd had a shitty week with getting a restraining order on Esmee and keeping her career afloat. She pushed her breasts in my face, and I used my free hand to pinch and tease her nipples, as I sucked her sexy, chocolate areola in my mouth. I deliberately did it slowly and watched her eyes lower as lust showered over her face.

"I want you to fuck my breasts," she said, nudging them out of my mouth, and crawling down and removing my underwear. She picked up my stiff shaft, put it between her tits, and stuck her tongue out to lick the tip.

"Shit, Kyla, don't play with it."

"I want you to come on my face."

Those words sparked a fire in my belly. She'd said I changed her in ways, but she did the same for me. My only mission was to keep a smile on her face. Thrusting upwards, she continued to lick and suck while her breasts cupped my dick.

"Fuck!" I growled and came a second later. I was still hard, and she climbed back over me and sunk down on my waist, bouncing up and down. I gripped her around the waist to help control her movement. The sounds in her bedroom got louder. Her lips moved toward me and trailed kisses to my chin and behind my ear. She knew that was my spot, and I growled feeling myself get heated in embarrassment.

"I'll make you pay for that."

She giggled as I flipped us over and pushed her legs back to her chest as I buried my face in her neck.

"Aghhh! Warren, you're so deep."

"This fat pussy can handle it, right?"

I taunted, switched my strokes from fast to slow, then went in a circular motion. She rubbed her clit, shuddered beneath me, and I knew she was about to come.

"What do you want, Kyla?"

"You!" she screamed. I maneuvered, let her legs wrap around my waist, slowed my strokes, and made love to her slowly, tenderly letting my release come inside her. I rolled off her to catch my breath, and she threw her leg over mine and kissed along my chest.

"I'm not the least bit scared of where this goes between us," she said.

I rubbed up and down her back, cupped her ass, and pecked her on the lips.

"So, we're a couple?"

"Are you cool with that? The spotlight I mean?"

"As long as we're together, I'm fine. Just be honest with me."

Kyla smirked, leaned over, and licked my neck, causing my dick to stand at attention. She went over to the drawer and grabbed the bottle bullet I thought I threw away and turned it on.

"What are you about to do with that?"

"How about a little sixty-nine before bed?" She passed the bullet to me and reversed around with her face over my dick and ass in my face. I smacked and spread her ass cheeks, and swiped my tongue from top to bottom.

"First one to come has to make dinner."

"Shit, I'll buy your dinner and breakfast if I can get this tight ass again."

I put the bullet to her lips, and she moaned, grabbing my dick.

"Baby," she weakly grumbled, her body shivering and convulsing under my touch. The sounds of her coming back to back spearheaded me to fit her snug walls again as the loud smacking in the room would capture our pleasure.

❧

A DAY LATER.

I walked next to Kyla in the grocery store while she ran off each item she needed for dinner. I loved when she was just plain Kyla dressed down in jeans, Vans, and an oversized t-shirt she took from my closet.

"What do you think of kale salad, baked chicken, and mixed veggies?"

I pushed the cart and stopped in front of the frozen food aisle. She bent over to grab a bag and toss it in the basket.

"That's fine with me."

"Perfect, have you heard anything from you know who?"

My phone would get random calls from an unknown number, and I figured it was Esmee trying to reach out, but I blocked her every time. When I went to visit her, I told her to never contact me again or Kyla if she didn't want more charges brought up.

Flashback before Vegas.

"What are you doing?" Esmee asked me and dropped our food on the desk. It was a busy day around the office, and I couldn't leave when I had to hire and get the estimates on the amount of team members to hire over to Barry.

"What do you know about Kyla Stevens?" I closed out the gossip blogs on my computer and went back to the payroll template before she could see my screen.

"She's an actress, why?"

"Nothing major."

"You see celebrities all the time. What's the big deal?"

"No big deal. I just met her the other day with Morris."

"Interesting."

"What does interesting mean?" I sat back in my chair and picked up the spicy rice and chicken from the Jamaican restaurant near the office.

"You don't seem like the groupie type."

I scrunched my nose.

"Groupie."

"I just expected you to be into more of a classier woman."

"Like who?"

"Don't take this the wrong way, but I seem more of your speed than Kyla," Esmee said.

Present.

"Are you listening to me?" Kyla asked.

"Huh."

"I asked, how did the visit go with Esmee?"

"Nothing you have to worry about."

Kyla looked at me and nodded.

"What?"

"You make me happy, that's all."

"My job, lil mama."

"Kyla Stevens! It's really you. Can I have an autograph?" A young woman approached us with her camera and notebook in her hand. I took the camera out of her hand, and Kyla mouthed thank you and stood next to her and signed her name. After taking the picture, we continued grocery shopping and packed the car up. I held the passenger door open for her to climb in, shut the door, and went to the driver's side. My phone vibrated, and I saw a number I didn't know.

Unknown: She'll never be me.

Deleting the message, I slid the key in the ignition and drove back home. We arrived fifteen minutes later and unpacked the food. I sat watching her around my kitchen, getting things prepared and talking about her upcoming premiere and my trip out of town for work.

❧ 29 ❧

KYLA

The bedroom door pushed open, and my mom walked in with Lisa and Chelsey behind her in their best outfits. The premiere was today, and I was excited to finally walk the red carpet and meet some of my supportive fans. Warren had to fly out to Vegas to handle business with the security firm, so the girls were my escorts tonight. Chelsey wore a floral gown with red gladiator shoes to match and wide pockets on the side. Lisa's outfit was just as pretty, showing her curves and fashionable taste in a baby-blue pantsuit and no bra. Red lipstick made the entire outfit pop. I smiled and stood, reaching out to hug them both while still wearing my robe.

"Are you almost ready, Ky?" Mom asked.

"Give me ten more minutes, Mom."

Lisa handed me a gift bag, and I pursed my lips.

"What did you do? I said no gifts."

"I know, but you deserve it after all the mess I got you involved in with the club," Lisa replied.

"Stop blaming yourself. I'm a grown woman, and I made my choices."

"She's right, Lisa. We all decided to join the club," Chelsey stated, holding a black gift bag.

"You two."

I shook my head, sat on the edge of the bed, and opened Lisa's gift first. I burst into laughter.

"I'll wait outside," Mom said, and all three of us laughed. Just like Lisa to gift me a taser for protection.

"What am I going to do with this?" I turned it around and rolled my eyes at the pink taser case in the bag.

"Duh, protection."

"I have Warren for that." I removed the wrapping paper from Chelsey's gift bag and giggled at the silver cuffs with the pink ruffled cover around them. I chuckled at both girls always thinking outside the box when it came to gifts. I stuffed everything back in the bags and stood to hug Lisa and Chelsey.

"Are you ready for your big premiere?" Lisa asked, checking herself out in the vanity mirror. I stepped out of my robe, wearing only a strapless bra and thong set. I treaded over to the bathroom, took my yellow canary dress off the back of the door, and slipped it over my head.

"Yes, and soon as we finish, I need to eat."

I nudged Lisa to move over and finished touching up my makeup, grabbed my purse and keys, and looked around the room to make sure I didn't miss anything.

"All right, ladies. It's time!" I squealed, clapping my hands together in excitement.

Lisa led the way out of my room, down the hall to my mom and dad waiting on us to head out to the limo.

"Ky... you are so beautiful, baby." Dad leaned over to peck me on the cheek.

"Thanks, Daddy."

My publicist ended her call, grinning at me.

"You ready?" she questioned.

"More than ready."

She hugged me, then looked me over, and gave me a thumbs up.

"You'll walk the red carpet and take a few questions," Janell informed me, texting away on her phone.

"Nothing about my personal life, Janell." I nodded at the driver. He held the door open for us to climb in, and I scooted in after my mom.

"They already know. Don't worry, today is your day," Janell replied and pushed her phone in front of my face to show me trending on social media.

"Stop stressing, Kyla. You have the man, the career, and family," Lisa reminded me and cuffed my palm to squeeze.

❧

"KYLA, WHO ARE YOU WEARING TODAY?" THE REPORTER asked.

I looked down at my dress and back up at the reporters as the cameras flashed.

"I'm wearing Diane Von Furstenberg."

More shutter clicks went off at my revelation. Some actors loved the red carpet, but I found it so exhausting and boring to constantly answer the same questions over and over again.

"Kyla has more questions to answer. Thanks, guys." Janell ushered me away to the next row of reporters. I posed with my mom and dad, then Lisa and Chelsey for a few more poses. I then waved to some fans waiting. I smiled while heading toward the doors of the theater. I was completely thrown off at Warren in a nice button-down jacket, black slacks, and dreads pulled to the back, showing off his shaped-up beard.

"What... How..." I was speechless, as tears pooled in my eyes.

He pulled me to his chest in front of the whole world, causing every reporter and photographer to film us.

"I took a flight to get back here in time."

"But I thought you needed to stay to cover for Morris."

Warren grinned and bent down to kiss my forehead.

"Everything is fine at the office; you're more important," Warren said.

"Thank you."

"No reason to thank me, lil mamma."

"Never had a guy go out of his way to do something this big for me."

"Stick with me, and you'll get something else big," he growled and kissed the side of my neck. I shook my head and stepped out of his arms.

"Save that for later."

"Warren, nice to finally meet you in person. My daughter speaks so highly of you all the time." Mom let my dad's arm go and hugged him. Warren greeted my dad, then the girls, while Janell led us into the movie theater.

"Excuse me, Kyla Stevens?" A guy, around five-ten, with low cut, black spiky hair, wearing a t-shirt with my name across it, walked up on me.

"Yes."

Warren tightened his grip around my waist and pulled me behind him, to put space between me and the gentleman.

"I think we all have some alpha men, but sweet at the same time," Lisa whispered for only me and Chelsey to hear.

"We have Maya to blame." I giggled, remembering how this all started by one invitation into a sex club that handled all of your desires.

"I'm a huge fan. Can I have an autograph?" he asked.

"Sure, baby. It's fine." I rubbed Warren's arm to relax him.

I grabbed the pen from the guy's hand, signed his picture, and thanked him.

"Thank you," he said, strolling out of the theater.

"I'm still getting used to that," Warren said.

"Used to what?"

"You being some big celebrity."

"Awww, you're sweet. But I'm just Kyla."

He placed a finger under my chin and stared into my eyes.

"To me, you're my heartbeat."

"I guess it was a good idea."

"What was?"

"Vegas."

"Anytime you want to go back, I have more toys for you." Warren winked and grasped my hand.

"Good, because I have a few of my own."

EPILOGUE: KYLA

Six months later.

My eyes watched as the scowl across his face deepened, and I wondered if we'd ever get to that happy place. How long had I been afraid, nervous, nauseous that this love wouldn't be enough for him? I looked away, turned silently, and wept as he wrapped his arms around my waist and held me close.

"Cut!" the director yelled, and everyone clapped in excitement at wrapping season two on a new project with me as the lead. After the premiere of my last leading role, I had to fly out to California for six months to film a secret project that would be airing in a year. My schedule only got busier with film studios wanting to work with me, calling my agent to send me scripts and audition. I missed my girls, but we talked on FaceTime a lot, and I told them I'd be back to Tennessee to visit as soon as things wrapped up here.

"Kyla, once again, you amazed me." Lee went to hug me, and I reciprocated. Our chemistry was off the chain, and he was a great sparring partner that I would miss acting with, but I knew our paths would cross again when the final product came around.

"Thanks, Lee. You weren't too bad yourself," I joked, and he blushed.

"Baby, you ready?" Warren came up beside me and kissed me on the cheek, and I smiled. To think he'd become my personal bodyguard on top of being my man for these last few months.

"Yes, I'm just finishing up with Lee." I motioned at him.

"Warren, did you get my email about the club opening?" Lee asked, and I was glad to hook Warren up with more clients. Lee invested in a club with his brother and needed help getting security, so I recommended Morris' company. Warren was taking the day-to-day lead over Vegas and West Coast in general.

"I have my people working on sending you the details," Warren replied.

"Great, you guys should come to the opening," Lee suggested and left the set. Warren followed me to my dressing room. Opening the door, I stepped in and sat on the couch.

"Super star, how does it feel?"

Warren bent down, removed my shoes, and sat next to me with my legs in his lap.

"Feels great."

"Good, you deserve it."

"What are your plans now that filming is finished?"

I sat up and straddled his lap, extending my arms around his neck. He palmed my butt. I took in his open chest in the black Ralph Lauren shirt that clung to his body, rubbing my hand up his chest.

"How about I go with you back to Memphis for good?"

"Are you saying you want to move permanently?" His brow raised.

"I am. What do you think about us living together?"

Warren ran a hand up and down my back.

"I'm ready."

"The best is yet to come." He smirked, flipped me on my back, and pressed kisses all over my face as I giggled at him roaming a hand around my body.

"Thank you for protecting me, Warren."

"You don't have to thank me, Kyla."

Our lips glued together, and my tongue rubbed over his bottom lip, pushing through it.

"You let me bare my soul and didn't run away."

❧

I HOPE YOU ENJOYED KYLA AND WARREN'S STORY. DID I forget to mention Xavier and Chelsey with **"Seek To Love Book 4"** is here https://books2read.com/u/mB2QvO

Check out Brother's BestFriend Romance here ***"Sensual"*** https://books2read.com/u/49lYYM

Don't miss out on ***"Love Don't Live here Anymore book 1"*** https://books2read.com/u/mBOWGZ a steamy enemies to lovers romance.

Have you checked out **"His Peace Her Pleasure"** click here https://books2read.com/u/3JJroP a billionaire, steamy romance.

SEEK TO LOVE

SEEK IN ROMANCE BOOK 4

SYNOPSIS

Chelsey

Sometimes in relationships things run their course, but I thought we would never be that couple. I wanted my Happily ever after to continue, but love isn't about the good times, and learning myself everyday in this relationship has brought out a different side of me.

Xavier

She's the one that approached me. I tried to leave her alone, but now we're too deep into things to let anyone come between us. I refuse to let her go and will work to stop anyone, even her own thoughts from causing us to end.

Note: These characters first appeared in (Wet Heat). Seeking in Romance series is dealing with Adult language, explicit content.

I snatched the door open, stomped into my office, and dropped my bag down on the floor. Exhausted from staying up late with Chelsey to make up for our busy schedules. She was at some girls' night, out having drinks and dinner. While I decided to come in and get caught up on some paperwork for my business. I was working for myself now, and that demanded a lot more of my time. The last time we spoke was at breakfast; she told me her day was booked up. I knew with me opening a second gym and possibly a third, depending on the negotiations, it would have a big impact on us spending time together. Chelsey was overseeing multiple banks now under her family's business. Her father still could be an asshole and barely spoke unless I initiated the conversation. Plus, having her new nephew around made me excited to want to try for our own kids. Jordan and Emma were constantly letting him stay over unless her parents requested for him during the week.

It was around eight at night, and my stomach growled from the lack of food. I'd packed a few items for the road to snack on while I went through the updated permits and leasing information. Ever since we became friends with Mason and his friends at Club Seek, my world had changed for the better, and my clientele had increased. No longer did I have to advertise to get people to come into my business. I still had a high ratio of single women or new moms who wanted to lose weight; everything came word of mouth. A knock at the door caught my attention, and I glanced up to see Chelsey push it open, stroll inside, and come around my desk. She leaned over with her hand on the top of my shoulder.

"When did you—"

She placed her middle finger on top of my lips to cut me off.

"No questions," she replied, removing the pen and paper out of my hand. She dropped to her knees, unzipped my pants, and pulled out her favorite toy.

"You really missed me, huh?" She licked her full lips, opened her mouth, gripped the base of my dick, and kissed the tip. I reached to grasp the back of her head, and she smacked my hand away. No longer the shy, soft-spoken girl I knew growing up. Peanut transformed before my eyes and became a woman who knew what she wanted.

"Shit... Chelsey."

I watched as her eyes stared back up at me, and I almost lost control. My blood pressure rose as she took control of my body, but the pressure of my seed rose to the tip. I gritted my teeth as my toes cracked, and I felt her hands roam across my thighs.

"Take all of it down your throat," I demanded, as her head bobbed up and down. I gazed at how she took the last remnants of my cum and wiped her mouth with the back of her hand. Chelsey stared into my eyes as she moved from her knees to sitting on the edge of desk, with her legs spread and her dress raised over her thighs.

"Come and eat." She threw her head back, anticipating my lips upon her sweet nectar.

I stood, stroking myself, and lined up to her entrance as her breath caught in her throat with my initial push. Our skin warmed as I picked up the pace, trailing kisses along her chest and taking both breasts in my hand. She palmed the back of my head, as I latched onto her erect nipples, flicking my tongue, groping, and pressing them together to feel the cozy full breasts I loved to call home. I nudged my head up, shoving my tongue in her mouth, and clasped a hand around her throat, rocking back and forth in her sex. The sounds of her cries and moans reverberated in my ears, letting me know the dominance I put forth paid off. Finally moving my hands to her plump ass, I squeezed tightly, speeding up my pumps.

. "Shit," I grunted, feeling her pussy holding me hostage, and gripped the side of the desk. I whispered in her ear how good she felt to me. "You've ruined me for anyone else."

Her eyes lustfully drew open, and her upper lip curved up. "You've damaged me from anyone else."

That saying sparked something in me, and I growled, thrusted faster, and moved a hand to her clit to get her to the end of the line. Her screams in my ear let me know I was right behind her.

"Xavier, I'm coming."

"Fuck! Right behind you, Peanut." I picked her up off the desk, and slipped out. She dropped to her knees and pulled my dick in her mouth, sucking out the last remnants of my seed.

"WHAT ARE YOU DOING HERE?"

I helped her stand, watching her put her clothes back on. I sipped up my pants and fixed the papers on my desk.

"Dinner with the girls was fun, but I missed you."

"Yeah."

She sat in the chair in my office.

"I feel like we've been working so much, we don't have time for each other."

"Same."

"So, what do we do about this?"

I sighed, not feeling up to an argument.

"I'm not sure."

Her brow cocked up.

"What does that mean?"

"Chelsey."

She held hand up to stop me.

"We just had a great time. Can we talk about this later?"

Her doe eyes blinked, with her lips poked out in a pout.

"Fine." She jumped up and gathered her shoes and purse to leave. I rose to stop her from leaving in a huff.

"Stop acting like that." I slammed the door before she could leave, with my hands wrapped around her full figure.

"Not acting like anything."

"You forget, I've known you since you were in middle school."

"Still pisses me off the same way."

"How is that?"

"I'm tired and not in the mood to argue."

I stepped back, giving her space so she could leave, and I watched her walk out, past one of my workers and waved at them.

"What's up with Chelsey?" she asked, pointing behind his back.

"Nothing."

"Seems like she was upset."

Not up for talking about my relationship, I grabbed up the inventory list and went to check on the supplies we needed to order.

"Did you need something?" I questioned.

She rolled her eyes and flipped me off.

"I should be offended, but I'm already dealing with an angry woman."

"Then you're not surprised if I stop talking to you."

"Go back to work."

"You don't pay me enough." She stuck out her tongue and skipped off to the front desk to check someone at the counter.

Next morning.

I carried the garbage down the walkway, opened the top, and dropped it inside, before waving over to the neighbor who constantly stuck her nose in anybody's business. Retta was in her late-sixties, widowed, and her kids lived out of the state. Since I moved to the area seven months ago, I'd gotten to know her, and she hung with my mom when she visited. Retta knew everyone's business; even Chelsey's parents came up in conversation sometimes when I was out here doing yard work or working out. I stepped back in the house, shut the screen door, and went to the kitchen to grab a glass of water, kissing the side of Chelsey's neck. She tried to move away, and I shook my head at her little attitude from last night.

"You're not talking to me today."

"Possibly."

"Peanut."

"Xavier."

"Somehow I think this has more to do with your father than me."

She dropped the spatula and turned around, glaring at me.

"My father is not the problem this time."

"What can I do to make it right?"

"We both need to compromise and spend more time together."

"I agree, but you know the second gym is taking up a lot of my time."

"And I'm happy for you but remember what matters."

"I will. So, how are things coming along at the bank?"

Chelsey shrugged and turned back around, picking up the spatula to plate the pancakes, eggs and place them on the table in front of me.

"I'm thinking of leaving the bank."

"You've always loved working there."

"I do, but my father is putting more pressure on me."

"Come work for me."

Her eyes lit up at my suggestion.

"Thank you for the offer, but that would be too much."

"Why do you say that?"

"Xavier, you ignore all the women flirting with you, but I see it, and I'd be ready to fight them."

I chuckled at her statement, and she hated the stories of how women come in the gym and want to get a one-on-one session. She even worked out in some of the class sessions. Some of the women knew she was my girlfriend, but they didn't care.

"Sorry, baby. I'll do better to put a stop to them flirting." I kissed her cheek.

"Thank you. What are your plans for today?" She scooped oatmeal in her mouth.

She wanted to go on a diet, and I often complained because in my eyes, she was perfect the way she was. I didn't care about her being a size zero or twenty. I loved every curve, stretch mark, smooth mound of her breasts, and sweet brown skin. The relationship we had was bumpy in the beginning. Her parents weren't too happy that she was dating a blue-collar type of guy with baggage from his upbringing. Plus, her family was well known in Tennessee, and my family was known as the black sheep. We made it work and became even closer, and things were looking up until recently.

"Meet up with Jordan and Mason at the gym."

"I have to see my mom, then run to the bank for a few minutes."

"Let's plan a date."

"Tonight?"

"Yeah, what do you want to do?"

Chelsey pushed her fork over into my plate and picked up a piece of pancake.

"Can we go to the club?"

"You can have whatever you want."

"What if I wanted to do something different at the club?"

"I don't share."

She snickered and stretched her hand out to palm my wrists.

"I know, but I was thinking we could try some new things out in the bedroom."

"Should have started the conversation off like that."

"Stop being so uptight." She rose, pecked me on the lips, picked her dishes up, and went to the sink.

"I told you long ago, you're mine."

I followed to put the leftover food in the trash and helped wash the dishes before showering and going off to work.

AN HOUR LATER, I WAS INSIDE MY SECOND LOCATION, teaching a class, and watched to make sure everyone was doing the steps correctly. I didn't teach as much as I used to in the beginning because the business side of things took up most of my time. I'd planned to have my assistant handle more of the workload, but I had control issues, and leaving anything up in the air would drive me crazy.

"Xavier, can you help me with my back?" LoriAnn called out from the second row. She was one of the ladies Chelsey had talked about flirting with repeatedly. rEver since she got her breast implants, she thought that would be a turn on for me, which was further from the truth. I liked my women natural, intelligent, and a great personality.

"You look to be doing okay to me," I said, standing next to her. I pushed the microphone up and turned the music volume low.

"I think I'm missing the correct pose; can you help me please?" She batted her eyelashes and smiled. I knew what she was doing, but I refused to fall into her trap, especially with Emma being here and staring. Jordan was planning on meeting me here soon, and Emma would run her mouth and say I was doing something I wasn't.

"Spread your legs a little further out. Overall, you got this," I replied, continuing to walk around the room. I checked to make sure everybody was comfortable and getting what they needed out of the session.

"All right, folks. Another great day. I hope you enjoyed it. Make sure to check the schedule for the next session."

"What if we want a private session?" LoriAnn blurted out, tossing her blond hair into a high ponytail.

"I no longer do private sessions, but my team can help you out."

"But I want you." She stepped in front of me and ran her finger down my arm.

"Xavier, have you talked to Chelsey today?"

I smirked, looking up at Emma as she stared at Lori-Ann's hand on my arm.

"Yes, we're planning a date tonight. Why?"

"You have a girlfriend?" LoriAnn asked.

"He does, so I'd advise you to knock off the flirting," Emma informed her. Out of the corner of my eye, I saw Jordan hold his finger up to his lips, creeping up behind Emma.

"Excuse me—"

"LoriAnn!"

Jordan bearhugged her from behind and twirled her in a circle.

"Put me down!" she snapped, clenching her fist and hitting him on the back.

I laughed and stepped around LoriAnn to gather my bag and clean up the equipment from the class. LoriAnn took that as her cue to leave, which I was grateful for. Emma was a spitfire like Chelsey when she was pushed.

"Man, what are you doing, messing with people." Jordan put Emma down on the floor.

"If Chelsey is not here, who else will have her back?" Emma replied.

"Not your job, Emma."

"Jordan, shut up and worry about yourself. I know you've been looking at other women," Emma fussed, took the keys out of his hands, and marched out of the room in a huff.

"Women, man." Jordan picked up one of the rugs off the floor to help me clean up.

"Is she still accusing you of stepping out?" I asked. Emma recently had a baby and worked on losing some of the baby weight, but she still felt like Jordan was cheating, even though they'd been married for a year.

"Same thing, different day. We'll be fine."

"I understand."

"My sister is acting funny."

"I think your father is starting up again."

"He was pissed about you guys living together?" Jordan asked.

"Probably, but it's mostly us not spending time together."

"You have to make it a priority. I'm taking Emma on a little couples trip."

"Where?"

I left the room, marked off the class, and blocked off the rest of my day with the front desk. Jordan went to the bar I had installed for the new location. A few minutes later, Jordan set the peach-lime smoothie on the desk, and I thanked him.

"We're heading to Jamaica for a few days."

"Who's keeping Jr.?"

"My parents."

"You guys deserve a little getaway."

"Being married comes with adjustments, so I'm not knocking Emma for feeling lonely."

My brow hiked at his admission.

"Is there something you need to tell me?"

"Bro, cut it out. I'm not cheating."

I raised my hands in shudder.

"I didn't say you were. Just need to know if I should get a spare room set for you," I joked. His eyes drew into slits.

"Not funny."

"I hear you, but what are you doing tonight?"

"Nothing but hanging with my kid and Emma."

"I'm going to the club with Chelsey."

"Spare me the details please."

"It's your fault we even know about the place."

"You always throw that in my face."

"Fuck you."

"But for real, my sister loves you. Ignore what naysayers throw your way."

"Thanks, bro." We shook hands, and I continued shuffling through orders.

"Have you thought of expanding the business more?"

"I am, and it's one cause of contention in my relationship."

"She thinks you'll have less time for her?"

"I've been on a kick of wanting everything perfect."

"That's understandable as a new businessman."

"Yeah, but I do stay here late at night sometimes, or come in extra early."

"Gotcha."

"Not good."

"Nope, especially if you want to eventually marry."

A knock at the door interrupted us, and I motioned for Mason to come in and take a seat.

"We were just talking about you."

"Whatever it is, leave me out of it please." He slugged his gym bag on the floor.

"Are you just getting in now?" I questioned.

"Yeah, I had an early meeting."

"We need a room reserved."

"Just called my assistant to hold one and tell her I said the top room."

"Thanks."

"No problem. So, how are things?" Mason picked up a piece of candy from the jar on my desk.

"Women."

"When are you planning to marry Chelsey?" he asked.

"More than likely after I have the next location up and running."

He and Jordan looked at each other.

"What?"

"All I'm going to say is that waiting too long can be disaster."

"Thanks, Oprah."

"Chelsey wants to get married," Jordan said.

"I know that, and I want to marry her, but not yet."

"Putting work before your relationship is not a good idea," Mason said.

Everyone knows I grew up poor and struggled to make ends meet once I got into what I loved to do and have the person I loved by my side. Att the same time, she came from wealth and was used to having money and her lifestyle. I planned to make sure it continued once we got married.

"I got this, guys."

CHELSEY

I lied and told Xavier I was only visiting with my mother and then some bank work, but I failed to mention I had an appointment with my doctor because I'd felt a little off lately. I was afraid it could be something serious and not knowing would stress me out even more. Dr. Abrams wrote in her notes as I sat up from the table and pulled the gown down.

"All right, Chelsey, so how long have you been feeling off?"

"About a month now."

"Have your periods been regular?" she questioned.

"Yeah, are you saying I'm pregnant?"

"No, I will have to wait and see what the test results are."

"Extra tired from working a lot."

"Are you putting in more hours than usual?"

"Yes."

She dropped the pen, removed her glasses, and sat back in the chair.

"We talked about your workload, Chelsey."

"I know, Dr. Abrams."

"Call me Chloe, but I think it's stress."

"Really think so?"

"Not to worry. Take a vacation or cut your workload down."

"I promise I will."

"Good, I'll call you in a few days with results."

We hugged, and I got dressed and set up an appointment to come back in a few months. I picked up my phone, walked to my car, and dialed Emma's number.

"Hey, lady."

"Hello."

"Where are you? You sound windy."

"Getting in my car, leaving the store."

"Well, I'm sitting here with throw up on my boobs from your nephew."

I laughed, turned out of the parking space, and headed through the green light. I propped my phone on the stand to talk on speaker.

"Leave my baby alone."

"Your baby is messy."

"Awww, Jr. is sweet."

"That's a lie."

"You need a girls' day out. What about lunch and the spa?"

"That sounds great, but your brother has planned a trip for us."

"What! When does this happen?"

"In two weeks, Jamaica."

"That sounds exciting."

"I can't wait to be buck naked on the beach." She laughed, and I chuckled at her statement.

"Have fun for me then."

"Why don't you come with Xavier?"

"He's too busy. Plus, my schedule is mounting."

"Too much work for me."

"Change the subject. How was class earlier?"

"It was fine, besides LoriAnn's ass."

"What she do now?"

"Her usual flirting and trying to suck Xavier's dick through his shorts."

We burst into laughter at her comment. I slowed through a yellow light and made it a block away from my job.

"Girl, LoriAnn is a mess."

"She really is and so desperate."

"Let her keep on with the mess."

"Why does she think she can have my man?"

"I don't know, but you better inform her before I do."

"You're right."

"Let me call you back. This boy is crying up a storm."

"No worries. Give him a kiss for me. I just made it to work."

"Sounds good. Call me on your lunch break."

"Okay. Bye, girl."

I ended the call and shut the door, holding on my brief-case and purse. I spoke to the security guard and staff, then sauntered to my office. I dropped my bags on the floor next to my desk and hit the answering machine for messages.

"Hey, Chelsey. You have an appointment."

"Who is it? I wasn't expecting anyone."

"A Ryan Barnes," she whispered, biting her nail.

"Candice, please be professional."

"Sorry."

"Send him back here." I bent down to open my brief-case and take out the banking loans I needed to approve. I heard someone whistle, and I jumped up fast.

"Sexy."

"Huh?"

"You're sexy."

A lump formed in my throat. The dark-brown eyes staring back at me looked like a lion ready to pounce on his prey. I would never cheat, but something about this man seemed odd and familiar.

"Ryan Barnes." He stuck his hand out for a shake.

"Chelsey, president of the bank."

"I know. You don't remember, do you?"

"No, have a seat."

He chuckled, opened his jacket, and sat with his legs gaped open. Ryan looked to be as tall as Xavier with all thirty-two teeth. Dimples on both sides of his cheek, light brown skin, low trim fade.

"I worked with your father."

"Oh."

"He told me I should meet with you about my company looking to do investments."

"Well, my father was mistaken, Ryan. We're not doing investments."

"He said you'd say that."

"My father tells a lot of lies."

"I think the last time we saw each other, we had a charity event together."

"That's where I know you from."

"Yeah, a children's charity my company helped sponsor."

"I hope you find the investors, but right now, that's not something I'm interested in doing."

"No problem, thought I'd ask. What about dinner?"

I stood, and he rose out of his seat. I rounded the desk and opened the office door for him to leave.

"I have a boyfriend."

"You're still with that handyman."

"Handyman?"

He nodded.

"Xavier's a businessman with two gyms that are very well known in town and across the country."

"Ouch! Sorry, didn't mean to step on your toes."

"I know what you meant, and you can tell my father it won't work."

"Touché."

He walked out of my office, and I slammed the door behind him and started to work. I lifted the phone to put in a lunch order, and Maya poked her head in my office.

"Am I interrupting?" she asked.

"Hey! I haven't seen you in forever, Senator Hill." I reached out for a hug.

"I know. I thought I'd pop in on my way to work to say hi."

"You look gorgeous."

"So do you. How are things going around here?" She motioned around my office.

My head tilted to the side in thought, and I pursed my lips.

"Exhausting."

"I told the girls that when I'm back in town, we all should get together for a girls trip or something."

"How is everything in politics?"

"Up and down as usual."

"How precious is this little one?"

"She's beautiful, funny, and sweet. How is your family?"

"You know my brother just had a baby boy, and he's married."

"Your parents must be happy."

"They've spoiled him so much."

"Probably waiting on you to have one."

"That won't happen for a while."

"You're not interested in having a family?"

"In the future, but we're living together now, and I like it being just us."

"I get it. Mason and I were just having fun in the beginning. Soon, we just became husband and wife."

"One day I'll get there."

"Well, I won't hold you up. Get back to work." Maya reached over for a hug, and I waved goodbye. I grabbed my cell and dialed my parents at home to talk with my father.

"Hello."

"Hi, Mom."

"Hey, Chelsey."

"Is Dad there?"

"No, he's at some busy meetings."

"What happened to him retiring?" I questioned.

"Your father will never stop working."

"Well, can you relay a message that he needs to stop trying to interfere in my love life."

"What did he do?"

"You remember Ryan Barnes?"

"That name sounds familiar."

"He owns a lot of real estate properties and has a charity we contributed to."

"Oh, right, I remember."

"Yeah, he just showed up here in my office."

"Maybe he wanted to do business."

"Mom, I'm not stupid."

"All right, I'll talk with your father."

"Thanks, please tell him this was the last straw."

"Chelsey."

"I'm serious. Get over it. Xavier is my forever."

❧ 4 ❧

CHELSEY

The club was crowded tonight, and I was happy Xavier reserved a room tonight and ordered us drinks and a light meal. I removed my jewelry and stood naked in front of him as he held onto anal beads in his hand.

"Turn around," he commanded, and I nodded, doing as he instructed and climbing on top of the bed. I felt his warm hands caress my ass. I watched him pick up the bottle of lube and pop it open to prepare for what was to come.

"Take a deep breath, baby," he said. I felt an intense pressure once he pushed each bead in slowly. Clenching my teeth, I squeezed the sheets in my hand as he came up behind me and pushed my legs close together as I lay flat on my stomach. Tonight, he'd wanted to be gentle and take his time exploring my body and giving into my desires. Feeling his kisses down my back to each ass cheek, he separated and pushed his large girth in my pussy. A lump formed in my throat, knowing how good he made me come at times. Sometimes, it became a game to see if I'd squirt on command.

"Fuck me... Yes, right there," I panted, trying to push back into him. Often, he'd tell me to bring him to his knees, but he couldn't imagine what it felt like to have him moaning and rumbling under his breath.

"Shit..." He buried his nose in the pillow next to me, grinding back and forth.

"Harder, X," I cried out, needing him to lose control.

"You feel that?" he questioned, giving me punishing deep thrusts. Our skin smacked against each other until he abruptly pulled out and turned me over. He lifted me around the waist halfway, bent his legs, and slid back in to pump faster. I propped myself up with my hands, barely able to control the orgasm that lingered in my core. Something about these new tricks turned me on even more.

"Mmmm... Ohhh God... .Xavier," I screamed when he lifted me up and stepped off the bed, still holding me around the waist. I reached out to grab the back of his head and smashed my mouth on his. The tingling feeling rose, and Xavier pushed my left leg down and propped my right leg up in his arm. He thrusted from the bottom, and I felt my soul leave my body at him slamming into me hard.

"The room is spinning... Ahh!"

"Your pussy is choking my dick."

"Please can I come?" I asked.

"Damn, come now," he grunted, moved his hand, and rubbed my clit.

"Ughh... Xavier." My head fell onto his shoulder.

His tongue snaked his way through my lips. I rubbed the back of his head.

"I love it when you get flexible," he whispered in my ear.

❧

Three days later.

Tonight, we had family dinner with my parents and my brother, his wife Emma. Xavier was dressed nicely, and I threw on a simple black, knee-length dress with wide straps. Xavier held my hand. and I knocked, leaning my head on his shoulder.

"Hopefully we don't stay long."

"Let's pray everybody is cool tonight." Xavier responded, knocking on the door again. The butler opened it and smiled.

"Miss Chelsey," Anderson said.

"Hi, Anderson."

I removed my coat, and he took it, hanging up, along with Xavier's. We headed into the family room and heard laughter. I smiled at my nephew in my brother's arms and glanced around the room full of guests. My mouth dropped open in shock.

"There's Chelsey," Gerald blurted out. All eyes looked at us.

Ryan was here with an older couple I assumed were his parents. He looked gorgeous with a fresh, trimmed beard. He wore a black Tom Ford suit, which I guessed from a glance because I had purchased the same thing for Xavier months back. I grew heated in annoyance that my father would stoop so low after everything we'd been through to become a family again. He promised to make an effort with me being in a relationship with Xavier, but that was all a lie from the simple fact Ryan showed up at my office. Now, he was here at their house.

"Peanut, you good."

I cleared my throat.

"Yes, I'm fine. Why do you ask?"

"You went blank for a second."

"Finally, Princess has arrived," Jordan joked, walked over to Xavier, and dapped, then gave me a hug.

"Shut up, Jordan." I pushed him in the shoulder.

"Not my fault you take forever to get dressed," Jordan complained. I rolled my eyes and grabbed my nephew.

"Come here, Auntie's baby."

Emma passed him over, and I kissed his chunky cheeks. I was planning to ignore everyone except Jordan and Emma. You would never catch me disrespecting my parents, but I was good with ignoring them to keep the peace and from keeping Xavier out of the games my father was playing. I walked down the hall to the kitchen to grab a bottle for Jr. and a drink for me.

"Are you planning to ignore me all night?"

My back stiffened. I felt my skin get warm, as my nephew continued sucking on his bottle without a care in the world. I turned around to face the culprit and put on a fake smile so the chef wouldn't freak out.

"Mr. Barnes, it's nice to see you again."

I pulled the bottle from my Jr.'s mouth and held him on my shoulder to pat his back.

"Is that your boyfriend?"

"Mr. Barnes, how is that any of your business?"

"You're cute when you're upset."

"I know. My man tells me that all the time."

He smirked and slid his tongue over his top lip.

"Chelsey, you good?" Xavier approached, stood to the side of me, and stared at Ryan.

"Ryan, and you are?" He reached a hand out toward Xavier.

"Someone you don't want to know about."

XAVIER

The guy looked from me toward Chelsey, like they held a secret that shouldn't get out, but I knew all her old boyfriends. If you want to call them boyfriends; we ran every guy away who tried to talk to her.

"No offense, but Chelsey was introducing me to her nephew."

"You see him. Anything else?"

"What's your name again?"

"I didn't give it."

Chelsey held her hand out, blocking me from charging at him.

"Ryan, I think you better go," she said.

The cockiness on his face went away. He seemed more nervous when my fists drew at my side. I tdidn't play about a lot of things, and Chelsey was one of them. I caught on as soon as we walked in that her parents were trying to set her up with him. All this time of him pretending to be cool with me was fake and phony. For Chelsey's sake, I never said a word, but tonight went overboard.

"You okay." She wrapped her arm around my waist and

leaned into my chest. I took Jr. out of her hold and held him in my arms.

"I'm fine, but your little boyfriend's going to get his ass kicked."

She slapped me on the chest.

"He's not my boyfriend."

"You sure, because he's really working on trying to be."

"I already have a boyfriend."

"What's his name?"

"Xavier."

"Good girl." I bent down, ran my tongue across her lips, pushed my tongue through, and sucked on her bottom lip.

"Eww... don't do that nasty shit in front of my son," Jordan barked, grabbing his son out of my hands.

"Shut up, Jordan. You act like you don't do worse in front of him." Chelsey pinched his arm. He stepped out of her way, as she chased him around the island in the kitchen.

"Jr., you see your auntie. Nasty, man," Jordan joked, and I chuckled and held my hand up to cover my laugh.

Chelsey's face grew into a grimace.

"Stop telling him that stuff. Babies retain the stupid shit you say."

"Chelsey, are you going to ignore your parents all night?" Jordan stopped running, passed his son back to Chelsey, and grabbed a bottle of water out of the fridge.

"Yep, so don't get on my bad side, or join my list." Chelsey strolled out of the kitchen, we followed as she played with the baby.

The dining room table was set for a large party, but it was a small gathering, so this told me her parents wanted to impress him and his parents.

"Xavier, I'm glad you could come, but Chelsey said your businesses have taken off?" Lynidas asked.

I pulled the chair out for Chelsey and sat next to her. Ryan sat across next to his parents.

"Chelsey wanted me here, so I make sure to spend as much time together as we can."

"He's even thinking of opening a third fitness center," Chelsey replied.

"Does that really bring in any money?" Gerald asked.

"Daddy, we talked about this."

"Tonight is about family, and new business. Mr. Barnes is looking to expand his business." Lynidas held her glass up for toast.

"I went by Chelsey's office earlier today, but she declined my offer," Ryan said.

I clenched the napkin in my hand, as he stared at Chelsey and smirked. Swiftly I glanced at her to meet her eyes, and she quickly handed Jr. to Emma.

"Xavier, let's go." Chelsey jumped up out of her seat.

"We haven't had dinner yet, Chelsey," Lynidas said.

"I lost my appetite," Chelsey replied and walked out of the dining room.

"Ryan, I apologize for my daughter's behavior. I will get you with the right people," Gerald answered.

I saved and worked to get everything I had now and to be with Chelsey I knew she was a prize. She was expected to date a guy on a certain financial level to provide for her. For him to stand in my face after we talked and made some type of resolution. Chelsey had no problems out of our relationship.

"Let's go."

"I'll call you tomorrow, Peanut," Jordan said. She kissed her nephew on the lips, and I grasped her hand and walked out together, not looking back.

THE FOLLOWING DAY, I HAD MORRIS AND WARREN follow up on Ryan Barnes and his business. Their work not only involved securing events but delved into background checks and private investigation if needed. I knocked on the door of Morris' office and waited to be let inside.

"It's open!" he called out.

I turned the knob and walked in to see Lisa sitting on the edge of his desk.

"Hey, Xavier!" Lisa said.

"How are you, Lisa?"

We hugged, and I sat in the chair across from his desk.

"I'm doing good. Actually, I'm meeting Chelsey later for shopping and lunch."

y"Try not to spend too much of my money," Morris blurted out. She rolled her eyes, pecked him on the lips, and grabbed her purse to leave. Morris opened the desk drawer, pulled a yellow envelope, and tossed it on top of the desk in front of me.

"What did you find?"

I flipped it over and took out stacks of photos and documents with Ryan's name on the label.

"He's looking to make a name for himself, working with a lot of big-time people."

"Looks like he's skimmed some money off the top."

"He's good, but most importantly, Chelsey was right to not work with him."

"Did you tell her?"

He shook his head.

"No, I thought it should come from you."

"Yeah, her father is adamant about doing business with him." I looked at the numbers and noticed a lot of money changing hands.

"You'll see even more photos of Chelsey there at the club and work."

My nose flared looking over the photos he had taken of my girl and me together. This was a game to him, and I wasn'tt one to play games when it came to my woman.

"What do you want to do?"

Irritation at him grew, and my pulse raced.

"I'll handle him."

I stood, and Morris jumped up and held his hand out to block me from leaving.

"I didn't give you that information to possibly end up in jail."

"Don't worry. I'll have a little conversation with him and be on my way."

Morris chucked his chin up.

"Just a conversation."

"I'm a businessman first."

"Yeah, but we both know how you are about Chelsey."

I growled at his comment, bringing up the past when Mason mistook her for someone else, and we almost got into a fight.

"Sounds like you're worried about me."

"Any friend of Lisa's, I have to protect. Chelsey is her friend, which means we look out for each other."

"Thanks, Morris, but I promise not to kill him. A black eye, now that's different."

I smacked the papers against my hand and marched out of his office to find Mr. Barnes and catch up on some things.

❧ 6 ❧
CHELSEY

The mall was crowded, and I held two bags in my hands from Lane Bryant. I needed some more comfortable clothing before the winter time got here and some rain boots I'd been eyeing for the longest time. My father tried calling me earlier today, and I ignored his call and met up with the girls for a day of pampering before Emma went on her trip.

"Let's go in here." Emma pointed at Victoria's Secret. We followed, and I saw a black silk robe with a matching bra set. I picked it up to check the price and look for my size.

"You ready for your trip, Emma?" Lisa asked.

"Yes, I can't wait to be on a beach with my boo." Emma picked through the row of red stockings and bras.

"How long are you guys going for?"

"A week," Emma replied, holding a bra up to show us.

"That's cute. Try a pink or lavender color," I suggested, going to the rack of tights and pajama pants.

"Why didn't we get invited?" Lisa wondered.

"For real, I'm done filming for two months. I need a

vacation," Kyla pouted, holding three pairs of socks and thongs.

"This is a reconnection trip for me and Jordan," Emma answered, and I nodded in agreement. She'd been working nonstop as a stay-at-home mom. Plus, with Jordan working nonstop, they needed time together as much as me and Xavier.

"Well, we can plan something for couples next time."

"I vote for that." Maya joined us, and we all screamed and crowded around her as security stood, blocking people off. I should have asked to have the store closed for us to shop privately since we had a politician and actress, along with Lisa in attendance.

"Maybe we should get out of here. The place is getting a lot of attention," Emma suggested.

"Are you done shopping?" I questioned.

"Just need these." She held up a thong set, switched over to the register, and I laughed.

"You won't even have that on long enough once Jordan sees you wearing them."

"That's true. Our love life has been in a little rut," Emma complained.

"Preaching to the choir." I raised my hand.

"Strong women with hot guys, and no time to fuck. What is the world coming to now?" Lisa joked, and I chortled and placed money down to pay on my nightgown set.

"I could go for something to eat."

"Where do we want to go?" Lisa asked.

"Try that pizza place on Third and Poplar Avenue," Kyla said.

"No, I'm tired of crowds. Let's go to my place and order food," I said.

All the girls agreed and finished paying for their items. Lisa and Kyla piled into my car, and Maya told the security team to follow her in mine since Emma drove her car, and she would ride with her.

⚜

THIRTY MINUTES LATER, WE SAT OUT BY THE POOL IN THE back with bottles of wine, fruit, cheese tray, with a variety of meals from salads, fish tacos, and pizza. I opened a bottle of wine and served the drinks, while Maya fixed the plates as they lounged near the cabana deck.

"So, Morris wants me to move to Vegas," Lisa blurted out, taking a gulp of her wine.

All of them gasped in response, and I sipped my drink.

"What do you want?" Maya asked.

"I might feel the same way." Lisa shrugged her shoulders.

"Warren and I are splitting time between Vegas and here. He's also expanding into Chicago," Kyla told me.

"I feel like Xavier and I are drifting apart."

"Wait! Why am I the last to know all this?" Maya argued.

"You're a senator, wife, and mother, Maya."

"We can't come to you with all our problems." Lisa walked up to the table and poured more wine.

"I understand, but I feel like our little group is growing apart. I just met Emma." Maya pointed toward Emma and bit into her pizza.

"We have to make a promise to stay in touch."

"No matter what, we'll always have our group chats." Lisa laughed and shimmied in her seat.

"This is like a full-circle moment."

"What do you mean?" Emma said.

"Because of you, we went to Club Seek, and they found men." I pointed at Emma.

"Ohhh, that's right. That's for helping me find the best pussy eater in the world." Lisa snapped her finger and held her glass up in the air. Everyone burst into laughter as Emma spat out her drink.

"Lisa, some things you can keep to yourself," Maya fussed.

"I know, Maya, but don't act like Mason doesn't have your toes circling," Lisa replied.

"I've been feeling a little off lately," I said, quickly draining my glass of alcohol. I reached for another bottle, and Lisa slapped my hand away.

"What do you mean off?"

"Tired, not able to eat. I went to the doctor."

"When did this happen?"

"A few days ago."

"When were you going to tell us?"

"Dr. Abrams is running tests."

"Call her." Lisa dug into her purse and pulled her cell phone out.

"Her office is probably closed. It's going on four in the afternoon." I looked down at my watch.

"We're best friends, almost sisters. Hell, she's your sister-in-law, and you kept this from her," Lisa argued.

"Maybe you're pregnant," Kyla blurted, grabbed some tacos off the table.

"I'm not ready for that."

"You're never ready," Maya and Emma said at the same time.

"What did Xavier say?" Lisa questioned.

"He doesn't know."

"Chelsey," Emma fussed.

"Our schedules are crazy right now, then there was the mess with my father at the house."

"What happened to that?" Lisa questioned.

Emma and I peered at each other.

"My dad tried to set me up."

"With another guy? Like a date?" Lisa asked.

"More like a marriage," Emma muttered.

"Had the guy come to my job, then my parents' house with his parents," I said.

"Wow," Maya said.

"I refuse to call them."

"Even your mom." Kyla passed Emma some of her food and sat at the edge of the chair.

"I'll call her in a few days, but it's mostly my dad."

"You're doing the right thing. Ignore him," Lisa said.

"Xavier was ready to kick his ass at the table." I chuckled.

"That plays no games about you," Kyla said.

"I know."

$$\maltese \quad 7 \quad \maltese$$

XAVIER

I pushed him up against the wall, held my arm up against his neck, and placed pressure with my fists balled up.

My thoughts went from talking to wanting to punch, then shoot him in my mind. I didn't need to be away from Chelsey, so I optioned for talking unless he got out of hand.e

"Mr. Barnes, Xavier is here to see you."

"Send him in, Rachel."

She waved me in, and I smiled politely and watched her close the door. I locked it and held the envelope in my hand. He stood, buttoning his jacket behind his desk.

"Xavier, what do I owe for this visit?" Ryan picked up the envelope I had tossed on his desk.

"You've been stalking my girl."

He chuckled.

"I don't need to stalk."

"Oh, because you have money, right?"

"Money, charm, world class."

"Look, you piece of shit!"

"I can have security here in a split second."

"Fuck your security."

"It's not my fault her parents want her with me."

"Chelsey doesn't want you."

"Did she say that?"

"I'm going to say this for the last time, because I know she already spoke to you. Leave Chelsey alone."

"Or what?"

"Find out."

"If we do business together, maybe I'll back off."

I chortled at his comment.

"The business you're stealing from me, right?"

"You can't prove that."

"Try me and see. If you come in contact with Chelsey or her father."

He blew out a breath and waved me off. I started to charge toward him.

"Okay, I'll stay away." He held his arms up in surrender.

"That's a safe bet."

❧

I DOUBLE CHECKED THE COLLAR AROUND HER NECK AND peered in her eyes as she watched my every move. Tonight, we decided to take it another step further with her chained by a spreader bar separating her legs and hands in suspension in the air. Her curvy full figure was a beautiful sight to see, and I decided to turn the video on. I needed a reminder of this for when we were alone again and needed inspiration. Chelsey moaned as my hand ran down from her ankle to her inner thigh. I smelled her sweet arousal, and my dick hardened and jumped, ready to dig into her walls.

"She's already screaming for me."

Chelsey nodded and gasped when I slid not one, but two fingers inside.

"Taste yourself, baby." I lifted my finger to her lips.

"Mmmm..."

"You're about to be fucked so hard."

"Please."

"You're my queen, remember that."

"You're my king."

I couldn't wait any longer and pushed forward to her asshole. I felt her tense up and lovingly tweaked her nipples, kissed her lips, and teased her clit to loosen her up.

"Just a little more, baby."

"Oh... Yes." She gasped.

"Oh, fuck!" I moaned and felt her rock back and forth, meeting my thrusts.

"Xavier!"

"I need you to come on my tongue." I suddenly pulled out, dropped to my knees, sucking, slurping, and twirling my tongue on her wet, gushy sex. Hearing her screams and shouts of pleasure gave me motivation to never lose sight of what I had in front of me. My past could never compare to what my future looked like before me.

"Shittt..." she moaned and squirted in my mouth, and I stood back up, shoved my dick in her tight pussy, and muttered more curse words under my breath once I came behind her. I bent over, deepened our kiss, and sucked on her tongue. Seeing the exhaustion on her face, I stood and reached for the towel from the back of the chair, wiped us off, and unhook the chains.

"You ready for bed?"

"I'm ready to go home."

"As you wish..."

I kissed the top of her forehead and helped her down, and we redressed and left for home.

❧

THE NEXT DAY, I DROVE WITH CHELSEY TO HER doctor's follow-up appointment to get her results. I was more nervous than she was, and I couldn't fathom her being sick and not waking up to her face every day.

"Stop worrying." I held her hand up, kissing her palm.

"Trying to stay positive, but what if…"

"No what ifs. We don't think like that."

"Thank you for coming with me."

"Never worry about me being at your side."

"So, something interesting happened early today when you were in the shower," Chelsey said.

"What?"

"My father called and apologized."

"Your father?" I turned at the light into the parking structure, went to a spot near the door, and cut the car off.

"Yes, I know."

"What did he say?"

"He loves me and said Ryan's not going to bother me again."

"I'm happy to hear that, baby."

"Xavier."

"Yeah?" I opened the passenger door to help her out.

"Did you do something to Ryan?"

"Chelsey, you know me, baby."

"That's the point."

"Stop worrying about somebody that isn't in her world view." I lifted her chin, pressed a kiss on her lips, and smacked her on the ass. Holding the door open, she swished in front of me, making me adjust myself.

"Hi Chelsey, the doctor is ready for you."

"Great, thank you."

"Follow me back." The office assistant pushed the door open and let us in to have a seat to wait.

"Are you nervous?" Chelsey questioned.

I reached over and grasped both her hands. She looked into my eyes.

"No reason to be nervous. We're good, and you'll be fine." I bent down, slid my tongue over her upper lip, and wrapped her hands around me.

With a knock at the door, the doctor stepped in and cleared her throat.

"Dr. Abrams." Chelsey giggled and wiped her lipstick off my lips.

"Xavier, good to see you again," she said.

"You too, Doc."

"Tell me the truth," Chelsey asked.

"I ran every test, and you're fine. You need to relax and take a vacation," the doctor replied.

"Seriously?" Chelsey said.

"No issues at all?"

"None. She's just stressed and needs to calm down. Her blood pressure is a little high," the doctor answered, pulling out her records.

"Thank you, Doctor."

"No problem. I like you, Chelsey, and want you to stay focused," the doctor said.

"I promise... self-care going forward," Chelsey promised.

CHELSEY

A month later.

I groaned, slamming the alarm off, and rolled over to feel Xavier's side of the bed was empty. I opened one eye and looked around the room. Then Xavier, wearing a pair of boxer briefs, sauntered back into the bedroom from the fog coming from the bathroom.

"Get up, sleepyhead."

"Why! This is supposed to be a vacation," I whined, falling back under the covers.

"As soon as you get up, we can have one." Xavier climbed on the bed and tickled me under the cover.

"Stop!" I screamed, trying to crawl away from him.

"Not until you get up."

"Fine, I'm up."

"Great, per doctor's orders, I want you to relax." Xavier jumped out of bed and extended a hand for me to take.

"What's the plan for today?"

"You shower, have breakfast, and then we head to the beach."

"It's gorgeous here."

"Jordan was able to get a great discount on a last-minute flight for us, so I wanted to fly you out and enjoy this weekend together."

"You didn't have to do that." I turned the shower on and stripped out of the pajamas I had picked up at Victoria's secret.

"I know, but I wanted to enjoy it all to myself."

"Well, Jamaica is the place to be."

"Might end up wanting to buy a place out here."

"Couldn't hurt to look around." I closed the shower door, grabbing the resort body wash and towel.

"Maybe not today, but we will."

"How about you come and join me?" I pushed the door back open for him to get a glimpse of me in soap suds.

"As tempting as you look, I need to get dressed and make sure breakfast is ready."

"Ugh... you're no fun," I shouted from the other side of the door.

"Later. I'll make it up to you."

⌘

Two hours after getting dressed and eating breakfast, we went out to the local shops and walked around, meeting new people and sightseeing. I wanted to go to the beach later, once the sun set, and possibly get a quickie in before we went to bed. Xavier didn't mind, but the shopping part annoyed him because of the amount of stuff I bought. We had to grab a car service to send it all back to the resort and come back to do a second round of shopping.

"This drink is amazing, babe."

"Don't drink too much. I need you ready and aware for tonight."

"Oh, I'll be ready."

"Listen, have you spoken to your father before we came on the trip?"

"Why do you have to spoil the day?"

"I'm not trying to spoil our day."

"Then leave my father out of the conversation."

"Chelsey, at some point you'll need to speak with him."

"I'll talk to my mom."

"Great, but don't isolate your father out."

"Why not?"

"One day, you may need him."

"I have my brother."

"Glad to hear, but a girl needs her father."

He was right. I stayed in touch with my mom cover the past few weeks after the dinner incident. Jordan said he argued back and forth with my dad on my behalf, and I thanked him for stepping in because that man always thought he was right.

I put the drink down on the table, stared out to the ocean, and decided to be spontaneous for once and run out to the beach and let loose.

"Chelsey! Chelsey!" Xavier shouted, ran behind me, and picked me up.

"Ahhh!"

"Woman, what are you doing?"

"I want to get in the water. Put me down."

"Don't scare me like that."

He put me on the ground. I looked to my left, then right, and smirked. I wiggled my brows, lifted my dress, and tossed it on the ground.

"Come catch me," I purred and ran off toward the ocean.

I splashed in, feeling the cool waters. Xavier's eyes darkened,, and I knew the beat was coming out. He'd make me pay for this little rendezvous.

"You're going to pay for that."

"You have to catch me first."

I swam out a little farther, away from any crowds, and he caught up to me, wrapped his arms around my waist, and pulled me into a kiss.

"Mmmmm...." he moaned, sucked on my lips, and gripped my breasts.

I threw my head back as he peppered kisses along my neck and shoulder. I locked my legs around his waist and felt him push in, stroking me slowly.

"Ughh... Xavier," I panted, tightening my grip to help balance my weight.

"Shit... We need to take this inside."

"Okay... Ahh."

Xavier pulled out of me, swam back to the beach, and led me back to the resort. We went to the shower and ended up back in bed, finishing what I started earlier. Later that evening, after going three rounds, I set up a nice dinner with all his favorites and placed everything on the deck. We sat under the stars and moon, eating and talking.

"You ever think about getting married and having kids?"

"Where did that come from?"

I cut into my calamari and took a piece.

"We never talked about the future."

"You're my future. Wherever you are, I'm there."

"I get that, but you have a booming business. It takes you away."

"Our business."

"Xavier."

"Chelsey, you know my past. It's not pretty."

"Let's drop it."

❧ 9 ❧

XAVIER

I'd been holding onto the news that my fitness center would be opening another location and the guys investing to expand it even further. They thought it would be great to open a division in New York, and I was planning to scout some locations. Telling Chelsey now would only start an argument, after bringing up the topic of kids.

"Listen."

"No, I don't want to fight. This is about us enjoying ourselves."

"We are, but I hate to see you pout, so we can shelve this conversation."

"Sure."

"What do you want to do tomorrow?"

"Maybe go scuba diving."

"We can try that."

"Something that gets us really engulfed in the scenery."

"Whatever you want, sweetheart."

"Are you full?"

"I'm stuffed. This was good," I said.

"It's getting late. You want to watch a movie?"

"Yeah, it'll probably put me to sleep."

We grabbed the bottle of wine and stepped in the living room tod set up a movie. She grabbed a blanket out of the bedroom, and I poured us another glass of wine and placed her feet in my lap.

"I could get used to this."

"What, being spoiled?"

"You love spoiling me." She poked her lips out for a kiss, I leaned over, pecked her lips, then rubbed a hand up and down her thigh.

"I do."

"Good."

Two hours later, we were startled out of a sound sleep at the ringing of a cell phone. I looked around and noticed it was her phone ringing.

"Babe, your phone is ringing." I nudged her in the shoulder.

"Huh."

"Your brother is calling."

"Oh... hello," she answered groggily.

She sat up quickly, with a perplexed expression.

"Is he all right!" she shouted.

"What's wrong?"

"Okay, we're leaving now." She hung up the phone and jumped off the couch.

"Chelsey, what's going on."

"We have to go back home; Dad is in the hospital."

I stopped her from pacing and pulled her in my arms to help calm her down. She started to hyperventilate.

"He's going to be fine; I need you to breathe for me, baby."

"Xavier, I can't lose my dad."

"You won't, I promise."

"We need to get a flight out."

"Just pack your things, and I'll handle everything else." I kissed her on the forehead, grabbed our phones, and made some calls to get us back to town fast.

❧

I STOOD OFF TO THE SIDE AS CHELSEY LAID HER HEAD ON her father's chest, while the monitors beeped. The look of relief on her face and his when we made it through those doors must have helped his recovery. He had a mild heart attack and needed to relax, cut out any stress for a while. Jordan stayed up here until we arrived and then went home to be with Emma and his son. Her mom was sleeping in the corner. Chelsey continued talking with her father, and some type of resolution was had because smiles crossed her face and his. Probably knocking on death's door helped him to see that he needed to change his ways and rethink trying to control his kids' lives.

"We'll be up here tomorrow, Daddy," Chelsey said and kissed him on the cheek. He nodded, letting her hand go.

"Xavier," he said.

"Yes, sir." I kicked my foot off the wall, treading toward the end of the bed.

"I'm sorry for everything."

"Me too."

"You're like a son to me, and I treated you horrible."

"No stress, Daddy," Chelsey said.

"Stop smothering me, Chelsey."

He waved her off, and Chelsey rolled her eyes.

He's for sure back to normal," Chelsey muttered.

I chuckled and clasped her hand, leading her out of the hospital room to head home for the night. The next morning, Jordan called to drop off Jr. with Chelsey to keep him while he and Emma helped their mom bring their father home. Standing in the kitchen, I poured coffee and set the table for breakfast, watching her stroll with him in her arms.

"He looks like your brother more and more."

I motioned for her to sit down.

"I know, it's scary."

"How's your dad doing?"

"Better. He has to change his diet and cut out stress."

"Something you know well about."

"I'm going to spend more time with you and my nephew." She lifted him in her arms, and he giggled.

"You look good with a baby in your arms."

She smirked and passed him over to me.

"He's a big boy." Chelsey kissed me on the lips, took her seat again, and poured syrup on her waffles.

"I'm still processing my brother having a kid and Dad almost dying."

"It's going to take time."

"Glad to spend that time with you."

"We already went for two rounds before he got here. Control yourself, Peanut."

"Ughh, I hate when you call me that."

"I know."

"Not the same little kid who had a crush on you when I was younger."

I placed the bottle in Jr.'s mouth and watched him stare into my eyes. I smiled at the innocence across his face.

"You mean the same one who approached me and said they wanted to F.U.C.K."

Her head fell back in laughter.

"He's a baby; he doesn't understand a word you said."

"Doesn't matter. I want to do what my parents didn't do."

"Which is?"

"Protected."

"You're going to be a great dad one day."

"Long as I have you."

EPILOGUE: CHELSEY

One year later.

I closed my eyes and pictured myself on a beach with all my family and friends, laughing and dancing together. The relationship I built with Xavier was a long time coming, and we weathered the storm.

"Chelsey! Push one more time," the doctor demanded. The sweat on my forehead and brow dripped down my nose and cheeks. I did the breathing exercises to keep steady and pushed one more time. I felt a lightness in my body when I heard the cries of my son.

"Chelsey, he's beautiful," Mom said.

I was in a daze and barely could keep my eyes open from the ten hours of labor to get our child here safely. Xavier held him in his arms and walked back over to me, placing him on my bare chest to do skin to skin.

"He looks just like you," I cooed and rubbed the back of his head. Xavier bent down and kissed me on the lips.

"Thank you, Peanut."

"Thank you for being an amazing friend, lover, and husband."

"I can't believe I wasted so long to make you mine."

"It was meant to be like this."

"You're right. Get some rest though; I'll stay up with him."

"What do you want to name him?"

"Michael Xavier."

"He's perfect like his mommy."

He yawned and opened his eyes briefly, and I teared up again, seeing the same ocean-blue eyes like his father. My son would be a heartrbreaker, and I needed to prepare myself to not hold on too tight.

"He's starting to cry; I think he's hungry."

"I'll feed him, then you can rock him to sleep," I told Xavier, who helped me pull the gown down and get Michael to latch on properly to right breast. It hurt a little, but I knew this was what I wanted in the beginning when the doctor said I was too stressed and needed to relax. I took her advice and cut my hours at work and spent more time with Xavier, going on trips together. One of those trips ended up being the night we conceived Michael. Now I had all the blessings and the man of my dreams, who I had loved since I could remember.

⚜

Two years later.

"Do you Xavier take Chelsey to be your husband, in sickness and in health?"

When I thought of my life after giving birth to my son, I never took that day for granted, even when I married Xavier. Here we were years later, and I stopped working at the bank. He opened up a chain of fitness centers, and I was a stay-at-home mom with Michael our little Angel. Xavier wanted more kids, we talked about waiting until

Michael is older, in school. After we had our first, I couldn't deny seeing the joy from my family growing.

"I do." Xavier smiled and held onto my hands. We stood in the backyard of our home he had built. Xavier became a multi-millionaire, and no one would ever know. We lived just as modest as we did before.

"Do you, Chelsey—"

"I do!" I yelled excitedly, and our friends and family laughed. The yard was decorated in white and pink with rose petals on the ground. A large sign with our names and the kids hung over the balcony.

"I now pronounce you husband and wife."

Xavier didn't even wait for him to finish, smashing his lips onto my mouth and palming my butt. I extended my arms around his neck. Xavier surprised me with renewing our vows, and I had a surprise for him later when we went to our own private club in the basement.

❦

I hope you enjoyed Chelsey and Xavier's story. Please also check out the bonus scene.

BONUS SCENE: XAVIER

Our relationship started here, so I wanted to celebrate at the place we frequented together and spark up what made us take the step to be together. The kids were home with her parents for the day, so I blocked off the day to spend time with her on our anniversary. She wore a sexy cross-body Ivy Park workout fit. All her curves and fat ass poked out that I loved to taste at night when we were alone.

"Xavier!" she gasped when my hand went to her lower back and peeled back the shorts. She kicked them off, showing only a red thong. I smacked her ass, watched it jiggle, and kissed each cheek.

"I want you to do five pushups."

"What do I get in return?" she questioned.

"I want you face down, ass up with me over you as you rise."

"Somehow I think this won't be an actual workout."

"It can be."

The smirk I held showed I was planning something else behind my little suggestion. I had the whole place locked down for the day and put on some music, brought drinks and food in case we needed them. She turned around, got in position, and started to drop to the floor, I pushed her legs together in the proper form. Then I removed my shirt and shorts.

"What are you doing?" She licked her lips.

"We're going to start with me behind you as you come up.:

"Your dick is going to be poking me."

"That's the point, my love."

"Somehow I knew you'd make these torturous."

"If you do a full push up, I'll give you a reward either with my tongue or my dick."

"If I can't?"

"You don't get either."

"That's not fair."

"I promise, by the end of this workout, you won't be sweaty from just pushups."

She rolled her eyes, turned around back into her normal form, and lifted, causing her ass to graze the tip of my dick.

"Oh, God."

"It's only me here, baby."

SEEK TO TRUST

SEEKING IN ROMANCE BOOK 5

SYNOPSIS

Emma's been happily in love with Jordan most of her life. Now, as parents to a little boy and working on her business, she's finding Jordan is spending less and less time with her as he navigates his family's business. Being his wife and his sister's best friend, Emma wonders if she made the wrong decision when her trust is broken.

"I hope you're enjoying yourself. I can't believe you, Jordan." I dropped my phone on the table, glanced around the food I made, and blew out the candles. Today was supposed to be about us reconnecting and making time for our relationship. He promised he would come home straight away, but once again, he lied. Jordan was a busy man, working for his family's business, but today was about his marriage. Chelsey was cool with watching our son tonight, which made my plans complete. Everyone knew I had the evening blocked off and not to disturb us unless it was an emergency with our son.

Since I became a mom, all of my time was focused on him and trying to stay on top of work. Jordan and I barely spoke to each other unless it was about our child. Our life was a routine of us getting up in the morning, getting dressed, and leaving for the day. No more breakfast dates or weekend getaways for just the two of us. We'd been together for a while, and I knew some marriages grew stagnant, but I never saw myself being one of those couples.

I lifted the plate of food, walked into the kitchen, and

dumped it in the trash; it wasn't even worth saving. He loved when I made marinated chicken, greens, baked potato, and spaghetti. Even his favorite dessert of strawberry shortcake would have been presented before we headed upstairs to the bedroom. Not up for washing dishes, I placed the leftovers in the fridge and grabbed my cell to march upstairs and turn on the shower. I scrolled through social media and saw he posted a photo of him with his coworkers out at a bar.

"That bastard," I hissed, put my phone on the counter, turned the shower up to the highest temperature, and removed my cocktail dress. Sliding the door open, I stepped in to reach for the towel and lemon body wash. I still remembered the day we met when I picked him up from the airport. We just hit it off from there. He was used to women falling over his charm, and I set him straight out the gate that I wasn't like most women. Now almost five years later we'd been together, and things slowed down since our son.

"He really went out with me," I hissed, dropping the bottle of lotion on the nightstand, slipped under the covers, and took a screenshot of social media before turning my phone off.

"Mmmmmm..." My eyes slowly flickered open when I felt kisses trail along my thigh.

"You smell so good, baby." Jordan groaned and rubbed my stomach. Finally focused on what he was doing, I slapped his hand away.

"What the fuck, Emma?"

"Leave me alone, Jordan." I turned my back to him and pushed my gown down.

"What's wrong with you?" His hand reached around to pull my chin toward him.

"Go to sleep or better yet, go back to your friends." I

pushed his hand away and peered at the clock. It was three in the morning.

"Baby."

"Go to sleep, Jordan."

He groaned, fumbled around, and rose out of bed. I fell back asleep and planned to ignore him.

❧

THE NEXT MORNING, I POURED THE COFFEE IN MY CUP and stared at the news program discussing the weather updates and reached for a piece of bacon. I stood at the island and wiped my hands when he stalked in and wrapped his arms around my waist.

"Morning, beautiful."

"Hey."

He dropped his hand, then turned me to face him.

"What did I do?"

In irritation, I twitched my nose

"Jordan, leave me alone please."

"Woman, I'm not dealing with the silent treatment all day." He reached for a coffee cup and poured himself a coffee. He looked around the stove and then me.

"You didn't cook me breakfast?"

"No."

"Emma, you're being petty."

I scoffed and bit into my toast in front of his face.

"Are you going to tell me what I did wrong?"

"What happened yesterday, Jordan?"

"What do you mean?"

"That's why you're getting the silent treatment." I trashed the rest of my bacon and eggs and finished my coffee before walking out of the kitchen. For him not to remember what yesterday meant for us as a couple hurt, and I didn't know what he had going on, but he needed to get his act together before I decided to leave.

❧

HOURS LATER, I CLOCKED OUT FOR LUNCH AND KNOCKED on Chelsey's door and waited for her to respond.

"The door is open."

I pushed it forward and smiled at her behind her desk. She'd taken on the role of manager of this branch and collaborated with her brother. The Hayden family was well known in Memphis, and I was surprised they didn't hold resentment the way they did with her husband, Xavier, after they made things official.

"Hey, sis." I sat on the couch in her office.

"Are you headed to lunch?"

I nodded and picked up the magazine on the table.

"Yep, are you coming?"

"Sure. I was waiting on Xavier, but I think he's held up with work."

"How was my baby last night?"

"Great as usual."

"I'll grab him when I leave here today."

"You don't have to. He loves staying with his aunt and uncle."

I laughed because we both knew they spoiled him with his own room at their place. Anything he wanted, they gave to him. I had to fuss with Xavier to not buy him more toys whenever they went out of town.

"You two spoil him so much." I leaned my head against the couch with my hand resting on its side.

"He deserves it though." Chelsey turned her computer off and reached for her purse and jacket.

"Between you and your parents, my baby will never have to lift a finger."

"Especially with my parents. Lily told me that my parents set up his own room, plus a playroom."

"He doesn't even have a playroom at home." I threw my hands up in surrender.

Chelsey laughed, and I jumped up to head out of her office.

"Where are we going today?" She tucked her hand in her jacket.

"Thinking about pizza."

Chelsey and I headed out of the bank to the local pizza joint around the corner.

❧ 2 ❧

JORDAN

"**F**uck!" I slammed the phone on my desk after Emma ignored my call for the fourth time. Once I checked my calendar, I saw I had last night blocked out for Emma. It was supposed to be dinner just the two of us, and I fucked up big time. I prayed she would forgive me. Last night wasn't purposely missed. I truly hoped she would let me make it up to her today. I would have my assistant schedule a getaway trip if she was free from the bank.

Knock! Knock!

"Mr. Hayden." My assistant stepped in my office.

"Yeah, Capri."

"Miss Asha is here."

I rubbed my forehead and sat back in my seat. Asha Knight was one of our biggest clients at the bank, and we'd done a lot of work with them over the years. Asha was a princess, and her father handed over most of his business to her. They were looking into buying a few properties. We not only had our family business in banking, but real estate as well. Signing a major deal with the Knight family would be huge for the city and us as the premier business for other corporations.

"Send her in, Capri."

The biggest problem with Asha was she wanted everything when she wanted it and fuck anyone else who refused.

She slid the door open further. Asha removed her shades and swished her hips into my office and smiled. Asha had a problem with flirting and not understanding we would never be an item.

"Have a seat, Asha." I motioned to the chair in front of me.

"No morning hug, Jordan?" Asha removed her coat and like I thought, she wore the skimpiest skirt with a slit on the side. Her breasts spilled over her white blouse. All she did was try to get my attention, and I laughed at her too many times to even care.

"Asha, how are you?" I extended a hand to keep it business related.

She didn't like my gesture with the weak shake she gave me.

"I was good until I heard you were thinking of putting someone else in charge of this deal."

"You have to understand, Asha, as the CEO of the company, I need to delegate certain deals."

"I have no doubt, but I only want you to handle me." Asha hovered over my desk, with her breasts right in my face. I peered from her eyes, down to her chest, and then her eyes again.

"See something you like?" she asked, and I cleared my throat.

Knock! Knock!

"Yeah, Capri."

"Sorry, sir. I have your mother here with your son." Capri stood at the door.

"I thought he was with my sister?" I jumped up. Asha stood and buttoned the rest of her blouse.

"She didn't want to disturb you, but Emma hadn't picked up her call," Capri explained, and I whipped my head toward Asha. Somehow, she and Emma didn't get along. Many times, I had to divert them running into each other, so the deal didn't fall through.

"Send them in, and I'll try Emma again." I grabbed my cell and dialed her number.

"This is Emma Hayden. I can't get to the phone right now—" I ended the voicemail and dropped my phone on the desk. My mom stepped into my office and smiled at Asha. I took Jr. out of her hands. He was two years old and looked exactly like me, with a little of Emma's features. I wanted more kids to give my son siblings like I had growing up.

"Hey, Mom."

"Hi, baby. Asha, I haven't seen you in so long." Mom extended her arm out for a hug.

"Mrs. Hayden, good to see you. Is this your little guy?" Asha pinched Jr.'s cheek, and he pushed her hand away. Asha was embarrassed, and I laughed as my mom corrected him.

"What are you doing up here?" I sat him on my lap.

"Emma didn't pick up my call, and I thought I would come here and drop him off."

"She's probably in a meeting."

"If I didn't have this charity meeting, I would have kept him longer. Daycare center said he wasn't feeling well."

I placed a hand on his forehead. It felt warm.

"Thanks for grabbing him," I said.

"No problem, son. Tell Emma to call me later."

"She's not talking to me right now."

"Why? You know what? Keep me out of this."

I learned from Chelsey and Xavier that it was safer to stay away from my sister's drama with my parents, and I did the same for me and Emma. Even though my parents came around to the idea of Xavier as her husband, it was a hard journey. Both of them could be judgmental, and Emma had it rough at the beginning, not only from me, but my parents when we officially started dating.

"Emma will call you later." She walked out of my office.

"So, I take it our meeting is over?" Asha asked, planting her hand on her hips.

"Yeah, sorry. I need to get my son home."

"You know if you ever need any help with him..."

"Asha." I groaned at her attempt to flirt in front of my son.

"All I'm saying to you, Jordan, is that you used to be happy." She winked, slid her black shades on, and lifted her jacket before strolling out of my office. Jr. laid his head on my chest, and I blew out a breath and thought of how I could fix things with Emma. I knew I was fighting a losing battle the moment she spoke when I first met her; she owned my heart. As short as she was, her confidence and brains pulled me.

"Are you ready to go see Mommy?" I asked, and he picked his head up and looked at me.

"I knew you were faking." I chuckled, and he giggled, falling back on my chest.

❧

I UNLOCKED THE DOOR, CARRIED JR. ON MY SHOULDER and his backpack on my arm, and noticed Emma on the couch in sweatpants and her hair up in a ponytail.

"How long have you been here?" I placed Jr. on the loveseat opposite her.

"An hour, why?"

"Your son is sick. You didn't think to call me back?"

"Why didn't you leave a message?" Emma put her glass of wine down, grabbed Jr. from the loveseat, and rubbed his stomach.

"Baby, you sick?" He slowly nodded his head, wrapping his arms around her neck.

"All right, you want to play games." I tossed my jacket on the couch and put his backpack on the floor.

"Jordan, you have the nerve to come at me. After what you did." She hissed.

"Emma, I messed up. Sorry I missed our dinner." I squatted down in front of her.

"Okay."

"Okay? That's all I get?"

"Okay is not what you deserve, but since my son is right here, I want to keep it about him." She popped her lips.

I knew this was a losing battle, so I walked into the kitchen and saw she had prepared dinner. I was grateful she even thought of me since I barely ate breakfast. Once I fixed a plate, I came out of the kitchen and saw she was gone, but the TV was still on. After I plopped down on the couch with the beer, she came back in with a pair of black tights and my white shirt. She rolled her eyes, and I smirked when she sat next to me on the couch.

"Baby, this food is good."

"It should be; it was left over from last night."

"Can you forgive me please? I'll do anything to get out of the doghouse." I put everything on the table, turned toward her, and caressed her thigh.

"I forgive you, Jordan. I'm just disappointed."

"Understandable."

"When did we become these people?"

"What people?" My brow bent in confusion.

"Roommates."

"All right, Emma, you're crazy. I'm not your fucking roommate." I gripped her chin.

She pushed my hand away.

"Could have fooled me. You used to be up under me all the time, and now it's like I can barely get a phone call from you."

"I have been a little extra busy."

"A little, Jordan?"

"Marriage is a two-way commitment. You've been missing in action."

"What is that supposed to mean?"

"When was the last time you sucked my dick?"

"Fuck you, Jordan." She jumped up, and I reached for her hand. She pushed me away and stormed off.

"Emma! Emma!"

The bedroom door slammed shut, and Jr. started to cry.

"Fuck, man." I checked on Jr. and rubbed his stomach to put him back to sleep. I came out of his room and glanced at our bedroom. I heard sniffles and tapped on the bedroom door.

"Please leave me alone, Jordan."

"Baby, let me talk to you." I felt like shit.

Ring! Ring!

"Hello."

I heard Emma answer the phone, but when I twisted the doorknob, it was locked.

"Really? She locked me out," I muttered to myself.

"Yeah, hold on," I heard Emma say. A second later, the door jerked open, and the expression on her face told me she was ready to kick my ass.

"Who's on the phone?" I asked.

"Your client Asha Knight. I guess you forgot your wallet last night." Emma shoved the phone in my chest and slammed the door again, which caused Jr. to cry again.

"Shit! This is Jordan Hayden." I forgot Asha showed up at the bar last night. We'd celebrated closing another deal, and she popped up. I forgot to even stop off at the bar that we went to because I wanted to get my son home. A few of my employees dropped me off, and I climbed into bed horny and ready to fuck my wife.

"Jordan, I have something you want." Asha snickered over the phone.

"Asha, you could have left my wallet at the office this morning."

"Oops. I forgot."

"Yeah."

"Don't be mad. I'll bring it to you now."

"Ugh, no that's not going to work."

"Why not?"

"Because I'm home, and you're a client."

"Jordan, you worry too much. Who answered your phone? Was that Capri?"

"Asha, I don't have time right now to get into a long conversation."

"Jordan, you seem stressed. Maybe I could take you out for dinner."

The bedroom door swung open, and Emma glared at me.

"You're seriously on the phone with another woman, Jordan. Get out of my way before I slap you."

She tried to walk around me, but I blocked her and grasped her waist.

"Asha, I'll have Capri schedule a meeting to discuss the building permits." Emma tried to push me back, but I tightened my hold and buried my face in her neck.

"Are you listening to me—" I ended the call before Asha could continue.

"That was a client." I rubbed her back.

"Could have fooled me." She avoided my eyes and crossed her hands over her chest.

"Come have dinner with me so we can talk."

"Not hungry."

"I apologize for missing our dinner. It'll never happen again. Also, I apologize for the comment I made. You're the most important person to me."

"Maybe we should do counseling."

"Have we gotten that far off the rails? Ignoring calls and counseling."

"Honestly, you've changed."

"How?" I let my hands fall.

"You're never here and when you are, it's to hang with Jr."

"You have to admit some fault, Emma. All you do is hang with Jr. or Chelsey."

She ran a hand through her hair and nodded.

"You might be right."

I captured her lips and sucked on her tongue.

"We both need to do better in this marriage."

"I agree, but you need to get your clients in check and tell them not to call here after five."

"That won't happen again."

"What did you do last night?"

"A few of the employees took me to the bar, and we celebrated a deal. I lost track of time and my brain cells."

"You did."

"Let's go to the living room and finish this movie."

"Our conversation is not over, Jordan."

"Didn't say it was, dear."

❀ 3 ❀

EMMA

Jr. ran fast to his friends in daycare, and I smiled looking at my little boy for how well I'd been able to transition to becoming a mom after many years of being single. I never thought I would be someone's mom. He slept through the night, didn't give us too many problems, and never cried at every moment. He was extremely quiet and thought before he did anything. Jordan and I were so blessed.

"He looks better." Sloan, his teacher, approached me.

"Yeah, I just kept him home, away from other kids, and let him rest."

"No need to worry. I think you're doing a great job." Sloan patted me on the shoulder.

"Thanks. Here's his backpack with his favorite book and food."

Sloan took the bag, and I turned to leave. I checked my watch and saw I had a few hours before I needed to meet the girls for lunch. I arrived at work and saw Jordan outside with a client. The way she leaned into him shot my anxiety high. I opened the door, slammed it shut, strolled over, and stood next to him.

"Hello, I'm Mrs. Hayden." I stuck my hand out.

Her lips turned up in disgust.

"Asha Knight, a client and partner of Jordan's."

"Partner?" My brow hiked at her statement.

She smirked. Jordan pulled me back behind him.

"Asha, I'll be in touch."

"Please call me when you decide, no matter the time." Asha winked at him, and I balled my fists up.

Jordan turned to me, and I glared at him and cocked my head to the side.

"Baby, it was a business meeting."

"Is she the one who called you that night?" I would be a widow real soon and find Jr. another father, depending on his lie.

He ran a hand down his head.

"Yeah, baby, it's only business."

"Did you sleep with her?"

"Emma, stop being stupid."

"Fuck you, Jordan." I stormed off, ran into the building, and stomped to my office. Chelsey was laughing with a coworker.

"Hey, Emma!" Chelsey waved, and I motioned with my hand up.

"Emma! Emma!" Jordan screamed behind me.

I slammed my office door and paced back and forth to calm my nerves.

"Will you calm down?" Jordan shut and locked my door.

"Get out." I grimaced, removed my coat, and walked around my desk, pulling the chair up.

"No."

I pointed my finger at him.

"If you want her, then fuck her."

"What are you talking about? I love you."

"Since when? You promised to make some changes, and I haven't seen anything."

"What can I do to show you I want you and only you?"

I scoffed and turned my chair around to look out of my window at the traffic.

He shifted my chair around, reached for my hands, and pulled me into his arms.

"I want you, only you. Asha doesn't mean anything to me."

"Jordan, move." I tried to push him away, but he didn't move.

"I want you to take the rest of the day off. Get your hair and nails done."

"Why? I have too much work here." I glanced at the pile of paperwork on my desk.

"That can wait. Take Chelsey with you."

"Jordan, if you're trying to get alone time with your girl-friend, you don't need me out of the way."

He slammed me on the ass.

"Shut up. Asha doesn't mean shit to me. I was telling her I moved her deal to another business manager."

"You did?"

"Yes, give me a chance to make this right." He started to trail kisses down my cheek and behind my ear.

"Well," I cooed, grasping him around the neck.

"I promise my life is you and Jr."

"Okay."

He slid his hand in his pocket, pulled out two hundred dollars, and placed it in my hand.

"Tonight, I'm taking you to the club."

"Seriously?"

"It's been a while, and we haven't played since Jr. arrived." He grinned and gripped both of my ass cheeks.

"Thank you, baby."

"You'll be thanking me later tonight."

"You think you know me." I laughed and slammed his chest lightly.

❧

THE MASSAGE WAS THE BEST I'D HAD IN A LONG TIME, and I couldn't wait to have Jordan's hands all over me. After our argument, I caught up on a little work and then left to come to the spa; Chelsey tagged along, and we met Maya here.

"So, she was in his face when you pulled up?" Chelsey wondered, finished with her massage.

"Yes, and I held my composure because I could feel myself ready to snatch her dusty wig off."

Chelsey giggled, and I rolled my eyes.

"That girl has beautiful hair," Chelsey said.

"So, whose side are you on?" I lifted up and tightened the towel around my body.

"Always on your side, boo. I knew something was wrong when you just walked by me earlier."

I slid my feet into my sandals and walked out of the room to re-dress and get our nails done.

"I was so heated. Maya, how are things with you and Mason?" She opened the door to the dressing room.

"Nice, we're doing good. I had a few days off from the senate this week, and Mason took time off with me," Maya explained.

"See, your husband makes you a priority. I can barely get mine to have dinner." I could feel my annoyance heighten.

"Relax, Emma. You're having dinner with him tonight, right?"

"Yes." I pouted, taking out my jogging pants and shirt to re-dress.

"Then give him a chance to get better. I know Jordan, and when he knows you're hurt, he'll spend the rest of the day or week trying to make up for his mistakes," Chelsey said.

I nodded and slid my purse out of the locker.

We strolled to the nail section, and they had our seats lined up for our feet and toes. I sat in the middle and grabbed the champagne glass.

"I know I should give him a chance, but I just feel like the Asha chick is doing too much," I fussed, gulping the rest of the drink.

"It's his job to get rid of her, not yours." Maya leaned over and picked out the color of their nails.

"You're right."

"Exactly, you have to remember Jordan has changed from the bachelor he used to be. I promise, you have my brother wrapped around your finger," Chelsey reminded me. I thought about his devious smile whenever he wanted to fuck, and the way his smooth hands rubbed against my large breasts. His six-pack abs and thick thighs were the first things I fell in love with. The bulge in his pants when I drove us back from the airport had my mind going crazy. Plus, his scent drew me in even though he was arrogant and charming at the same time.

"All right, I'll let him run the show tonight, but if I see Asha again, I need you to make sure you get me out on bail."

Maya laughed and slapped hands with me.

❧ 4 ❧

JORDAN

Xavier lifted the beer and tossed his head back in laughter. I came to his house to let off some steam after we played ball in the backyard with Warren and Mason. The girls went to the spa, and that gave me time to get things in order for my night with Emma. Asha tried to call me nonstop after I had one of my business managers contact her about leading the renovations. He told me she was pissed and cursed him out because I let my wife carry the balls. At first, I wanted to call her back, but the fellas said it would be pointless, and I agreed.

"So, what are you doing tonight?" Warren opened another beer.

"I reserved a room at the club. It's been a while." I picked up a slice of pizza.

"Emma knows you reserved it tonight?" Xavier tossed his napkin in the trash.

"No, I mean she is getting ready for a date tonight. I had her get her nails and shit done."

"You better eat a lot of pussy, man," Xavier joked, and I chuckled.

"Shit, who are you telling? That's my baby though."

"You started all this when you didn't get rid of Asha," Mason reminded me.

"Here he goes." I burped and sat back in the chair.

"He's right. I never let a woman even get a hint that something is going to happen," Warren informed me.

"True, and I never let her down. Asha's just spoiled."

"Hopefully, you set her straight." Xavier flipped open the box of meat lover's pizza.

"The client account was switched to another bank manager."

"Good, you had Chelsey pissed at me," Xavier hinted.

"What the fuck? Why?"

"You know those girls stick together," Xavier said.

"Emma knows I've never cheated. She's the only woman for me."

"But are you consistent in showing her?" Mason brought up.

I rubbed my chin, thinking over the past few weeks and months. Emma did bring up that I worked a lot more and skipped out on events.

"You got me there." I threw my hands up in surrender.

"Tonight, make it all about her." Mason washed his hands and opened a bottle of water.

"Anything else I should do to get out of the doghouse?"

"Eat a lot of pussy," they said at the same time. We burst into laughter.

❧

EMMA HAD A CAR PICK HER UP AND BRING HER TO ME, and I held my breath and prayed we would make a step forward after tonight. I didn't see her when she came home, but I left instructions for her to put on a dress I had delivered. Once lunch was over with the guys, I came here to the club, showered, and helped to set things in motion. The Red Room—or VIP, as they liked to call it—was opulently decorated with its own bathroom, fireplace, TV, and living room, separate from the bedroom. All of the toys would be used tonight, and I made a commitment to keep us locked until we both agreed to keep better communication open moving forward.

Knock! Knock!

I checked myself out in the mirror and brushed my waves again. I wore a black silk robe and pants to match her black dress. I opened the door, and her beauty blew my breath away. She peered at me with a grin on her face, and I reached a hand out for her to come inside.

"Damn, baby."

"You picked this out." She ran a hand down the silky black dress with spaghetti straps. Her full figure had my dick hard as a rock. The way her breasts filled the bodice and the extra weight on her ass after having my son, forced my mind into dirty places.

"What do you have up your sleeve?" She walked around the room in awe.

I came up behind her and lifted her off her feet.

"Jordan, put me down!" She screamed in laughter, and I chuckled.

I laid her on the bed, pushed my legs between hers, and hovered over her chest. Emma's breathing heightened, and her eyes locked on mine.

"You love me?"

"Yes."

"Say it."

I love you."

"I promise tonight is about us, and no one can take your place."

"Not even Asha?" she teased, and I slid my hand up her chest to pull down a strap on her gown. I did the same thing to her right breast and licked my lips.

"Asha who?" I asked.

"Good answer."

She tried to reach up and pull me on top of her, but I moved back. She pouted.

"Stop playing, Jordan."

"You stop playing. We haven't done this in a while. You remember the safeword?"

"I do and what about you?" Her brow hiked in suspicion.

"Fuck, yes." I picked up the oil on the side of the bed and brought it closer to me.

"So, what is the safeword for tonight?"

"Blue, and all you need to do is relax and let me handle you."

"Handle soft or hard?"

"Both." I sucked her bottom lip, squeezing her right thigh.

She moaned and tried to arch into me.

"Can we do some nipple play tonight?" I questioned.

"Yesss…" she cooed, squeezing her breasts together.

I removed my robe and grabbed the clamps and oil. She watched me climb back on the bed. I caressed her cheek, moved my hand over her right breast, and licked her nipple.

"Ohhh… Jordan."

"Love when you're responsive, baby."

I rubbed some oil between her breasts, down her arms, then her legs. Then I rubbed her lower lips and watched her facial expressions as I put clamps on each nipple.

"How was the massage today?"

"Goodddd," she dragged out.

I stared at both clamps and then ripped her dress in half.

"Ugh, Jordan!" I slid a finger in and out of her pussy.

She arched her back, as my tongue locked on her nipples.

"You taste so good, baby."

"Fuck me!" she cried out.

"Not yet."

Emma wound her hips and tried to stick her hand inside her pussy, but I slapped it away.

My stiffness was ready to pound her for trying to take charge of what I had planned.

"Please, can I... arghh."

I stuck my tongue in her pussy and latched onto her clit.

I used my left hand to rub her breast. She shook underneath my hold, and I was ready to slide in and give her what she wanted. I pulled back, and her head popped up in anger. I smirked.

"What are you doing?"

"Before we go any further, I need you to swear that you'll never get an idea of me stepping out on you again."

"Jordan, this is not the time to bring something like that up."

"Actually, it's the perfect time."

I stroked my dick and waited for her answer.

She cut her eyes at me.

"Jordan."

"Come on, answer the question."

I tapped the head against her essence.

"Yes, Jordan. You feel so good," she purred

"That's not the question."

She squeezed her eyes shut and bit her bottom lip when I slid just the tip in and didn't move.

"Okay, baby, I swear. No more foolish thoughts. I trust you."

Her breasts heaved up and down. I thrusted, slamming my lips on hers. Our moans of pleasure emitted when our skin clapped together.

I placed my hands on her waist and watched my dick disappear. The night was still early, but the way she gripped me around my pole had me biting my tongue.

The bed shook, and I moved in long strokes for the next few minutes before I pulled out and switched places with her.

"We aren't leaving this room, so prepare to ride my face, baby." I lay on the bed and tapped her thigh to get up, and she sluggishly rose and crawled on top of me. She held on tight to the headboard, and I eased my tongue inside, with my finger in her asshole.

"Ooh, shit..." she groaned.

Hours later, we had used most of the toys, from the cock ring to the floggers and a swing. I stared at her beautiful face as she slept peacefully next to me.

A month later, conversation flowed at the dinner table with my parents. They wanted us to join them along with a few of our friends for dinner. Normally, family dinner would be just us and the kids. Maya was high-profile, and my parents loved the attention when she came to visit. News reporters would put our family in the paper when she showed up. Emma rubbed my thigh under the table, and I placed my hand on hers as we ate. Jr. sat in the high chair next to me while I fed him off my plate.

"How is the senate going for you, Maya?" my father asked.

Maya picked up her glass of water and took a sip.

"Fine, just busy with trying to push bills through and balance married life." She chuckled.

"Back in my day, all we had to do was stay home with the kids. Women nowadays, I give them praise with how much pressure they have," Mom said.

That was funny coming from her because she didn't feel like Xavier was good enough for Chelsey since he didn't come from money. She'd evolved over the past few years now that we had kids; it made her see the world differently.

"Some women," my dad said and glared at Emma.

He found out Asha and I weren't working on the project together because of Emma's concerns. Her father talked to my dad about the situation, and he was pissed with me for letting a woman run me. I told him we respected each other when something made us uncomfortable, and Asha flirted too much for my liking, but he didn't care.

"Mr. Hayden," Emma started to say, but I shook my head.

"Pops, it's over. We still have the deal. She just has another person handling it as a point of contact."

"Our reputation is a big deal, Jordan. You shouldn't let anything confuse that," he spat.

"Daddy!" Chelsey shouted.

"It's okay, Chelsey." Emma clasped her hands together.

"Chelsey, stay out of this."

"Mr. Hayden, we've never had an issue, and I respect you as a grandfather to my son, but please stay out of my marriage."

He scoffed and marched out of the room. My mother jumped up and followed him.

"I like that shit," I whispered in her ear.

"What shit?"

"You being a badass."

Emma laid her hand on the back of my neck and kissed me. Dinner continued without my parents, so we decided to head out to a bar together. My dad apologized to Emma and agreed to let our son stay the night.

Emma bent over and grabbed her ankles, popping her hips with me behind her on the dance floor. It was like we were young and in love after the other night together. All we did was replay the events at the club and her screams all night as I thrusted inside her. I hoped to have her pregnant again.

"Let me see how low you can go." I smacked her on the ass, and she twerked before rising up. I laid a hand on her stomach and pulled her back to my chest.

"You look sexy tonight."

"Can't wait to take you home."

"Take me home and do what?"

"Suck your dick." She whirled around, extended her hand out, and we slowed to dance to an old Keith Sweat song.

"I want you forever. I want more babies."

"The crazy part is I want the same thing."

"Glad you didn't let my father push you away."

The music changed, and I escorted her back to our booth with the rest of the couples.

Chelsey sat on Xavier's lap. Maya couldn't come because of her job, so they went home, but Kyra came with Warren.

"Did you film today?" Emma hugged Kyra.

"Yes, it was a long shoot," Kyra complained. I hugged her, and we sat down.

"Baby, what do you want to drink?" I rubbed her back, and the bottle girl approached our section to take her order.

"A bottle of Jack." Emma fidgeted in her seat.

"Can she get a Jack, and I'll have a cognac?"

The DJ played the latest from Lizzo, and I scanned the crowd as my eyes caught an annoying face. Asha watched us from the bar, and I chuckled when she rolled her eyes at me.

"What's funny?" Emma asked.

"Some people can't take a hint." I pointed at Asha.

Emma glanced around the crowd and saw Asha with some girls and started to jump up.

"That bitch!" Emma shouted, and I grabbed her hand.

"Sit down. She's not worth a fight."

"Like hell she ain't."

"Emma, the girl is bitter and jealous. Calm down because you are a queen and never have to stoop to her level."

She relaxed, sat back down on my lap, and turned to straddle my lap. I laughed at her antics.

"You're petty."

"Call me Petty Betty, because she's going to learn." Emma forced her tongue down in my mouth.

"Hmmmmh," she moaned.

We danced and drank for the next hour before going home.

❧ 6 ❧

EMMA

"Do you like my new hair color?" Jordan closed his eyes tight and growled his pleasure. I was in control after the other night at the club and felt his big hands rub against my ass. I knew I needed another session in the playroom. Right now, I had his balls in my mouth, and I popped them out as he grabbed the back of my head.

"Stop playing, baby."

I scraped my nails against his thighs and made eye contact with him.

"Shut up." I popped his dick back in my mouth, moved up and down, gagged a little like he liked, and fondled with my breasts.

I rose off the bed and grabbed the beads then oil and got in position. Took a small amount in my hand rubbed across my ass, plus the beads.

"Fuck me on my side, baby." He grabbed the beads out of my hands, ran the oil along my pussy, asshole, and kissed both cheeks. I threw my head back in pleasure.

"Arghhh, Jordan! Baby, keep going."

My essence covered the bed, as he stuck the beads in his mouth, pushed them up to mine, and slowly eased through the barrier.

"Ummm. God." I felt my body tremble. His dick slowly pushed home.

His balls slapped against my skin. I reached up and gripped the pillow. Jordan gasped, then lifted my leg a little higher and went deeper.

"Damn, I love you, Emma."

Roughly cuffing my breasts with his other hand and thrusting faster, I felt my orgasm rise and my vision get blurry.

"Emma! Fuckkkk, I'm about to explode."

"Me too!"

Jordan pushed me onto my stomach and hammered me as I convulsed from my orgasm. He came and fell on top of me, kissing down my back. He rolled off to the side of the bed.

"That was amazing." We tried to catch our breaths.

"Sinful, you know that."

I giggled and turned my head toward him.

"I bring that side out of you, huh?" He grasped my hand and kissed my fingernails one by one.

"I'd do anything for you. Just never leave me, baby."

"I'd never do that."

"Let's head to the shower, and then we can watch a show." He reminded me of the scene with one of the couples we liked to watch when they had sex. They loved the public to watch them, and it turned Jordan on even more. We would probably come back to the room afterwards and go another round in bed.

CHELSEY PARKED BEHIND US, AND I UNLOCKED MY SEAT belt and slid out of the car while Jordan helped Jr. out of his car seat. Today, we reserved the kids' playhouse for the next three hours and brought all of our kids. Maya and Mason were right behind us, as I pulled the door open and looked around at all of the play sections for each child range. Jordan and I held hands and headed to the front counter. They pointed to the section we could start with as I paid for the coins they use.

"Are you ready to go play, baby?" Jr. clapped his hands in excitement, wiggling to get out of his father's arms.

"Watch him while I get us something to drink," Jordan said, walking to the food counter.

Maya and Chelsey helped the kids on the playpen. I laughed at Jr.'s giggling and throwing balls back at the other kids.

"You seem chipper today?" Chelsey nudged me in the arm.

"Feel good, and my baby is happy."

"Probably has to do with you and my brother joined at the hip."

Chelsey's booty bumped me. I lifted my shoulders in a shrug.

"Look at Jr. help the girls climb out." I pointed. He was already a gentleman.

"My nephew is already cute. Wait until he turns sixteen."

"Please don't remind me."

"I talked with Mason about our baby growing up. He's already talking about keeping a gun ready." Maya chortled.

"I hope you reminded him that you're the senator in Memphis. He can't go around threatening people."

We watched the kids laugh and enjoy themselves

together. Jordan planted his arm around my shoulder and winked.

"I was thinking..."

"About?"

"We renew our vows."

I jerked back in surprise.

"Huh?"

"The guys and I talked. We think that maybe in a few months, we do a little vow renewal and a getaway trip."

"Are you my Jordan, or did someone kidnap your body?" I ran my hand across his forehead, and he laughed.

"All me, baby. No, seriously, you scared me there for a while, and that got me into a different headspace."

"Like where is this going?"

"Maybe with my parents, we do something that's just close friends and family, but I want to take you away first."

"Did you forget about our son?" I pointed in the direction of Jr. playing in the train station with Xavier.

"Chelsey and Xavier are willing to keep him for a few days."

"Since you have all the answers, I can't say no to you."

"Perfect. I can't wait to get you alone."

"Same, honey."

Finally, we had peace and quiet in the house. After all the kids ran around at the playhouse, they didn't want to leave each other, so we took them for ice cream. I rubbed the lotion on my hands and lifted the scarf over my hair. Jordan lay in bed with a book, and the game played on the TV. I slipped under the covers in a t-shirt and panties and pulled his free arm around my waist. I yawned, picked up the remote, and switched through channels.

"Tired?"

"Kids wore me out today." I placed a hand on his chest.

Jordan closed his book and focused on me with his back against the headboard.

"I'm serious about us renewing our vows."

"I believe you."

"Tell the truth. How close were you to kicking my ass out of the house?"

"Very close, and a possible stepdaddy on speed dial," I joked while he bombarded me with tickles.

"Sorry, stop! Jordan, sorry." I laughed for a long time, until tears gathered in my eyes.

"Maybe I should go find Asha."

I slapped his chest.

"Get cursed out."

He gripped my chin, pushed me on my back, and sucked on my neck. I raised my arms around his waist and inhaled the warmth of his body against mine.

"Trust me, she's not in your league," he remarked, and I felt him ease his dick in slowly, and we made love for the rest of the night.

EPILOGUE
JORDAN

The pilot explained we needed to put our seat belts on as we were prepared to land. I picked up her hand, kissed the back of her palm, and relaxed my eyes. Our trip was planned without her knowing any of the details, and she was completely surprised when we drove to the landing strip. Our family's private jet flew us to Costa Rica, and we rented out an entire villa for just the two of us. Chelsey didn't hesitate to watch our son. A few seconds later after we stepped off the plane and loaded in the limo with our bags, the driver headed to our villa.

"Baby, this is beautiful."

I pulled her to my chest.

"You deserve it, baby."

She poked her lips up, and I cupped her chin, peppering her with kisses.

We drove through the streets, and I pointed to different landmarks I'd love to visit.

"I'm starving."

"Lunch is being served on the beach. We'll get there, unload our bags, and change."

"You're in the running for best husband of the year with this vacation." Emma removed her phone and took photos.

"I'm working on husband of the lifetime." I grinned. When the car arrived at the villa, the driver put in the code and drove to the entrance. The place was over twenty thousand square feet, with a pool, a private beach, basketball court, and a theater. Our driver opened the passenger door, and I helped Emma to step out, and he grabbed our bags. The butler and house manager opened the front door. I shook hands with them, and Emma scanned the high ceilings.

"This is incredible, Jordan." Emma walked to the double stairs in the front, turned to the open-space living room, then she found the kitchen.

"Baby, we should shower and change for lunch."

"Welcome again, Mr. and Mrs. Hayden," the house manager said.

"Thank you. We're excited to be here." Emma hugged her, and I grasped her hand. We started upstairs to our room. Emma released my hand and ran to the double doors of the balcony. I removed my jacket and lay on the bed.

She came over to me and straddled my lap.

"I'm going to have to reward you for our trip."

I grinned and planted my hands on her thighs.

"I have ideas."

Emma bent down and buried her face in my neck. I groaned and slid a hand up her back to grip her neck.

"We have lunch, baby."

She slid her hand down to my chest.

"Thank you for making us a priority." She interlocked our hands.

"Thank you for not giving up on me. Promise, you come first."

"First lunch, then I want my dessert with you naked on

the bed." She brushed her lips across mine, and I gripped her hands tighter.

"Fuck lunch."

Emma giggled, and we stayed like that for the next hour or two.

BONUS SCENE
EMMA

Six months later.

"Taste this." I slid some strawberry cheesecake in his mouth, and he smashed his lips to mine. Today was our anniversary dinner with our friends and family. Earlier, we had a small ceremony and renewed our vows. Most of the food was catered except the dessert that I handmade because he loved only the cheesecake that I made. I wiped remnants of my lipstick away from his lip and pulled back to the cheers of our friends and family.

"Congrats again, Emma and Jordan. You both look so happy." Kadence leaned in to hug me, then Jordan.

"Thank you, Kadence. Is Kyrin having fun?" I peered over to the table she sat on. Now a single mom, she was still dealing with grief. At first, she didn't want to come. It would have been too much for her with the death of her husband.

"Kyrin was happy the minute he saw the dessert table." She laughed, and we watched him eat a piece of cake with some other kids his age.

"Don't forget if you're still looking for a job to let me know."

"Thanks, I will. Still waiting on a few interviews to come back."

"Kadence, do you mind if I steal my bride for a dance?" Jordan grasped my hand.

"Go enjoy. We'll talk soon."

"Come on, wife. They're playing our song."

The DJ played an old-school ballad from the sixties. Jordan knew I loved old R&B that really told a story of a guy and girl in love. We swayed on the dance floor in my in-laws' backyard and grinned as he licked his lips.

"How does it feel?" he asked.

"How does what feel?"

"To have me so deeply in love with you, I would walk through fire to make you happy."

"I would walk through fire to make you happy." We rubbed our noses together.

"I got lucky." Jordan placed both hands around my lower back. We didn't do anything traditional, from my red strapless cocktail dress to only including our closest family and friends, to serving a barbeque buffet, and Jr. standing as his father's best man. Our route after six years had shown me more love, devotion, and trust in the people we'd become through the storm.

"How about we slip out of here and head to the club?" Jordan trailed kisses down my neck, lifted my hand, and caressed my palm.

"You remember your safeword?"

He groaned, lightly biting my neck, and I felt his dick get hard between us.

"Fuck the club. We can go upstairs to my old bedroom," he said, and we burst into laughter.

I hope you enjoyed Emma and Jordan's story. Please also check out Kadence and Gunner in **"Seek to Earn"** next.

READER QUESTIONS

1. What's the name of the club?

2. What's the name of Mason's business partner?

3. Did Mason forgive his father too easily?

4. What's the name of Maya and Mason's daughter?

5. What's the name of the reporter that interviewed Maya? 6. Who worked with Mason's father to destroy Maya?

SEEK TO EARN

SEEKING IN ROMANCE BOOK 6

SYNOPSIS

Falling for him would be a mistake, my heart can't take more pain.

Kadence:

I lost my husband, and my entire world turned upside down. All I could think about to keep from breaking down at night is my son.

Gunner comes into my life and shakes things up.

Can I keep my heart in check and avoid another heartbreak all over again?

Gunner:

Kadence is something I wasn't looking for, but I knew I needed her in my life.

We work together, but I don't think she really notices me. I can see the kindness in her eyes, but something is missing, and I want to make her smile again.

Will I be able to convince her that what she's missing is standing right in front of her?

❧ I ❧
CHAPTER ONE
GUNNER

Tonight, Club Seek was crowded, and the atmosphere was full of couples and singles ready to dive into unfiltered pleasure for the evening. I stood off to the side of the bar and lifted the bottle of Aces to pour two glasses for the waitress to take to the VIP room. Mason had been short-staffed, and I volunteered to handle the bar for a few hours. Normally, I'd give a refund to my clients, but Mason wasn't worried and knew how I did business. As the owner of Gunner Vishon Signature Bar and Staffing Services, I prided myself on having professional people work alongside me. To hear someone had taken advantage of my business relationship by constantly calling out or leaving early pissed me off. After Xavier introduced me to Mason, we became fast friends, and then he hired me to exclusively take on the bar upkeep and hiring for all of his clubs. Rosaline probably thought since we'd messed around in the past, she could get away with anything. I tried to be patient and understanding of her situation of not having family or friends in Tennessee, but I was done being nice to her ass.

A bottle girl approached and slipped a credit card on the bar with a receipt to pay the bill. I gave her back the card and saw another hand go up for a drink. I turned to pick up the bottle of scotch.

"Empty," I grumbled and tossed it back in the crate.

"Oops. Sorry." I heard a soft, angelic voice. I released one end of the crate and wrapped my hand around her elbow to prevent her from falling.

"Sorry, you okay?"

Her bottom lip curved into a sweet smile. She pulled her soft coils behind her ear.

"I'm fine. Sorry, I wasn't paying attention. My first day."

"What's your name?" I looked deeply in her eyes, wanting to know how to whisk her away from here.

"Gunner! Where's the vodka?" I swiftly turned my head at the stretched voice.

"Give me a second," I let Wendy know and released my hold on the newbie's arm.

"I should probably get back to my station." She shifted to walk around me, but I wanted to block her and get her name. The bar filled up, and Wendy pissed me off with her annoyed expression. I walked down the hallway, then pushed open the employee section and loaded up more scotch, vodka, and bottles of champagne. For a good moment, the girl I bumped into consumed my thoughts with her beautiful rich brown skin, the subtle lift of her full lips, and large brown eyes. I knew people said love at first sight and from that split second, I wanted to stare at her long lashes, curvy frame, and supple cleavage in the corset outfit all the bottle girls had to wear.

"You're still here." I gazed around to see Mason at the door.

"Rosaline called out again." I grimaced, lifted the crate up, and left the stock room.

"You need to fire her," Mason kidded, and I grunted and stepped back behind the bar to unpack the alcohol on the shelf. Mason reached down to grab a few bottles, placing them on top, and I poured the drink for Wendy so she could get going.

"Who's the new girl?" I asked.

"What new girl?"

I tapped him on the shoulder and pointed at the girl I ran into a few minutes ago.

"That's Kadence."

"What's her story?"

Mason grinned at me, and I clicked my tongue.

"Why?"

"I bumped into her by accident."

"She was hired two days ago, but I don't know much about her."

"Damn." She smiled in the face of a customer, and he reached a hand out and patted her on the ass. I wanted to say something, but she wasn't my girl. It would look suspicious if I punched him in the face.

"Listen, I need to get going before my wife calls and yells."

"We don't need Maya up here going off. How is she and the baby?"

"Great, it's nice to come home to a family."

"Family is what's important." My eyes went back to the new girl as she turned from taking an order, and we made eye contact. She smiled and then turned away when another customer grabbed her attention. Since everything seemed to be in order, Mason stepped from around the bar and headed to his office. I blew out a heavy breath and continued to help get the bar caught up. An hour later, I managed to get relief from another bartender and went to let security know I planned to leave for the evening. I pulled my phone out to check notifications as I walked out when Rosaline sent a message.

Rosaline: Sorry, babe. I'll make it up to you.

"Selfish," I mumbled and slammed in the back of someone.

"My phone!" she screamed and bent down to pick up her things.

"Shit, my fault." I reached down to help her, and she stood.

"You make it a habit of not paying attention when you're walking?" she asked, and I held her keys out.

"Only to beautiful women."

She shook her head and chuckled.

I held my hand out.

"Gunner."

She looked down at my hand and back up to me.

"Kadence."

We shook hands, and she whirled around to slide the key in a blue Kia Optima.

"Nice to meet you, Kadence."

"You too, Gunner."

I stared as she opened the car door and closed it behind her before putting on her seat belt. I debated if I should even try to question the flutter in my chest when this was only the second time we'd been in each other's presence. Most of my life had been about work and nothing else as I grew up wanting to be like my Dad and just focus on building a business. I had plenty of women in my life, but nothing was ever permanent or seemed to be fulfilling. Now to have this stranger completely cause peace and want inside of me had me second-guessing the future plans I laid out for myself.

"Have a nice evening, Kadence."

She backed out of the employee parking lot and drove

off as I watched until the taillights of her car faded away. Tomorrow, I had plans to hit the gym and maybe find out more about Kadence and her reasons for working at Club Seek. I slid into my car and headed in the opposite direction to my place. At the light, I picked up my phone and blocked Rosaline's number.

$$\text{❀ 2 ❀}$$

CHAPTER TWO
KADENCE

"Mommy, can we get pizza for dinner?" I pressed my lips together because this little boy loved to spend money he didn't have when I already had plans to cook dinner.

"Kyrin, I told you we have food at home, baby."

He groaned, and I tittered at the little attitude. He was like a grown man in a little boy's body sometimes. Other times, he was protective over me.

"Can we have it tomorrow then?"

"Boy!" I cackled and turned into the parking space of my mom's building. I'd spent all day with him before I had to work tonight at the club. Tonight would be my second night working there, and it wasn't for the bashful. I found out about the place through Emma because our kids went to the same daycare. She knew that with me rebuilding my life, I needed a job. My husband died suddenly a year ago, and I'd been struggling since to take care of my son. Kyrin, at four years old, reminded me of his father every time I looked at him. It took me a while to accept that his father was gone. Everything I planned for myself went into being a wife and mother. When the path changed, life spiraled out of control. His parents never liked me, and it showed after his death when they basically disowned their grandson. They didn't give my son anything from the insurance money and refused to even tell me any of the plans. I managed to say my final goodbyes at the funeral before all hell broke loose when his mother tried to fight me.

"All right, we're here." I shut the car off and went around to grab him out of the car seat.

"I hope Granny has pizza."

I covered his mouth with my hand.

"Kyrin, you will eat whatever she cooked and maybe if you're good, I'll take you for pizza this weekend." I squatted down in front of him.

"And ice cream?"

The front door opened, and I stood.

"You finally showed up." Mom grumbled and leaned against the door with her arms crossed.

She wasn't a big fan of my new job and told me every chance she could. In her mind, I was stripping and needed something respectful.

"Hi, Mom."

"Hey."

Kyrin ran toward her and hugged her legs.

"Kyrin, be good for your grandmother." I grabbed his bag from the back seat and handed it to her.

"Okay, Mommy." He ran inside.

"When are you coming back to get him?"

"Tomorrow, if you don't mind." I felt a knot form in my stomach. Usually she'd complain once I picked him up.

"Kadence, you need a nine-to-five job like everyone else."

"Can we not do this today please?" I blew out a frustrated breath and got back in the car.

"Kyrin needs a stable environment." My lips parted and then closed.

"What do you mean a stable environment?"

"All this moving from my place and from job to job. Maybe you should think about contacting Kelvin's parents for help."

"Do you remember how they acted after his death? They don't want anything to do with me."

"I don't know what to tell you, Kadence, but I can't keep doing this with you." She turned to march back to her door. Growing up, she'd had men in and out her life after she broke up with my dad. He eventually remarried and had another family. He barely stayed in touch with me because she didn't like the fact he wanted someone else. I couldn't blame him because my mom was too judgmental and aggravating.

"I need to get to work."

Ring!

"Hello." I backed up out of the space.

"Hey, Kadence."

"Hi, Emma."

"You do remember me." She scoffed, and I laughed, stopping at the red light.

"Sorry, friend, life has been kicking my ass."

"Where are you?"

"Leaving my mom's house after dropping Kyrin off. Going home to nap and eat before work tonight."

"You sound like an old woman."

"I feel like one."

"You should come to lunch with me."

The light changed, and I sped up.

"I wish I could, but I have to save every dime I can get."

Emma's husband came from money, and they'd recently gone through some stuff. She told me at one point she was ready to leave her husband. I told her to make sure she had a backup plan. I knew firsthand that raising a child on your own was difficult if you didn't have a foundation in place.

"Lunch is on me, so stop stressing."

I checked the time on my watch.

"Okay, when is this lunch?"

"In thirty minutes."

"I'm not even dressed, Emma." I pouted and honked at the car that suddenly slowed down in front of me.

"Anything you wear shines. Stop pouting." Emma giggled.

"Fine, send me the address." We ended the call and a few minutes later, the address came through. I looked down at my shorts, crop top, and boots. My hair wasn't too off-putting, but I grabbed a little gloss and mascara to do a little touch-up.

Twenty minutes later, I arrived at a cute little bistro and parked my car. Emma told me she'd be near the back with some of her girlfriends. I shut and locked my door, strolled inside, and the hostess greeted me.

"Hi, How many in your party?"

"Actually meeting someone." I pointed to the three women sitting near the rear of the restaurant.

"Perfect! The waitress will be right over," the hostess said, and I nodded in answer.

"Hey, thanks for coming." Emma rose out of her seat and extended her arms for a hug. She shifted to the other women and introduced them.

"Nice to meet you, Kadence. I'm Chelsey."

"You too, Chelsey."

"Emma said you were cute, but, honey, you're gorgeous." Her other friend was named Maya and was a senator.

"Have to say the same about you, Senator." I smiled.

"Please call me Maya," she replied.

I scooted up to the table and placed my purse on my lap.

"What is my boyfriend doing?" Emma questioned, and I rolled my eyes. Emma spoiled Kyrin and whenever he went over to her place and spent the night with her son, he'd come back with more toys.

"Driving me up a wall."

Emma giggled.

"Her son is in the same daycare with my baby," Emma explained.

"You spoil him too much."

Emma waved me off.

"Don't hate on his swag," Emma joked, causing the entire table to burst into laughter.

"Where do you work, Kadence?" Chelsey asked.

"Club Seek." I dropped my head, embarrassed that I admitted it in front of a senator.

"Pick your head up. That's where I met my husband," Maya said, and my eyes widened at her comment.

"Mason owns Club Seek," Emma informed me, and I thought of Mason when I interviewed with him a few days ago. The man was cute, but the one I bumped into twice that day was insanely sexy. He was taller than me by a few inches, with short, wavy, golden hair, full bushy brows, and piercing gray eyes.

"I started a few days ago, and Mason's been really great."

The waitress came over and set their drinks down on the table.

"Are you hungry?" Emma asked.

"A salad would be fine and whatever they're drinking."

"A peach bellini," Emma said.

Chelsey and Emma started to drink, and mine showed up a second later.

"I know Maya is a senator. What do you do, Chelsey?"

"I work at my family's bank."

"That has to be exciting. Does your husband work there too?"

Chelsey's small, toothless grin formed on her face.

"He is a fitness trainer and owns his own gyms."

"Nice! But do you have to deal with women throwing themselves at him?"

Chesley snorted.

"All the time." She chuckled, and we laughed. For the rest of the afternoon, we exchanged numbers and went shopping, but I didn't purchase anything. My goal was to build up my money to get a new house one day. After my late husband's parents kicked us out of our old house, I lived with my mom until I could save up for an apartment. Once I fully had enough for a down payment, I wanted to get back in a home and focus on going back to school to get a degree in business.

CHAPTER THREE
KADENCE

I'd been working for a month now at the club, and I was late today because Kyrin started crying when I tried to leave him with my mom. I felt guilty, so I stayed until he fell asleep. I'd made enough to pay for school registration for a few classes, so we were in a routine now. In the mornings, we had breakfast, and I dropped him off by nine at daycare. Three days out of the week, I went to class and then came home to clean and sleep. Then it was time to pick him up and drop off with my mom. I put my purse in the locker, checked my makeup in the mirror, and went to grab my tray and notepad. The outfits we had to wear weren't my favorite, but they were necessary when working in a place that alludes to sex and mystery. I worked on the main floor, but a few girls said when they had to work upstairs or in private sections, they'd come across a lot of naked bodies and had been invited to join. I was curious about the overall practice when someone joined, but being dominated during sex didn't appeal to me that much.

"We meet again."

I shut the locker and whirled around to find Gunner, a business friend of Mason's.

"Hey. Gunner, right?"

"It is, how are you?"

Another girl walked between us and left us alone.

"I'm fine. Just running a little behind."

"I'll put in a good word for you, Mason owes me."

Those thick lips curved into a smile, and his long tongue made an appearance when he swiped across his upper lip.

"If I let you do that, then I'd owe you." I crossed my arms.

"Nah, just a friend doing a favor."

"Oh, we're friends now."

"I mean we bumped into each other twice."

"So that makes us friends?" My brows dropped in confusion.

"Yes. and soon best friends. Then we will go out."

"Huh." I laughed at his statement.

"You're beautiful, Kadence. I'd like to take you out."

"Uhm, what makes you think I'm single, Gunner?"

"I don't, and I really don't care." He walked closer to me, and the laughter left my face. I cleared my throat and shook my head.

"You're too cocky for me, Mr. Vishon, and you're my boss."

"Call me Gunner, and I'm a silent partner."

"Which means, based on the rules, I shouldn't even be talking to you."

His eyes narrowed in on me.

"Mason found his wife here at the club, plus Warren and a few other people. Employee and employer relationships happen."

"They do, but I'm not in the habit of being the type to fall for the boss."

"Good because I'm not your boss." My heart was beating out of my chest at the look he gave me.

"Gunner."

He waved me off.

"One date, that's all I ask."

"You don't even know me."

"I know you're a single mom, in school, and focused on raising your son."

I stuck my hand on my hip.

"How do you know all of that?"

"Go to dinner with me, and I'll tell you," he said, stretching out a beckoning hand.

"All right, one dinner."

He smiled and kissed the back of my palm and walked out. For the rest of the night, I worked, but my mind was on Gunner and our date. I was afraid it would open a can of worms with Mason.

◈

THE NEXT MORNING, I FINISHED CLASS EARLY AND decided to go to the mall to do a little shopping with Emma and her other friend Kyra, who I found out was a famous actress. In each store, a crowd of people would take pictures of us, and photographers stood outside the building.

"Tell me I'm crazy for even agreeing to this date." I stood in front of the mirror with a gold shimmery dress.

"No, I told you Maya and Mason got together there, plus me and Jordan."

"Emma, that's different. I'm a bottle girl, and he's practically my boss."

"From what you've said, he seems like a good guy," Kyra noted.

I sighed and put the dress back, flipping through the rack.

"He's—"

"Cute, sweet, and knows what he wants. You've been alone for almost two years. Time to get out and do something for yourself," Emma said.

"I feel like I'm betraying Kelvin."

"Kelvin wants you to be happy."

"What if he hates the date, and we end up back at work, and it's weird between us."

"You've created this entire situation in your mind, and the date hasn't even happened." Emma stood next to me.

I felt goose bumps rise on my skin.

"What's the real problem?" she asked.

"I will end up falling for another person, and they leave me."

"Life is about living. You can't think like that, Kadence. Just one dinner, promise me you'll go." She held up her pinky finger.

"Are we ten years old or something?"

Kyra laughed at me.

"Yep, and you're going on this date. Who's watching Kyrin?"

"Mom, and I need to hurry up and get home and get dressed."

"If she acts crazy and says no, then bring him to me."

"Thank you. I like the light cream floral dress." I pointed to the dress on the second rack.

"With your hair pinned up, that would be cute," Kyra said. I nodded in agreement.

We all walked to the register and paid for our clothes. Afterwards, I went to get my nails done. Even though I wasn't planning on sleeping with him, I needed to be refreshed and glowing. It took me two hours to get dressed, do my hair, and finalize my makeup. Plus, I had to get Kyrin a bath at my mom's place and tuck him into bed. It was now nine-thirty, and I waited for Gunner to pick me up.

Ding!

The doorbell rang, and I jumped up and ran to the front door.

He whistled when he saw me, and I found myself blushing.

"You look beautiful."

"Thank you. You look handsome. I didn't know where we were going for dinner, so I hope this is okay." I motioned up and down at my dress. It wasn't too revealing, besides showing off my legs. I had on three-inch heels with my hair up, half of it hanging with flowing curls.

"The perfect dress for the perfect lady." He held a hand out and I extended for him to hold mine as I reached to close the door behind me.

"A limo!" I gasped in shock.

"I didn't want to lose focus tonight. All my attention will be on you, and driving would hinder that."

"But that's too much, Gunner."

"Let me worry about that." He opened the back door, and I climbed in. He followed and directed the driver to the restaurant.

"Why me?"

"Look, before we even get to the dinner, you should know I don't do things out of pity or to show off. I like you and want to get to know you. It's that simple."

"So, you're not looking to save me or lock me up as your sex buddy?" I watched him peer down at my lips, then back up to my face.

"Sex is easy to come across. I would like to know Kadence Wilkes and what makes her happy."

The limo arrived at the restaurant a few seconds later and parked.

"We'll call you when we're ready, Elliot." Gunner reached for the door handle, stepped out, and helped me next. We reached the front door and found it to be completely silent inside. I wondered if we came on a closed night.

"Uhm, are you sure the place is open?"

"I paid to have you all to myself and rented out the place."

"But—"

"Mr. Vishon, we have your table ready for you." The hostess escorted us to the middle of the dining room.

"You seem shocked by this, Kadence."

The table was decorated with candles, and a bottle of rosé sat in a bucket of ice.

"Speechless honestly."

"You shouldn't be. As we get to know each other more, you'll find that I don't half ass when I make someone my girl."

"What makes you think I'm going to be your girl?" I teased and cupped my chin with my hand on top of the table.

"I see you're intrigued by me, and I promise the night we ran into each other, I was intrigued by you."

He reached for the bottle and poured a glass for me, then him.

"This is the first date I've been on since my husband died. Before that, we were married for six years."

"Do you mind if I ask how he died?"

"Cancer. It's one of those things you don't prepare for.

Then his family never liked me in the beginning, so it only caused a bigger strain."

"They're the fools." He covered my palm.

"Thank you. I have my son, so he's been great to keep my mind distracted."

"Kids can be the best things to bring you joy."

"Do you have any?"

"No. I've never thought of myself as a father."

"Oh." I didn't lie when I told him I hadn't gone on a date. I didn't want to bring different men in and out of Kyrin's life. If Gunner was to stick around, and he didn't like kids, this would end before it even started.

"Hey, I like kids. Just never thought of being a father until I saw you."

"Kyrin is my baby. If I brought anyone around, it would need to be someone special."

"Then I'm your man."

I laughed.

The waitress brought over appetizers of salad and mussels.

"Cocky."

"Confident."

"Tell me about you." I said.

"I invested a lot in business and became a small partner at Club Seek. Also, I run a staffing agency for clubs and events."

"Wow, that's exciting."

"I grew up with parents who worked and instilled that in me. When I went to school, I brought liquor and the girls."

"Frat boy." I smirked, and he fed me some of the mussels.

"Actually a nerd in school."

"You're lying."

"No, girls liked me, and I'm not playing innocent, but nothing made a lasting impression."

"Until me."

"Until you."

"Doesn't it bother you that I was married and have a child? Not looking for a stepdaddy."

"I wouldn't expect you to, Kadence. I know I come on strong, but something is brewing, and I've seen you come to work. You seem to be on the go. Never take the time for yourself."

"Wouldn't even know what that feels like."

"How is working at the club for you? I mean it's an adult membership only."

"At first, I was hesitant. I'm not the most sexually outgoing person."

"So, I have to earn your pleasure."

"Well, we have to see how this first date goes."

"What do you do outside of work?" He changed the subject, as our food came out. We dove into the salmon avocado salsa and risotto.

"I went back to college to get my degree. I have two years left."

"That's amazing, smart and sexy." His words made me nervous and tingly all over. The words he spoke to me gave me confidence and strength to not let anyone's actions put me in a bad place.

The dinner was amazing. Then we walked around talking and ended up back at my apartment alone in front of my door. We stood face to face and held hands, and I felt like a teenager home from her first date.

"I had fun tonight." I spoke low.

"Me too, and I want to see you again."

"Maybe." I grinned, and he chortled, stepped closer to me, and rubbed right cheek.

"Can I kiss you, Kadence?"

Before he could even get the words out, I leaned forward and closed my eyes. We collided together, and his tongue opened my mouth. His moan caused me to pull him closer to my chest, and his hands went to my lower back. Our kiss went on for another few minutes before he pulled back.

"I'm sorry. I shouldn't have," I said, wiping the lipstick off his lips.

"I'm not. Get inside, and I'll call you tomorrow." He pecked my lips and waited for me to unlock the doors. I waved good night and leaned my back to the door and closed my eyes.

"Woah."

CHAPTER FOUR
GUNNER

"You went on a date?" Xavier asked, lowered the weights, and wiped his forehead. I got up extra early and came to the gym to release the tension from my date with Kadence. Her moans when I kissed her had me ready to fuck her right on the porch, but I didn't want to disrespect her home and son. So, I forced the kiss to end. Then I came home and jacked off in the shower and tossed and turned with her on mind.

"Yeah." I lifted myself up and did some sit ups.

"You and Rosaline only have sex. Since when do you take her out on dates?" Xavier chuckled.

"Never. It was with a bottle girl at Club Seek."

"Who?"

"Kadence, a friend of Emma and Chelsey."

"Awww. Gotcha." Xavier, like me, didn't care what the world said about who we should and shouldn't date because of different backgrounds. He came from a working-class family and married into a rich family. Her parents, at first, objected because he wasn't from wealth. I came from money and dealt with the pressures of people wanting me to fit into a box based on my family's status. But I liked to use my own mind, and my parents understood even though my grandparents came from money.

"Is she cute?"

"Hell yeah." I smiled at the thought of her.

"Are you ready to date after being single for so long? Especially someone you work with?"

"I want her."

He stopped lifting and turned to me.

"She a bottle girl or..." I stopped him before he even threw it out of his mouth. Some women did have experiences with men, and Mason had strict instructions on the type of people allowed.

"She's a bottle girl."

"Can't imagine dating a girl from the club."

"You fuck Chelsey at the club."

"That's different."

"How?"

"We're married, and she doesn't work there to see around-the-clock fucking."

"Kadence isn't like that. She's sweet, smart, sexy, and funny."

"Well, if she makes you happy."

"Besides, Rosaline doesn't mean anything to me."

"Does she know that?"

"I had a few texts from her come through the other night, and I told her it was over if she called out again."

"You fired her."

I nodded.

"What did Mason say?"

"He doesn't run my business."

"The man hired you to staff his bars at most of his clubs."

"Rosaline is good at her job, but she's not dependable."

"Good luck with that."

"Knew you two would be slacking off in here." Warren and Mason strolled in and laughed.

"That's him." Xavier pointed at me.

"He's still high on his date with Kadence." Mason laughed, and I flipped him off.

"Yeah, I heard the girls on three-way about you," Warren joked.

"Fuck y'all." I smirked.

"Does she know about the private rooms?" Xavier asked, and I shook my head. One of the reasons I kept Rosaline around was because she liked BDSM and what the club represented. We could explore each other and not have to worry about someone freaking out when they saw bar spreaders, whips, and cuffs. This world started for me in college, and I continued throughout and knew when I got married, I'd want someone compatible, who was open to the lifestyle just as much.

"I haven't talked to her about it yet."

"If you're really into her, you should start that conversation."

He was right, and I knew after one date, when we kissed, I wanted her for myself.

"Focus on someone else's love life," I blurted and stood to spot him on the weight bench.

"Kyra and I are trying for a baby," Warren said. We all hugged in excitement and congratulated him.

"Guess I'll be the sexy uncle to y'all kids," I joked, and they laughed.

❧

A WEEK LATER, KADENCE AND I WERE ON A FOURTH date, and it was a simple picnic at my house. I put on the fireplace and a movie with our food laid out in front of us. I wanted to have her alone to myself so we could continue to talk and learn more.

"Here's to you." Kadence held the glass of red wine up in the air.

"A toast for me." I watched her pull her bottom lip in and ran a hand through her long hair that she left down.

"I can admit you've been a pure gentleman through our dates, and you've grown on me."

"That's good to know. Anything else is love." I tapped her on the nose.

"Well, I have to admit I haven't had sex in a while besides a vibrator and my hand." She nervously shifted.

My eyes darkened at her confession.

"What's a while?"

"At least a year and a half since my husband died."

I was ready to take her right here but calmed my thoughts of bending her over the table.

"Have you ever been to the club as a guest?" I needed to see what her level of intimacy would be.

She choked on the wine, and I gently clapped her back.

"Are you okay?"

"Yes, so-rrrry... Uhm," she stuttered.

"Are you into the BDSM lifestyle, Kadence? Ever had a desire to join?"

"I mean, I'm not really sure. Mostly been into the regular smack on the ass and tug my hair."

We laughed at her comment.

"Would you ever like to go? With me of course." I put the glass down on top of the table.

"As a guest?"

"We'd take it slow and introduce you to my world."

"I don't want you to be disappointed."

"Unless this isn't what you want. But you could never disappoint me, baby."

"All right."

"All right." My dick got hard, and I pressed a kiss on her forehead, inhaled her hair, and trailed kisses along her cheek and shoulder. She caressed my chin and slid her tongue in my mouth. I trailed my fingers down her arm. She moaned when my hand went under her shirt. I inhaled her perfume and removed my hand.

"Tomorrow."

"I have work."

"I'll deal with Mason."

"But I need the money, Gunner." Her expression was annoying.

"Love, you'll make the same amount from me. Don't stress about that."

"I can't believe I'm actually doing this." I kissed her ear and down her chin to her lips.

"Already done, baby." Slowly, I kissed her while she talked about introducing me to her son.

She closed her eyes and interlocked our hands together. Then she pulled back, so I turned the movie up, and we continued to watch and hang out all night. She spent the night until the early morning, and I cooked breakfast, then drove her back home.

CHAPTER FIVE
KADENCE

Today, Kyrin decided to not drive me crazy, so I took him out for ice cream after we came from the library to pick out some books. He kicked his feet back and forth on the chair, and I saw specks of his father in his face and demeanor.

"Kyrin, how is daycare going?"

"Fun." His eyes rose with chocolate syrup on his chin. I cleaned his face with a napkin.

"I'm glad."

"Mommy, how is your school going?" Amusement glinted in his eyes.

I chuckled at his question.

"Mommy is doing good, baby."

"Then you should pick out some books for yourself."

I chuckled.

"Next time, baby."

"Grandma said you work too much at night."

I blew out breath. My mom and I didn't see eye to eye still with my job choice.

"Grandma shouldn't worry you, baby."

"Do you like your job?"

"Yes, and it pays for this ice cream. But you don't have to worry about that."

"Okay."

I watched him move the ice cream around.

"Hey, how would you like to meet a friend of mine?"

He shrugged.

"I know we haven't talked about your dad in a while."

"He's in heaven, right?" I cradled his face in my hands.

"He is and looks down on us every day." I wiped his hands clean.

"I miss him."

"He misses you too, baby."

"Can we go see Grandma and Poppa?"

I hated to be the bearer of bad news and have them shut the door in my face. I'd avoided this conversation for a year, but Kyrin remembered everything.

"Maybe in the future. Kind of hard for Grandma and Poppa to see us right now."

"Because Daddy is gone."

I nodded but wanted to say because they never liked me and thought I trapped their son.

"Finish your ice cream, and then we can go home and watch a movie."

"Okay, Mommy." Kyrin grinned, showing off his beautiful little teeth.

I GLANCED AT THE FRONT DOOR OF MY MOM'S APARTMENT and saw the curtain move, so I knew she was here. I hadn't spoken to her in a few days. After I took Kyrin out for ice cream and the library, I asked Mason for a few days off to spend time with my son, and he agreed. After a month at the job, I was more comfortable with how things ran. I got along with the staff, and Gunner came in some nights when I worked even though he didn't need to be there.

"What are you doing here, Kadence?" Mom held her robe closed, moved to the side to let me in, and shut the door behind me.

"I wanted to see you."

"Where's Kyrin?"

"Daycare."

"No class today?"

"No."

"Surprised you aren't at work."

"How have you been?"

Her eyes scanned me up and down. Gunner bought me a nice bracelet and shoes. I wasn't the material type of girl, but he was spoiling me beyond my dreams.

"I met someone."

"I hope you're not pregnant, Kadence.

"What? No."

"Thank God. You've always been flaky and never listened to me growing up."

"How can you say that? If anything, I watched you and my father go back and forth arguing until all hours of the night."

She waved me off.

"Your father wasn't shit."

"Here we go."

"Listen to me, I did the best I could, and he just left."

"Mom, you have to let it go."

"Try to not run this one off."

"All I wanted to do is hang out with you and have lunch or something."

"You got some money."

"That's all you care about is money."

"I mean if you're coming in here with diamond bracelets and your hair all done, you must have a sugar daddy."

"Gunner is nothing like that." I reached in my purse, pulled out some money, and slapped it in her hands.

"When is Kyrin coming back over?"

I jumped off and stalked to the door.

"Tomorrow and try to keep my business out of your mouth." I slammed the door behind me and strolled to my car. I couldn't wait for my night with Gunner to let off some steam and deal with my mother. She tried to dictate my life and make me feel miserable, the same way her relationship with my father caused her misery.

❦ 6 ❦

CHAPTER SIX
GUNNER

I blocked out the red room for tonight, turned the low lights on, and talked to her about what we would be doing for the evening. She walked in wearing a long, black lace gown with a matching black bra and panty set. We watched a couple have sex first; then I pulled her to the private room and pointed to each item that I wanted to try with her tonight. The look in her eyes was interest, but she was nervous. Once her clothes came off, I placed a sinful ball in her mouth, then set the sex bench up for later. I held the spank paddle up and rubbed it over her smooth flesh and lightly tapped it against her right cheek.

"Ohh gosh, mmmhhmm." Her eyes closed, and I loved how she submitted to me easily and was open to testing her limits.

"Baby, remember your safe word if you feel over-whelmed."

I leaned over and swirled my tongue over her nipple, and slid an index finger inside her pussy, her wetness showed against my fingers.

"Kadence, love, you're so fucking beautiful," I whispered, warm breath against her chest.

Smack!

I moved my hand over the sting and kissed both cheeks. Spreading them apart, I dropped to my knees and slid my tongue in her pussy.

"Arghhh, Gunner." Her moans filled my heart, and my dick got hard. I spat in her ass and slowly slid my finger in and out. I sucked and twirled my tongue at the same time, moving my finger in again.

"Yes, baby." Her lips fell apart.

Her moans filled the air, her juices covered my beard, and she couldn't touch me while her hands were cuffed. Finally, I removed my pants, slid the condom on and eased into her tightness. I felt like I was home.

"Love, you're killing me."

I removed the ball gag and thrusted forward. She looked over her shoulder as I kissed up her back, then captured her lips.

"Arghhh... Shit!" I grunted and dug my hands in her waist and stroked her faster.

"Gunner, I'm coming," she screamed, and I felt her nectar cover my dick. I pounded until I came and my breathing was out of control. I slid out of her and removed her hands from the cuffs. She steadied her breathing, lying flat on the bench.

Thirty minutes later, I brushed a thumb over her soft, plump lips and glanced up to her eyes in need of a sign this was what she wanted. I got my answer when she rested a hand on my cheek, leaned forward, and crashed her lips to mine. I pulled her bottom lip in my mouth, sucking on it slowly, and she moaned, leaning her head back as she closed her eyes. I put on another condom, and she straddled my lap, and we made love almost all night.

TWO MONTHS PASSED, AND WE HAD A SCHEDULED DAY for me to finally meet her son. I was at her door holding a train set and flowers. A part of me was nervous because most of the women I dated didn't have kids. Now, I was in a full-blown relationship, and I loved that her son was the top priority when we made any types of plans.

Knock! Knock!

"Here I come." I heard the door unlock, and Kadence stood in a pair of biker shorts and a long shirt, which brought back memories of our first night together.

"Hey, love."

"You didn't have to bring anything." She invited me in, and I kissed her and passed her the roses.

"For you."

"Thank you, Gunner. Is that train set for Kyrin?"

"Mommy! Who's at the door?" A little boy ran from the back and stood behind his mother's leg.

Kadence bent down.

"Baby, this is Mommy's friend. Can you say hi, Mr. Vishon"

"Hi, Mr. Vishon."

"Gunner. Nice to meet you, Kyrin."

"You know my name."

I bent down in front of them.

"I do. Your mom told me."

"Oh. What's that?" He pointed at the train set.

"I brought you a gift."

"Really!" He jumped up and down in excitement.

"I did. Hopefully, your mom says you can keep it."

She pursed her lips.

"I can't take it now, since it's here." Kadence and I stood.

"Yayy! I'm going to play."

"First you need to finish your food."

"But Mom..." he whined.

"No, Kyrin."

She pointed to the back, and I assumed the kitchen. Kyrin's face dropped in defeat, and he walked back to the kitchen with the train set.

"Hi." She leaned into my chest, and I wrapped an arm around her waist.

"Hey, baby." I kissed her on the lips.

"Mhmmmm. Come on, you hungry?" She pulled back before we got started and took my hand.

"Sure, I could eat." I stared at her ass.

"Food, Gunner."

Her eyes blazed with emotion, and I chuckled.

Kadence put the flowers in water, and I removed my jacket and sat down at the table across from Kyrin. He bit into the piece of fish, then mac and cheese.

"Kyrin, I hope you like the train set. I had one growing up just like that."

"Cool. I love trains and fire trucks."

"I'll remember that for next time."

"How do you know my mommy?"

Kadence put a plate down in front of me.

"We met at work."

"Kyrin, you remember I told you Mommy had a friend?"

He nodded.

"This is Mommy's special friend. I wanted him to meet you and get to know the number one guy in my life."

"That's me!" Kyrin stuck his hand in the air and laughed.

"Yes, you are, sweetheart," Kadence replied, and I winked. The way she talked and took care of him made me even more enthralled with her.

"Are you going to marry my mommy?" Kyrin asked, and we both froze.

"Where did that question come from, Kyrin?"

"Grandma said—" Kadence motioned for him to stop.

"Grandma shouldn't have brought that up to you. I'm not getting married. We're dating, baby."

"Okay."

"When or if that time ever comes, I would talk to you first, okay?" Kadence explained and I knew she was the entire package of what I needed in my life.

"The food is good, babe." I cut into the fish and took another bite.

"Thank you. After this, I have cupcakes for dessert."

"What are your plans for tomorrow?"

"Class and hanging out with the girls."

"How about we have dinner with everyone?"

"That could work. I only have two classes tomorrow."

"Great, then just come to my place afterwards."

"Can I come?" Kyrin asked and looked at his mom.

"No, baby. This is a grown-up dinner," she answered, and I wanted to say yes.

"We can take him to the park another day with just the three of us."

"Yeah, the park!" Kyrin clapped his hands.

"I can see you two stressing me out already," she said and helped him off the chair. He ran back to the living room with his train set.

"He's a good kid, Kadence."

"Thank you."

"You're doing a good job with him."

"I needed to hear that."

"You never have to worry."

Buzz!

When I felt my phone vibrate, I removed it from my pocket and saw a message from Rosaline.

Rosaline: Gunner, you really fired me!

Rosaline: Baby, call me back.

"Everything all right?"

I deleted her messages and placed my phone back in my pocket.

"Fine, babe."

"You sure?"

This was the third time Rosaline texted. I made it clear the last time not to be late.

"How is school?" I changed the topic, continued to eat, and listened to her goals.

"Good. My teachers are great and so far, I've passed my tests."

"You'll have a degree real soon, babe."

Kadence smiled and picked up her plate, along with Kyrin's, and took them to the sink.

"Are you ready for cupcakes and movies?"

"I'm ready for something sweet, but not cupcakes." I came up behind her and wrapped my arms around her waist.

She moaned when I nuzzled my face in her neck.

"Behave, Mr. Vishon."

"I can't promise you'll wear those shorts." I slapped her on the ass.

I helped her carry the cupcakes to the living room. We sat and watched *Spiderman* and a few Pixar animations for the rest of the night with Kyrin.

CHAPTER SEVEN
KADENCE

The teacher explained the next quiz would be on ethical violations and SEC rules. I closed the book, and he dismissed the class for the day. Finally, I could relax and grab a cup of coffee before I went home to study until dinner. Gunner's planned a nice dinner with our friends, and I wanted to be rested after the night we stayed up with Kyrin. That boy of mine loved his Marvel movies, and I could remember every line that Thor said with the amount of times we watched his movies. I hopped in my car and headed to the coffee shop next to the school. It was fairly quiet, and as I moved up in line to place my order, I felt a tap on my shoulder.

"Rosaline."

"I thought that was you, Kadence." Rosaline extended her arm for a hug.

"What are you doing here?"

"I saw you come in when I passed by. How are things at Club Seek?" Rosaline tossed her blond hair to the side, and I whirled around to give my order.

"Can I get the vanilla latte please? Things are good. I haven't seen you around."

Rosaline's eyes racked over me.

"They weren't paying me enough, so I left."

I found that hard to believe, because Mason and Gunner said the place had the wealthiest clientele, but I didn't question her further.

"Sorry to hear that."

"No worries. I'm making a ton of money at my new place. But how is everyone?" She walked alongside me to wait for my order.

"Everybody is good." The barista passed me my drink order, and I grabbed a straw.

"Is Gunner seeing anyone?" she asked, and my face scrunched up in confusion.

"Gunner?"

"Yeah, we were talking a little, but after I left, he got mad and cut me off," Rosaline lied, and I wanted to mention our relationship. I didn't like confrontation in public.

"Huh, I have to go, Rosaline. It was good to see you." I rushed out of the cafe and ran to my car.

Ring!

I saw Emma's number flash across the screen.

"Hello." I drove out of the cafe.

"What is Gunner planning for dinner? I need to know what I should wear."

"Uhm, Emma, I can't really talk right now."

"Why? What's wrong?"

"I think Gunner is cheating or was seeing someone."

"Huh, slow down. Where are you?"

"Driving. I just left school and ran into Rosaline."

"Who's Rosaline?"

"I used to work with her at the club." I came to a stop sign and placed my drink in the holder.

"Okay, and how does she factor into your relationship?"

"She asked if Gunner is dating anybody."

"What did you say?"

"I was surprised when she said they dated, and I rushed out of there."

Emma got quiet.

"Look, Kadence, some women are jealous. She probably knows you're seeing him and set that meeting up."

"Rosaline wouldn't do that."

"How close are you to her?"

"Not really close, but we've talked at work a few times."

"Then you have no loyalties to her, only Gunner. I say ignore her."

"Emma, you say that about anything." I chortled and drove toward my apartment.

"Anyway, do you think casual jeans and blouses would work?"

I picked up my things, climbed out of the car, and locked the door.

"Yeah, that should work. Nothing major. We'll have drinks and dinner on the patio." I unlocked my apartment door, reached for my mail on the ground, and picked it up.

"Sounds good. See you in a little while, babe.

"You too, crazy lady."

I dropped the mail on the table and blew out a breath. I sat on the couch, rubbing my temples.

"Gunner and Rosaline dated," I muttered to myself.

Conversation flowed and drinks poured as Emma continued to talk about the way her son acted in daycare today. Jordan came out, and I was glad to see them reconnect again and make their marriage a priority. In the past, my marriage had a bumpy road, but we came out on the right side of things until his death. My head whirled around to Gunner when he rubbed my neck and kissed me on the shoulder.

"You seem quiet tonight."

"I'm fine." I lifted my glass and drank the champagne.

"Come with me." Gunner stood and grabbed my hand. I looked at him in confusion.

"Where?"

"We'll be right back, everyone," Gunner explained, and Emma peered at me. I waved her off and put my napkin down. Gunner walked me to his massive kitchen, and I removed my hand and stared off. His eyes were on me.

"Are you upset with me?" He pulled my hands apart and laid them on his chest.

"Rosaline asked about you."

His mouth turned downward.

"Where did you see Rosaline?"

"Are you still sleeping with her?" My body went tense with shock.

"Kadence."

"You know what? Don't answer, I need to go." I felt a clutch of panic in the pit of my stomach.

I angled around him and stormed out of the kitchen, passing our friends to get my jacket and purse. Emma and Chelsey jumped up to follow us.

"You told him," Emma commented, and he looked between us.

"I'll call you later, Emma. Nice seeing you again, Chelsey."

"Kadence! Kadence!" Gunner yelled after me. I raised

my hand up to protest him from following, hopped in my car, and left.

"Ring! Ring!

I switched my phone to Do Not Disturb to stop his incessant calls and sped into traffic. If he couldn't answer a simple question, there was something to them dating. When I finally pulled up to my apartment and parked, my door was yanked open.

"Oh my God!" I jerked back, and Gunner stood at my door. "Get out of the car. Gunner, go home." I grabbed my purse and stepped around him. All of a sudden, I was lifted off the ground and thrown over his shoulder. "Gunner! Put me down." I smacked him on the back.

"Shut up." He smacked my ass, took my keys out of my hand, and unlocked my apartment door.

We walked inside, and he put me on his lap. I avoided eye contact until he gripped my chin to face him.

"Listen to me," he shot back, his eyes glittering with anger.

"I told you I needed a minute."

"No, you just left without hearing me out."

"It doesn't matter."

"It does to me, and you're listening to someone I haven't spoken to in months."

"She's..."

"She's irrelevant, Kadence. A girl I hooked up with a few times in the past."

He laid a hand on my thigh and squeezed.

"Based on how she questioned me earlier, I doubt you're irrelevant to her." I nudged his hand off my leg.

Gunner smiled and sat back on the couch.

"Are you scared?"

"What?"

"Of what we could be?"

"Gunner—" He stopped me.

"No, you and I click, and you're trying to force the Rosaline thing to end us before we really get started. I know you lost your husband, and your in-laws aren't reliable. But I'm not them."

His words were true, and I did keep people at arm's length after everything I'd gone through in life. Plus, my parents weren't the best example of commitment.

"All right, so Rosaline is in her head about you two being more than you are?"

"She and I had no real ties, baby. It's been you from the moment I saw you."

I smirked and leaned up against his chest. We kissed, and I jerked back in thought.

"Your dinner."

He chuckled.

"Come on, let's head back to my place."

"I know they probably think I'm crazy."

"Emma wanted to come with the girls and drag you back, but I said to let me handle it instead."

I covered my face in embarrassment.

"I'm sorry."

He kissed my forehead.

"No apologies necessary. I like this jealousy on you."

I smacked him gently on the chest.

"Whatever, Mr. Vishon," I joked, and he smacked me on the ass.

❦ 8 ❦

CHAPTER EIGHT
GUNNER

Knock! Knock!

"It's open!" I shuffled some papers on my desk and piled them for my assistant to file when Rosaline stepped into my office. Two days ago, Kadence came to me upset and ready to break things off. I was pissed off at the time, but I didn't want to show my hand and have her think I was a crazy asshole. Rosaline pushed me too far in contacting Kadence, like we had a relationship.

"I knew you'd call again."

Rosaline started to walk around my desk.

"Have a seat." I motioned to the chair in front of my desk.

"You seem upset, baby." Rosaline crossed her legs and bit her bottom lip flirtatiously.

"Rosaline, what's the problem?"

"Huh?"

"You told Kadence we were in a relationship?"

"Kadence, Kadence at the club?"

"Yeah."

"Why do you care what I told her?"

"She's my girl."

"Since when?" She jumped up with a frown on her face.

"None of your business, but you and I have never made any commitment to be together."

"Not in words, but the way you—" I stopped her before she could lie.

"Have I taken you to dinner?"

"No."

"Have I introduced you to a friend?"

"No, but Gunner…"

"Rosaline, I'm only saying this once. We are done."

Her nostrils flared, and her fists balled up.

"Fuck you, Gunner!" She snatched up her purse and stormed out of my office.

I fell back in my chair and ran a hand down my face. Rosaline knew what was best for her. She'd move on. I picked up my cell and made plans to show Kadence I was serious about us.

"Hey, baby."

"How are you?" Kadence asked.

"Wonderful. How are you doing? You didn't sleep in my bed last night. I missed you."

She giggled through the line.

"Kyrin had a fever."

"Do you need me to bring anything?"

"No. He's almost over it now. How is work?"

"Work is work, same shit different day." I kicked my feet up on the desk.

"Sounds like you're busy."

"I was, but not anymore."

"Maybe you want to come over for lunch."

"I'd like that, but how about I take you and Kyrin out for lunch? My treat."

"You don't have to do that, Gunner."

"I want to. Besides, I haven't seen my bestie."

"Here you go."

I laughed. Kyrin and I had a secret handshake and became best friends. Kadence hated when we would watch cartoons and play with his train set scattered over her living room.

"Is my baby jealous?"

"Shut up, Gunner, and I'll see you soon."

"What do you think about the club tonight?" With both our schedules, we hadn't had time to indulge, but I wanted to make up for the situation with Rosaline and devote all my time to Kadence to show her I was serious about us.

"I'd love to go," she cooed, and my dick stiffened in my pants.

"See you in a few."

☙❧

Kyrin was much better after being sick, so after lunch, we took him to the park. He climbed up the play ladder and slid back down to follow some more kids.

"He's better." I pointed at Kyrin jumping on the swing.

"Finally. These last few days were crazy."

I covered her palm.

"I talked with Rosaline."

"And what did she say?"

"She couldn't say anything. I told her to keep my name out of her mouth."

"I guess you're stuck with me then." Kadence laid her head on my shoulder.

"The best person to be stuck with."

"Gunner! Come push me on the swings," Kyrin yelled from the swings.

"What about me?" Kadence joked as she stood.

"Mommy, you're always here. I want Gunner to push me."

I laughed at their back-and-forth, raised my arm around her neck, and kissed her forehead.

"Sorry, love. He wants the best." Kadence pushed me off, and I laughed, jogging to Kyrin to push him on the swing.

"Smile. I want a picture," Kadence called out, and I held Kyrin in the swing. The rest of the day was spent with Kyrin in the park. Then we went to grab ice cream and his favorite pizza for dinner.

❧ 9 ❧

CHAPTER NINE
KADENCE

Gunner secured the private emerald room tonight. My arms circled his neck, and I deepened the kiss; then he leaned back.

"What's wrong?"

"I'm running the show." He removed my dress and helped me take off his clothes.

Gunner hungrily kissed me, then released me and captured my hand to walk me to the bed we often used when I had a night off. I went to sit, and he shook his head and turned me to face him.

"Tonight's a little different."

"How so?"

"I want you lying on the spreader over in the corner."

I smirked and reached out to grasp his dick.

"Is this pleasure or punishment tonight?"

"Both."

Gunner helped me to climb on top. I raised my arms above my head, and locked them in place. He did the same to my legs and had them at an angle that he could stand in the middle with his face directly in front of my pussy.

"Gunner..." I felt my stomach stir in anticipation.

"Shussh."

He picked up the vibrator, held it up to my face and then lifted the flogger. I licked my lips, ready for his games.

"I want all of you tonight."

"Yes."

He gripped his dick and stroked himself.

"Fuck! You're lying down like that, sexy and willing."

"I want you in my mouth."

"It's coming." Gunner turned the vibrator on to a medium setting and pushed around my nipple, then my breast. He used his other hand to jerk off in front of me. I hated not being able to touch him.

"Gunner, please." He moved the vibrator to my mouth and pushed it in and out. Our eyes connected and I felt my wetness.

"Mmmmm," I moaned. He maneuvered the vibrator to my pussy and replaced it with his dick.

"Oh fuck, baby. Take it slow."

He caressed my cheek and watched the vibrator enter my lower lips. Gunner turned the vibrator up a little, and I felt an overwhelming sensation. Warmth swarmed through my body.

"So wet."

I was so ready to pass out from all of the sensations. Gunner removed his thick shaft and kissed me on the lips.

"I want to touch you."

"Not yet."

He removed the vibrator, slid into me, and buried his face in my neck. Sucking on my ear, I felt his warm breath along my neck and shoulder. We made eye contact, and I saw the satisfaction in his eyes. His hand went to rub my clit, and my eyes rolled to the back of my head.

My back slightly arched, and we fucked for the next two hours.

જીસ્ટ

WE WERE COMING UP ON SIX MONTHS OF DATING, AND I hadn't been this happy in a long time. After dropping Kyrin at daycare, I told the girls I wanted to catch up. All of us had busy lives, and I wanted to show them the progress I'd made with school plans and Kyrin. I waved at Kyra when I approached the table and reached down to hug her and Emma.

"You're all done up. Did you have a shoot today?"

"Yes, and Warren is taking me out to dinner tonight, so I have to stay ready," Kyra teased.

I sat in the booth, opposite to Kyra and Emma.

"What is this glow on you?" Emma questioned.

"Life is good."

"Life or dick?" Emma joked.

"Girl!" We high-fived.

"Both, and my baby is doing well. Plus, my classes are going well."

"So happy to hear that. Has Kyrin been okay with having a man around the house?"

"He has. I made sure to take it slow and not just spring a new person on him."

"What about your mom?"

"Haven't talked to her in a few weeks."

"Why not?"

"She's been standoffish. Plus, Gunner and I have Kyrin most of the time."

"Oohh."

"Never would replace his father, but Gunner has shown himself to be a great friend."

"I like him for you," Emma said.

"I like him too." I smiled.

"Are you planning on staying at the club?" Kyra questioned.

"Not forever, but once school is done, I can look for a job in the administration field or start my own business."

"I'm surprised Gunner hasn't said anything about you quitting," Kyra said as she sipped her strawberry soda.

"He never brought it up like it was a bad thing." I shrugged.

"He can't say anything. He found his fling there," Emma commented.

"True, but how are you and Jordan doing? Enough talk about me."

"Happily married and ready for more kids." Emma raised her hand and showed off the new wedding ring.

"Jordan showed out on this ring."

"Yes, my husband is fabulous, isn't he?" Emma joked.

"What about you, Kyra?"

"Working and dealing with Warren's crazy self."

"What did he do now?"

"Driving me crazy about having a baby." Kyra sighed.

"He just loves you and wants to have a mini diva running around." I laughed.

❧ 10 ❧

CHAPTER TEN
KADENCE

The next day.

Kyrin ran inside my mom's house, and I laughed at him. Bypassing her toward the TV, he pulled out his toys. The talk with the girls helped me to get the courage to visit my mom and try to get on the same page, for Kyrin's sake at least.

"Hi."

"Hey, is he staying?" She shut the door behind me.

"If you want him to."

"He's my grandbaby, why wouldn't I?"

"Can we talk without the sass, Mom?"

"Kadence, shut up."

She pulled out a cigarette and lit it up.

"Why are you so angry with me?"

"I'm not angry with you."

"Then what is with the attitude all the time?"

She glanced at Kyrin, then back at me.

"You look just like your father."

"Here we go."

"See that's your problem now, always rolling eyes."

"Ma, I'm not Daddy."

"You think I don't know that."

She headed to the kitchen, and I followed. I climbed up on the counter and watched as she washed the dishes.

"He was an asshole."

"To you."

"You too. You just don't remember."

"You have to get over him."

"Who's the mother in this relationship?"

"Okay." I picked the towel up to dry the dishes.

"I just didn't have the life I wanted, and I do have some regrets, I took out my anger on you," she mumbled.

"I figured."

"You're doing great for yourself, and I guess I envied you."

"You can always go back to school."

"I'm too old."

"You're never too old to follow your dreams, Mom."

"How is that boyfriend of yours?"

"He's fine."

"He's cute."

"Thanks. When did you see him?"

"When you dropped Kyrin off months back, he was in the car."

"Oh."

"I'm glad you've opened your heart, Kadence."

"Thanks. I wish I could say the same for you."

She waved me off.

"Men are only good for one thing."

"What's that?"

"Money." She burst into laughter.

"Not even sex?"

"Honey, I got a toy upstairs that does me fine."

"All right, I don't need to know that." I pretended to throw up.

"Are you working tonight?"

"Yeah and some studying."

"Well, get on out of here and get to work. Tell that boyfriend of yours don't be a stranger."

I jumped off the counter and kissed her cheek. We hugged; and then she walked me to the living room. I bent down to kiss Kyrin on the top of his head and told him I was leaving. I strolled out of her apartment and grabbed my phone to call Gunner.

❦ II ❦

CHAPTER ELEVEN
KADENCE

"**O**h, fuck!" I cried out, trying to grab the back of Gunner's head. As my hands were tied, he snaked his tongue in my lower lips. I squeezed my eyes shut as the feel of his large hands ran across my stomach. Gunner flicked my nipple, pinched, and moved to my right breast. The ice chips sat in the bucket, and I knew the torture was about to begin.

"What are the rules, Kadence?"

"Pick up when you call." I looked down at his hand gripping my thigh.

"What else?" He smacked, then squeezed my left breast.

"Stop allowing people that don't matter in my life to upset me."

"What did you do today?"

He stopped sucking on my pearl, and I was pissed.

"I reached out to Kyrin's grandparents."

"They ignored your calls once again, baby."

"I know."

"So, what should your punishment be?"

He crawled up my body and hovered over me.

"Two orgasms minimum," I joked, and he chuckled, reaching for a piece of ice from the bucket.

"I should say no orgasms, but that would deprive me as well."

"They don't deserve me."

"Exactly. You're special, and anyone who doesn't see that can fuck off." He pressed the ice against my bottom lips and rubbed against my top. I stuck my tongue out and licked his finger as he held it in my mouth.

"Gunner." I gasped when he pressed the ice on my nipple and rubbed around my areola.

"She's pointed right at me, waiting to be sucked." Gunner stared at my breasts.

"Fuck me."

"We're together. You're everything to me, and no one will change that."

"I know, baby!" I cooed. He ran the ice down my stomach, circled my navel and then against my lower lips.

"Shit, she's ready for me." He pushed the ice in, lowered his head, and sucked on the ice. It felt so good as it melted with his mouth combating the coolness of the ice.

"Wet and ready, baby."

"Ouu... Shit! Yes, Gunner," I hollered, twisting my head back and forth. My chest rapidly rose and my breathing heightened.

"Your pussy's calling my name, Kadence." He slid a finger in and out.

"Gunner! Please put it in and make love to me."

He smirked, stood, and removed his pants and shirt. He grabbed the blindfold from the nightstand and placed it over my eyes.

"What are you doing?"

"Making our night special. I want you to just remember

through my touch." He lifted my legs and spread them out more. I felt the head of his pole tap against my slit.

"Shit, you're already soaking the sheets." Gunner didn't just slide in, but grinded slowly back and forth. My swollen clit screamed for him, and he teased me for minutes, but it felt like hours.

"I need you inside me."

"I like when you beg." His husky voice whispered in my ear. When he thrusted forward, he buried his dick deep between my walls. We stayed like that for a few seconds, and his groans against my ear only caused me to get wetter.

"Never again will I allow anyone to hurt you." He sounded pissed and ready to fight all my battles as he pounded with long strokes. My mouth stretched open at a loss for words.

"Yes! Baby, Fuck!" I cried out when he pushed my legs up to my chest.

"Fuck! You. Are. Everything. To. Me. Kadence." Gunner slowed his strokes, lay on my chest, removed the mask, and pulled my lips to his. We made love for the rest of the night at the club.

CHAPTER TWELVE
GUNNER

"Did you tell them about Kyrin?"

I parked the car and turned to face her.

"Babe, you need to relax."

"Gunner."

I lifted her hand and kissed the back of her palm.

"I know your other in-laws aren't supportive."

She scoffed at my words.

"Try evil." She leaned her head against the headrest.

"My parents aren't like that. I promise, and if they were, I wouldn't bring you around."

"They fooled me in the beginning."

"Billy and Katy Vishon aren't good actors." I lifted her chin and pressed a kiss on her lips.

Kadence turned her head and smiled.

"Well, they better be nice because I'd hate to lose this." She reached over and gripped my dick.

"Maybe we can reschedule this dinner and go back to my place."

She laughed, and I sucked her bottom lip.

"Nope, dinner first."

I opened the door and jogged around to help her out. We strolled to the front door, and my mother opened it and outstretched her arms.

"I was wondering when you'd show up."

After giving my mom a hug, I moved to the side and introduced Kadence.

"This is Kadence, my girlfriend."

"Nice to meet you, Kadence. I'm Katy," Mom said and leaned in for a hug.

"You too, Mrs. Vishon."

She waved her comment off.

"Please call me Katy."

"Katy."

"Come in. Are you thirsty? I have wine, water, beer, or soda." Our family was the typical family that let all the kids hang out at their house. Most parents had rules and never let their children experience anything, but Mom and Dad kept the communication open and explained about what drugs and alcohol could do if we abused them. I followed in my dad's footsteps when it came to business and became an entrepreneur. Mom worked as a paralegal, and Dad owned an investment firm and his own sporting goods store.

"Water is fine."

"Gunner, are you having beer?" Mom asked.

"Please. Where's Dad?" I removed my jacket and laid it on the seat of the couch.

"Should be coming in from the store any minute."

"How is the store doing?" I took the beer out of her hands, and Kadence thanked her for the glass of water.

"The store is busy. He might open another one." She sat on the opposite side of us.

The door opened, and Dad walked in with a newspaper in his hand.

"Gunner! Who is this lovely lady?" Dad dropped the

newspaper on the table and leaned over to kiss my mom on the lips.

"Kadence, my girlfriend. You look like a tired old man." I stood and shook his hand.

He went into a boxing stance, and I laughed.

"Your old man can still last a few rounds." He chuckled.

"Hi, Mr. Vishon. I'm Kadence."

"Please call me Billy. Sit back down."

"I was just telling Kadence to call me Katy."

"My son tells me you're in school." Dad grabbed the beer from my mom's hand and took a sip.

"I have about two years left. Then I get my degree in business."

"Nice. I like a smart woman. You did good, Gunner." He winked.

"Tell us about yourself, Kadence. Gunner mentioned you have a son."

"Yes, a little boy. After my husband died, I'm raising him on my own."

"Sorry to hear that. You'll have to bring him around. We have a huge pool in the back," Mom explained.

"I think Kyrin will probably never leave your house," Kadence kidded.

"We've been wanting grandkids for the longest time, so this will give us practice." Dad took another sip.

"So, you're a widower?"

Kadence encircled my hand.

"It's only been a year and a half, so it's tough for me to bring up."

"Understandable. I can relate," my mom said.

"How?" I questioned.

"We never talked about this, Gunner, but I was married before your father." My eyes ballooned.

"What? I never knew this."

"I was young and met your father a few years after. But he was a good man who died from a car accident," Mom explained.

"Yeah, I met your mom years down the road. We became friends and eventually, I fell in love with her," Dad said.

"Learn something new every day."

"Come on, let's go eat. Then we can show you pictures of Gunner when he was younger." We all stood and walked into the dining room. I stopped Kadence and wrapped my arms around her waist in the hallway.

"Any regret?"

"None. What about you?"

"None."

"Then let's go eat with your parents and plan our future family nights together. I bet Kyrin is going to like your parents more than me." Kadence cupped both sides of my face and kissed me.

EPILOGUE
GUNNER

A year and a half later.

Kadence held up her diploma and took pictures with her friends, then with her son and mom. It was great to stand back and watch her finally get everything she deserved and not have to struggle or fight for support. The promise I made and committed was to be there for her throughout, and so far, it'd been that way. Kyrin didn't seem fazed about moving in with me and starting a new life as long as he had his own room and pizza night. I laughed at the thought of him trying to negotiate pizza night every day before he agreed with the move. I respected how Kadence handled everything with her in-laws when they tried to come back into his life and demanded they work on earning her trust before she put Kyrin in a situation to be disappointed. My parents came up next and stood for a picture with her, and I chuckled at how much I loved that Kyrin embraced my family. Already he enjoyed spending time with my dad because he let him have all the candy he wanted when he visited.

"Babe, you ready?" Kadence approached me.

"Yeah, do we have to swing by the house for anything?"

"No, the restaurant has everything organized." Kadence slipped her hand in mine. Kyrin ran to us, and I bent down to pick him up.

"Do you want pizza Kyrin?" I asked.

"Yes! And—"

"No pizza, Kyrin! We're having a real meal as a family," Kadence replied, reaching for him.

Kyrin threw his hands up in the air, and we both laughed.

"He's so spoiled." Kadence rubbed his head.

Kyrin would try to run anything if you let him. It was funny to see how Kadence interacted with him. Something I could see for our future children. We walked to my car and gathered everyone to announce the plans for the rest of the day.

"Follow us to the restaurant," I said to my parents after I helped Kyrin in the car seat.

"Babe, I have a surprise for you." Kadence grabbed my hand across the seat.

"Today is about you and your graduation."

"I know, but I couldn't wait."

"What's the surprise?"

"We can save it for later, but just be prepared for the club."

My heart fluttered at her request. The last time we went, she allowed me to explore her for hours, and I was waiting for her to officially quit working at the club and feel more comfortable with being a member.

"So, you're ready to become a member?"

"I'm ready for anything."

We ended up at the restaurant, and Kadence had reserved a private section. It was nice to see her with a smile on her face and a glow on her skin from accomplishing her goal. Emma stood up with her champagne.

"I want to make a toast," Emma said.

"Don't make me cry, Emma." Kadence poked out her lip.

I raised my arm on the back of her chair.

"Too late," Maya joked.

"Hush, Maya." Emma cleared her throat.

"We love your speeches, babe," Jordan responded, rubbing her back.

Emma grinned.

"To Kadence, you've shined and overcome obstacles while raising a beautiful young boy. You're an inspiration to us all." Emma held her glass up, and everybody clinked glasses.

I pulled Kadence into my arms and kissed her on the cheek.

"You've earned this, babe," I whispered in her ear.

"I know, and I appreciate you for being patient with me."

"Trust me, you're worth being patient for, baby."

Kyrin ran over to us, and I pulled him on my lap, and we played with his trucks. Kadence talked with her friends, and the evening was like a reunion of family and friends. Once the dinner was finished, Kyrin went to Emma's for the night, and I planned to take Kadence on a getaway with just the two of us as a present for all her hard work. She wasn't only a mother, friend, daughter, and girlfriend, but hopefully, she'd become a wife again. In life, we lived for the moments and experiences. When death hits, it shocks us into not wanting to love again. For Kadence, I wanted to show her that it was about the memories one made that mattered and carried on. Even though she lost a love, I would never replace him or take away that experience. I only wanted to add more memories of joy.

❧

I HOPE YOU ENJOYED KADENCE AND GUNNER'S STORY. Also check out where it all begins with **"Wet Heat,"** a best friend's brother's romance.

Don't forget if you love Fling romances, bodyguard, forced proximity then check out, **"Protecting Chanel"** https://books2read.com/u/mqwPB8

If you love brother's best friend romance, then you'll love **"Sensual" here** https://books2read.com/u/49lYYM with a dash of steamy romance.

Check out Bodyguard Romance, military, romantic suspense here ***"Protecting Bria"*** https://books2read.-com/u/bQJkjd

How about a steamy, medical romance? Check out ***"Haven"*** https://books2read.com/u/4jAvyZ a steamy enemies to lovers romance.

Have you checked out **"His Peace Her Pleasure"**? Click here https://books2read.com/u/3JJroP a billionaire, steamy romance.

Please also check out my ***"Love Don't Live here Anymore"*** https://books2read.com/u/mBOWGZ a steamy enemies to lovers romance.

SNEAK PEEK PROTECTING YANIRA
SPECIAL FORCES OPERATION

Yanira ~

As a journalist, I need to remain objective, but that doesn't mean I don't have opinions. When I find my boss dead in the office, I'm more determined than ever to find answers. But my investigation leads me down dangerous territory and exposes a threat that's too close to home.

Bishop ~

A night out with friends sometimes comes with surprises, but when a woman literally lands in my arms, that's only the beginning of what will be the biggest surprise of my life. She's in trouble and I know what to do to keep trouble at bay. But it would be a whole lot easier if the woman wasn't as bossy and uptight as she is beautiful and irresistible.

Will the sexual tension help or hinder the search for the killer?

ORDER OF SERIES

Seek To Please Book 1
Seek To Touch Book 2
Seek To Bare Book 3
Seek To Love Book 4
Seek To Trust Book 5
Seek To Earn Book 6

WHAT'S NEXT?

WANT TO KNOW WHAT HAPPENS next?

Follow me on Bookbub and social media today.

Reviews are the lifeblood of the publishing world. They're read, appreciated, and needed. Please consider taking the time to leave a few words on wherever you buy books. Sign up for updates and sneak peeks at the site below.

304 PUBLISHING COMPANY

WE SHOWCASE AUTHORS writing African American, Interracial, Women's Fiction, Urban Romance, Erotic, and Contemporary Romance novels. Along with Thriller, Suspense, Poetry, Beauty, and Style Books. Thank you for taking the time out to visit. Join our mailing list to stay updated with new releases and blog posts.

CATALOGUE OF RELEASES
BY KEKE RENÉE:

Catalogue of Releases by Keke Renée:

•Wet Heat (Wet Heat Series Book 1)

•Every Time We Touch Novelette (Wet Heat Book 2 Series)

•His Peace, Her Pleasure

•Baby, It's Cold Outside

•Love Don't Live Here Anymore, Vanessa Andrew Book 1

•Love Don't Live Here Anymore, Isabella Andrew Book2

•One Night Only-A Novelette (Love by Design Book 1)

•Cassian and Savannah (Love by Design Book 2)

•Deidra's Love (Love by Design Book 3)

•Protecting Bria (Special Force Operation Alphas)

Thank you so much for reading.

If you enjoyed the crazy ride and decide to leave a review, we'd appreciate the support.

I WANT TO THANK FIRST readers for loving these characters, supporting me from the beginning.

ABOUT THE AUTHOR

A Tennessee native and CA dreaming Author Keke Renee is living and striving to continue her passion of writing Short Story romances from Erotic, Women's Fiction, Romantic Suspense, Paranormal and Urban fiction.

www.ingramcontent.com/pod-product-compliance
Lightning Source LLC
Chambersburg PA
CBHW011157190726
48286CB00009B/2813